By the same author

The Hengest
A Brother's Oath
A Warlord's Bargain
A King's Legacy

The Arthur of the Cymry Trilogy
Sign of the White Foal
Banner of the Red Dragon
Field of the Black Raven
Drustan and Esyllt: Wolves of the Sea (novella)

The Rebel and the Runaway
Lords of the Greenwood

Dreams of Dark Lands: 13 Tales of Terror
The Unconquered Sun: Tales of Yule, Christmas and the Winter Solstice

https://christhorndycroft.wordpress.com/

As P. J. Thorndyke

The Lazarus Longman Chronicles
Through Mines of Deception (novella)
On Rails of Gold (novella)
Golden Heart
Silver Tomb
Onyx City

Celluloid Terrors
Curse of the Blood Fiends

https://pjthorndyke.wordpress.com/

Field of the Black Raven

CHRIS THORNDYCROFT

Field of the Black Raven
By Chris Thorndycroft

2020 by Copyright © Chris Thorndycroft

All rights reserved. This book or any portion thereof may not be reproduced or used in any manner whatsoever without the express written permission of the publisher except for the use of brief quotations in a book review.

For Maia for her constant encouragement and my parents for their unwavering support.

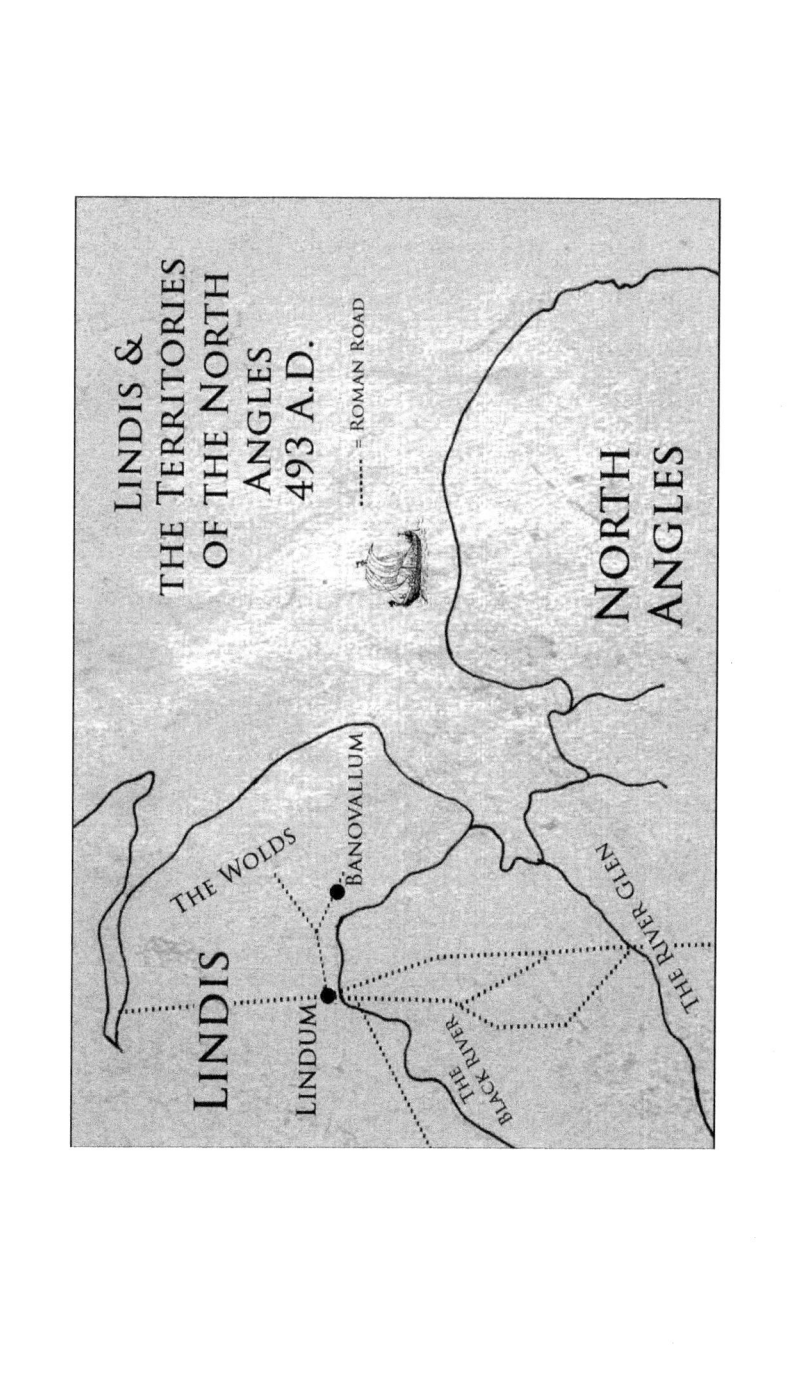

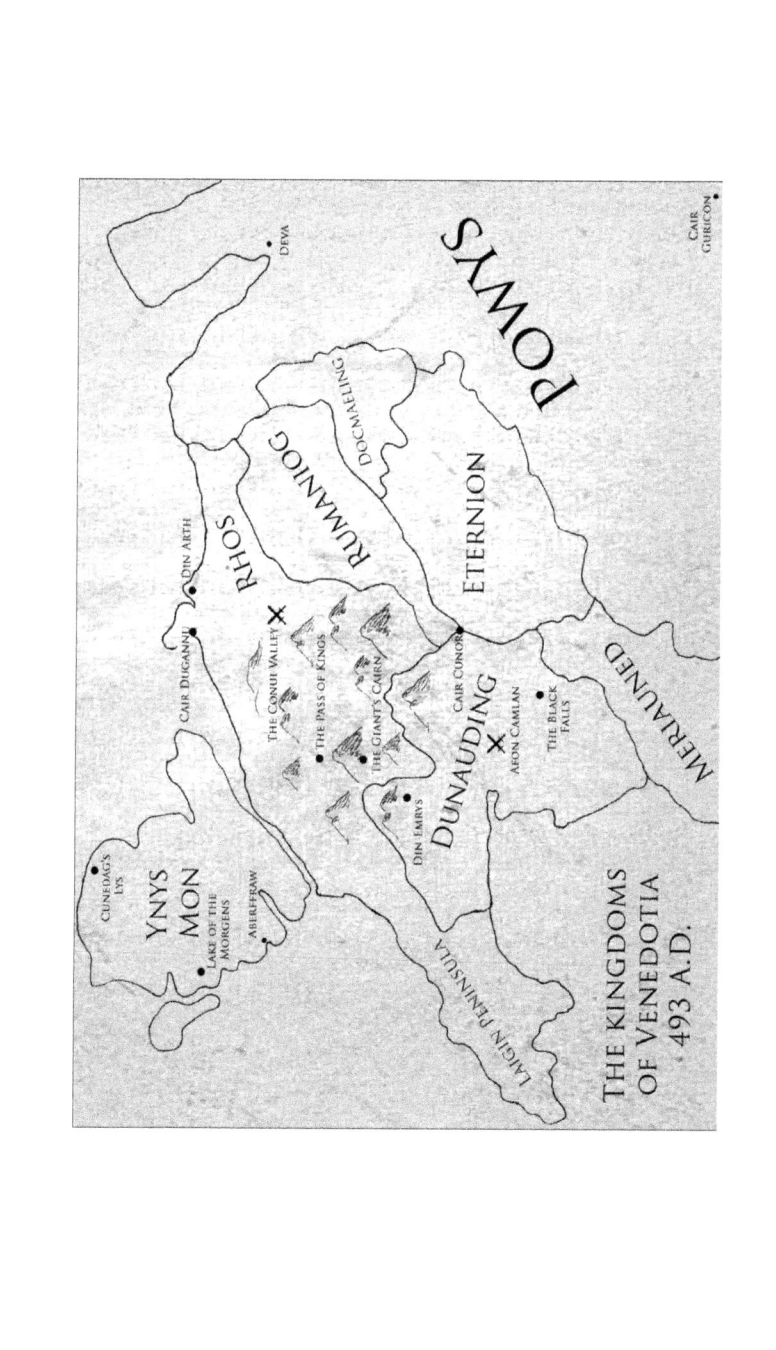

"537: The battle of Camlann, in which Arthur and Medraut fell: and there was plague in Britain and Ireland."
- The Welsh Annals

PART I

"Thereupon they heard a call made for Kadwr, Earl of Cornwall, and behold he arose with the sword of Arthur in his hand. And the similitude of two serpents was upon the sword in gold. And when the sword was drawn from its scabbard, it seemed as if two flames of fire burst forth from the jaws of the serpents, and then, so wonderful was the sword, that it was hard for any one to look upon it."
– The Dream of Rhonabwy (Trans. Lady Charlotte Guest)

South-west Britain, 486 A.D.

Arthur

The shape of the peregrine falcon was etched against the clouds as it wheeled overhead. Arthur watched it spot the lure and fold its wings to begin its lightning plummet; a black teardrop against the leaden sky.

Cundelig, the scout, swung the lure in a wide arc and Hebog snatched at it mid-air with talons of death. Missing the lure by an inch, the falcon skimmed the long grass and wheeled about. Cundelig held out his gauntleted hand with the tantalising piece of meat. Hebog settled onto the gauntlet and snatched his reward.

Arthur smiled. From Cair Cador's palisades he could see for miles around; rich farmland dotted with small clusters of roundhouses. Smoke drifted from thatched roofs while people stockpiled firewood and salted meat in preparation for winter. There was an air of tranquillity to the scene; a calm borne of an optimistic feeling of safety.

It had not been so three years past. Arthur had to keep reminding himself of that. Three years ago these lands had been in the very darkest peril. Three years ago King Aelle of the South Saeson had cast his shadow over the southwest of Albion and all the lands from the eastern tip of Ceint to the Sabrina Sea were under Sais rule. Arthur had led the Teulu of the Red Dragon south from the mountains of Venedotia to push Aelle back and reclaim at least a little of what had been lost.

It was hard to stay positive when all that three years of hard fighting had yielded was less than fifty miles of territory. Aelle may be dead, but his people still ruled swathes of Albion. There were not enough years in a man's life to win; Arthur knew that now.

And the years weighed on him heavily. He was only twenty-two. Ambrosius Aurelianus had been at least seventy when he had died and he had fought the Saeson for most of his life. Arthur was determined not to let this war consume him as it had consumed Aurelianus. Home beckoned to him across the mountains.

He had spent one winter in Venedotia out of three. He had been forced to remain at Cair Cador for the past two winters as the campaigning season had dragged on until the roads north were blocked by heavy snows. But that first glorious winter burned like a beacon in Arthur's breast. The teulu had returned home victorious after smashing the South Saeson at the battle of Badon. They had been hailed as heroes and Albion seemed to be on the verge of a great change with Venedotia as its proudest and strongest kingdom. Optimism crackled in the air as the darkness that had plagued the island for more than a generation seemed to dissipate at least a little.

The memory of that homecoming had kept Arthur and his men alive through the frozen mud and lean months of the following two years. For Arthur's part he remembered lying with Guenhuifar beneath wolf pelts while the snow-laden winds made the skin-membrane at the window rattle. That first winter had produced a son, Amhar. A son Arthur had carved a wooden horse for. A son he had not yet seen.

He climbed down from the rampart and crossed the muddy ground towards the Great Hall. Cabal, his faithful hound, got up from where he had been waiting at the foot of the steps set into the embankment and came to heel, following him closely, red tongue lolling.

Cabal had been the runt of his litter. His owner had been a farmer they had encountered in one of the hamlets at the foot of the great tract of forest to the east. The man had been rearing hunting dogs and had planned to drown the mewling pup rather than waste its mother's milk on it. But when Arthur had seen the small, furry ball, all paws and ears, he thought of the son he had not yet held in his arms and his heart broke at the thought of so brief and innocent a life snuffed out at the onset of another winter. He had taken the pup, kept it warm and fed it with milk from a bitch at Cair Cador who had just whelped. In no time at all, it seemed, the pup grew big and strong. But every day that Cabal grew, Arthur knew that so too did the Saeson beyond the forest.

The dense wood had become something of a natural boundary between Dumnonia and the new kingdom of the West Saeson on the other side of it. After the Battle of Badon, the domain Aelle had hammered together began to break apart. His sons ruled the lion's portion to the east of Ambrosius Aurelianus's old headquarters of Guenta Belgarum but, to the west of that, the splinter kingdom of the West Saeson had emerged, a new, green shoot from the old tree.

The West Saeson were ruled by Cerdic. His name was a bastardisation of the British name 'Caradog'; evidence of the warlord's British heritage. It was said that Cerdic's mother had been the daughter of some Sais chieftain who had married a British nobleman. If that was the way of it in the Sais kingdoms, Arthur thought, perhaps Albion was doomed already. This new generation of Sais considered Albion their homeland for they had been raised on its milk and wheat and called no other place home.

It was said that Cerdic had fought at Badon and had been one of Aelle's highest captains. Now it was Cerdic who barred Arthur's way to reclaiming Aurelianus's lands. It was Cerdic who had kept him here these three years.

Cei and Beduir approached him and threw up salutes. Arthur acknowledged his captains. "How go the preparations?" he asked them.

"Ready to set out tomorrow at dawn," said Cei.

"Cador wants to give us a send-off tonight," said Beduir. "The kitchens are heaving and they're already rolling the mead barrels into the Great Hall."

"Is he frightened we might not return?" Arthur asked, throwing them a wink. "I want no drunkenness tonight. Tell your companies. It's a long ride tomorrow and we need clear heads."

"Aye, you know the lads, Arthur," said Beduir. "They're as keen to get home as we are. They know that if a treaty can be reached with Cerdic tomorrow, they can taste Venedotian meat this winter."

"Where is Gualchmei?"

"Overseeing the breaking of the colts behind the stables. He'll miss those animals when we're gone for we can't take them back with us. They'll be needed here for Cador's warriors."

"Let's not skin the wolf before we've killed it," said Arthur. "Whether or not we *do* return home depends on Cerdic's willingness to establish a recognised border between Dumnonia and his own lands."

Cei and Beduir fell into a melancholy silence. The thought that a treaty might not be reached with Cerdic did not bear thinking of. They stopped at a fence and gazed at the white clusters of sheep that grazed on the flat patch of green between the houses and the wooden palisade.

The massive fortress had been abandoned for generations until Arthur had talked Cador into refortifying it. The circular hill with its earthen embankments that enclosed eighteen acres stood watch over the eastern marches of Dumnonia. With the West Saeson consolidating their power not fifty miles away, and Dumnonia still weakened after civil war, Arthur's suggestion had not gone unheeded by its new king.

The ditches were re-dug and a wooden palisade was constructed around the plateau set in a drystone wall and backed by an earthen rampart. Strong gatehouses were set at intervals, each crowned with a tower in the Roman style. It was a monumental fortification and stood as a testament to all Arthur had achieved. Seen from miles around, the fortress was a bastion of hope for all who had learned to fear the Sais warbands in recent years.

But, as its name suggested, it was not to be Arthur's fortress. He was but its guardian just as he was the guardian of all the west. When Cerdic and his horde were placated or defeated, these lands would be relinquished to Cador's control. That was an arrangement Arthur was only too happy with. He had no intention of remaining in the south a moment longer than he had to.

The hearth fires roared that night as the fat from the boar meat sizzled and spat in the flames. The iron rims of the painted shields that hung on the walls of the Great Hall reflected the warmth and colour below. The benches heaved with people and there was barely enough elbow room for eating.

"Companions!" shouted King Cador from the high table, a horn of mead held aloft. "It fills my heart with joy to see so many good friends around my hearth. I should really call it *our* hearth as this fortress has been as much your home as it has been mine and so shall it remain for all time. If the morrow brings us the success we have long prayed for then this fortress will mourn the loss of many beloved brothers as you depart for your homeland. But your legacy will be long remembered here in Dumnonia, indeed as it will be remembered across Albion! Drink with me now as I wish you every success!"

Benches and stools scraped on the flags as all rose to toast the teulu.

"Where is her ladyship?" Gualchmei asked Arthur, as they sat back down.

"Probably suckling Dumnonia's heir," Arthur replied.

Esyllt, the Gaelic princess whose illicit affair with her husband's nephew, Drustan, had thrown Dumnonia into a civil war, had shown remarkable adaptability. Not long after the Battle of Badon, Drustan became convinced that his lover was being unfaithful (and few could blame the man seeing as Esyllt had left her husband, March, to be with him).

Whether or not Esyllt had been having an affair was irrelevant for Drustan was slain in the brawl with his perceived rival for her affections. Arthur had been the one who had held the young Pict in his arms as his body bled out in the Great Hall of Din Tagel. It had been a futile fight which had stripped Dumnonia of its newfound stability in the wake of the civil war.

Esyllt found herself the sole monarch of a new and rather unpopular kingdom at the furthest extremity of Albion. Her husband, March, who had been licking his wounds in Armorica since the civil war, surely began entertaining notions of reclaiming his lost kingdom, not to mention his wife, upon receiving news of his nephew's death. So Esyllt had shown that canny Gaelic wile and quickly found herself a new husband; one who could not only protect her kingdom but even legitimise her rule of it.

The candidate was March's cousin. Cador was older, less handsome and considerably duller than March, but his most important attribute was that he was nearby and ready to hand while March was drinking away his sorrows and putting down rebellions in his territories across the channel.

The issue of bigamy was a thorny one but the Church was willing to agree that overlooking certain technicalities was preferable to another civil war while the Saeson sharpened their knives on their eastern borders. Besides, Cador had the support of Arthur and, despite the Church having their own bone to pick with Venedotia's penteulu regarding certain 'taxes' he had levied from their coffers, the likes of Abbot Piran and Abbot Petroc grudgingly admitted that Arthur was a handy man to have on their side.

Esyllt hastily bore Cador a child – a little too hastily thought some – but if there was ever any question that baby Constantine's eyes looked a little on the Pictish side, well, if the Church could overlook certain technicalities, then so could everybody else. Besides, for the first time in a long while, Dumnonia had an heir.

Menw, the bard, struck up a tune on his harp and the hall fell into a respectful silence. Words escaped his lips – an old song of home – and, for the Teulu of the Red Dragon, a tear welled in many an eye as the mountains of Venedotia and the women and children they had not seen in two years demanded to be recalled that night as the promise of homecoming hung in the smoky air above their heads.

They rode out as dawn was stretching the shadows across the plains surrounding Cair Cador. The mist of the new-born day retreated into the wooded valleys as Arthur and his three companies galloped east beneath the fluttering banner of the red dragon.

The great willows of the eastern forest enveloped them with gently flailing arms as they trod the loam. The arranged meeting point lay deep in the forest and had been chosen for its surrounding of dense trees. No cavalry could charge through such foliage. Both sides may fear treachery and with good reason, but there would be no open battle this day.

Arthur glanced sidelong at the rider who brought his horse up alongside of him. It was Peredur. The lad had proved himself a dozen times over during the past few years and had developed in to a proficient rider and warrior.

"This war could be over by sunset, sir," said Peredur.

"Aye, it could," agreed Arthur. "Or it could drag on for another three years."

Peredur's eyes fell to the ground ahead. "I pray to God that it will not be so," he said.

But Arthur detected a forcedness in the youth's words, like he was saying what was expected of him while his heart lay elsewhere.

"What's troubling you?"

"Well … many of the men miss home."

"We all miss home, lad," said Arthur. "Myself included."

"Yes. And many of the men have women back home who miss them."

"Are you such a man?" Arthur knew the lad had some noble woman tucked away in a villa somewhere. Whatever it was that had Peredur's mind in such turmoil, he was having trouble expressing it.

"Yes," said Peredur, his face colouring. "Her name is Angharad. Her family villa lies to the north of Cair Badon."

"Surely you have seen her during the winters we have spent here in the south?"

"Yes, sir. And in that I know I am lucky. Not many in the teulu have womenfolk nearby. My thoughts rest more on what will happen should a treaty with Cerdic be reached and the teulu goes back to Venedotia."

Arthur understood at last. "You fear that the tables will be turned," he said, "and, that as the others return to their sweethearts, you will be carried far away from your Angharad."

"Yes, sir."

"You are intending to remain in my service?"

Peredur's face looked shocked. "Of course, sir."

"You know that it is forbidden for men in the ranks to marry."

"I know that, sir. And I don't think she would be content to swap her life of comfort as the head of a household for the life of a soldier's wife anyway."

"If she loves you, Peredur, she'll wait," said Arthur.

"Wait? For what?"

"Horses approach, sir!" cried Beduir.

Arthur had sent Cei and his company forward to scout ahead. They returned with news that the warband of Cerdic lay not a league away.

"I will lead us in," said Arthur. "Standard bearer! By my side!"

"Is that wise, Arthur?" asked Cei. "You'll be presenting them with a mighty fine gift if their hearts are set on treachery. Let Beduir and I ride in front. A show of force should tell them we are not to be trifled with."

"A show of force may be our undoing if they suspect us as much as we suspect them. No, we need to show them that we come in good faith. I will ride in front but I want you close behind to get me out of a tight spot if it comes to it."

As they came upon the Saeson camp they could smell woodsmoke on the air. It hung between the trees like a blue mist and through it Arthur could see many hide tents. They dismounted and led their horses by the bridles as a further show of their peaceful intentions.

News of their approach had been carried to the camp by perimeter guards and a host was assembling on the westernmost fringe of the camp. Many thegns came forward, dressed in highly-polished scale armour with boar-crested helms that caught the sunlight through the treetops. Arthur wondered which of them was Cerdic. Did the self-proclaimed king dress in the Sais style or had he retained the customs of his father's people?

The identity of Cerdic became clear as a tall, slim man strode forward flanked by two thegns. He wore a helm the like of which Arthur had never seen. It seemed to be gold plated and was surely a ceremonial piece only. It had a great red crest, cheek flaps and a wide neck guard. The Roman influence was obvious for its shape differed little from Arthur's own more utilitarian helm but every inch of Cerdic's was covered in Germanic designs of running beasts, warriors and riders. It was a symbol of what Cerdic represented. The new generation – part Briton, part Sais – centuries of Romano-British heritage fused with an unconquered barbarian flourish.

"Arthur, bearer of the dragon standard," said Cerdic, as he approached. His British was flawless, native.

"Cerdic," Arthur replied, refusing to use any titles the warlord laid claim to.

Cerdic smiled. "Let us talk."

As chairs were brought forth for the two leaders to sit in, Arthur glanced up at the two banners that fluttered gently in the muted breeze of the forest. The red dragon of the Britons and the white dragon of the West Saeson. *We can talk all we want, but how long can any peace last between two such beasts?* he wondered.

Guenhuifar

Guenhuifar was startled by how old her father looked now. He had always seemed old to her during their many years living in the ruins of Cunedag's Lys. That was when he had been stooped under the weight of a dream that she had never believed in. And when it came true and the Llys was rebuilt and her father was reinstated as the Pendraig's steward, Gogfran had been as a man reborn. Years had melted away from him like autumn leaves to reveal fresh, green buds of spring. But after six years that burst of vitality had started to fade at last and Guenhuifar saw the deepening lines in her father's face, the whitening of his hair and the gradual returning stoop in his posture.

They were sitting in the Great Hall with King Cadwallon and Queen Meddyf as Guenhuifar related the recent news to the Pendraig and his wife.

"If a treaty with Cerdic is reached," Cadwallon said, "does your husband expect the Saeson to abide by it? They have not exactly inspired trust in the past …"

"I do not know my husband's mind on the matter," said Guenhuifar. "The reports come from one of his clerks and speak only of facts: numbers, inventories, that sort of thing."

She tried to keep the bitterness out of her voice. It had been two years since she had shared a private word with her husband. But Arthur did not know his letters and so she, like the rest of Venedotia, had to make do with the sterile reports of the teulu's progress in the south and tried to mentally construct a picture of what was going on down there, filling in the gaps between the statistics as to the men's morale, their hopes and fears as well as any words of comfort they may have for their loved ones at home.

As the southernmost fortress in Venedotia, Cair Cunor was the first to receive reports from the frontier and Guenhuifar felt it prudent to carry the news to the Pendraig herself. It was a good excuse to visit her father and sister as until now she had always been constrained by her duties at the fortress. It wasn't just the overseeing of Cair Cunor, she had little Amhar to think of. She couldn't bear to leave him and he was only just old enough for her to risk taking him with her on the arduous journey by horse and ferry to Ynys Mon.

If she was perfectly honest, it had been a glorious return to a sort of freedom that had been denied to her of late. She loved Amhar more than anything in the world but a baby had a way of sapping every waking moment from its mother along with the lion's share of her attention. For two years now she had felt the claustrophobia of being penned up within Cair Cunor's walls constricting her, making her feel like she was going mad. To ride north, even with Amhar sitting sideways on her lap and clinging to her cloak the whole way, had been an exhilarating breath of fresh air.

"And there is no indication that the teulu might winter at Cair Cunor?" Meddyf asked.

"We can only hope, my lady," said Guenuhifar.

"Yes," said the queen, smiling a little in sympathy to the anxiousness she surely detected in Guenhuifar's voice.

"Well, I don't suppose there is anything else we can do but await your husband's word," said Cadwallon. "And now, I imagine you wish to spend some time with your father and sister."

"Yes. Thank you, my lord," said Guenhuifar.

The small council dispersed but Guenhuifar's father remained with Cadwallon. "Go and visit your sister," he said. "She's planning something special for dinner. I'll be along shortly."

Meddyf followed Guenhuifar out. The sky was leaden and the leaves on the trees that grew close to the Lys's palisades were crisp and dry, the wind peeling them off, one by one.

"How have you been?" the queen asked her.

"Well, my lady," Guenhuifar replied. "Though I miss Arthur terribly."

"I know. Our suffering is often overlooked for we are but wives to great men. God will bring him back to us; I am sure of that."

Guenhuifar smiled, appreciating the sentiment.

"And how is little Amhar? He certainly has grown since I saw him last. Are the years really passing by so quickly?"

"He should be growing since he's eating everything in sight. He manages three bowls of gruel a morning! I don't know what he'll be like after a week or so with my sister. Guenhuifach does like to spoil him. He'll probably be as tall as his father by midwinter!"

They laughed as they wandered over to the training yard. A friendly tournament between the royal guards of Cadwallon and his brother Owain's men was underway. Owain bellowed in triumph as a spearman of Rhos sent one of Cadwallon's men tumbling at the end of his blunted spear.

"And I see your eldest son is turning into quite the handsome young man," said Meddyf, glancing over at the tall, dark-haired youth leaning against a nearby wall.

Medraut was watching the tournament with his usual combination of calculating silence. Officially Guenhuifar had brought him along as her bodyguard but in reality she had wanted to curry a little favour between him and his uncles. The last three years had done little to reconcile him with his newfound family and Guenhuifar suspected that Cadwallon and Owain were secretly glad he was kept at Cair Cunor, well away from court life. But being so far away had done nothing to heal old wounds not of his making.

"I worry about him sometimes," said Guenhuifar. "He has no real friends at Cair Cunor and keeps far too much to himself."

"Hardly surprising, considering his childhood. It must have been hard for him to get used to other people after having lived such an isolated life. It really was good of you to take him in and for Arthur to officially adopt him."

Guenhuifar nodded. That had taken some doing. Arthur had nothing against the boy but she still detected a reluctance in him to have anything to do with his half-sister's bastard child. It was that same reluctance and suspicion she saw in Cadwallon and Owain's eyes. In fact, everybody seemed to be unable to get past the fact that Medraut was the son of Anna and Meriaun; the two traitors whose scheming had torn Venedotia apart six years ago.

He had grown up on the Isle of the Dead and the only mother he had known had been his grandmother; a half-crazed exiled priestess. Guenhuifar often wondered what old Cerdwen had done to him on that island. What poisons had she filled his head with? But in truth he showed none of the hate that had consumed his mother and grandmother. He was a quiet boy, not shy exactly, but deeply thoughtful while other boys his age were as overexcited pups, never thinking before they spoke or acted. Everything was a game to them but not for Medraut. He took to his lessons with a seriousness that defied his age and stood him in good stead with his tutor if not his peers.

Owain had entered the lists and was sparring with a younger man in Cadwallon's guard who desperately fended off the bigger man's attacks.

"Owain's really putting that poor lad through his paces," said Guenhuifar, as they watched.

"Men and their pride," said Meddyf with a slight shake of her head. "It's all fun until someone gets hurt. And then we'll be a man down for a few weeks."

"It keeps them on their toes. Stops them getting sloppy."

Meddyf laughed. "I forget you are something of a warrior yourself. No doubt Arthur approves of your philosophy."

As predicted, the young guard made a mistake and Owain's blunted blade caught him in the belly, making him double over and grimace for air. A knee to the face knocked him to the ground, blood streaming from his nose to the accompanying groan of sympathy from the crowd.

"Does he have to be so bloody brutal?" Meddyf asked under her breath.

Owain paraded around the yard with his arms outstretched, daring anybody to step forward and try their luck against him. Nobody seemed interested and Cadwallon's guards huddled together, visibly edging away. It was shameful cowardice from the Pendraig's own men but Owain paid them no heed. His attention was fixed on Medraut.

"How about the son of our illustrious penteulu?" he asked. "You're a man now, surely? Care to test your mettle against a real warrior?"

Medraut raised his head and fixed a glare on Owain. A thin smile crept over his lips and he strode forward, accepting a blunted sword and a battered old shield from one of Owain's men who grinned in his wake.

"Is he any good?" Meddyf asked, her face concerned for the lad's fate.

"Oh, I think he might give Owain a run for his money," said Guenhuifar.

Meddyf glanced at her sidelong. "You seem rather proud. He's that good, eh?"

"Caurtam speaks very highly of him. That's the tutor of all the boys at Cair Cunor. Apparently Medraut is his best pupil."

"He certainly has confidence."

They watched as Medraut squared off against Owain. Then, all was a flurry of blows, each trying to outdo the other by working through their defence and scoring a winning blow.

Owain was a big, heavy man and although his swings were wide and slow, they were devastatingly powerful. Every time his blade crunched into Medraut's shield, Guenhuifar winced. But he kept up a good defence, only taking a blow on his shield when absolutely necessary. For the most part he danced around the big man, dodging and feinting, seeking to both wear Owain out and catch him off balance.

"Your boy has skill indeed," said Meddyf. "I expect he'll be keen to join the teulu and take his place alongside real warriors."

"Yes, he *is* beginning to chafe at the bit a little."

"How old is he?"

"Sixteen this summer. Old enough for me to give him his first spear. But, with Arthur away in the south, he'll have to wait until the teulu returns before he can join."

Sixteen was a restless age for a boy who had outgrown his lessons. Arthur had been sixteen, Guenhuifar remembered, when he had been sent to Ynys Mon to steal the cauldron from the Morgens. Medraut craved such responsibility as a newly-weaned wolf pup craves its first taste of blood. That was also why she had brought him along on this trip. To give him a little taste of responsibility and to let him stretch his limbs a bit.

The crowd voiced their excitement at impending triumph as Medraut crumpled under a particularly savage downwards chop from Owain that beat the strength from him. Down on one knee, Medraut glanced up as Owain's blade came down in a finishing blow.

He sprang to the side, his legs propelling him with a hidden strength that carried him out of the way of the whistling blade. He had been shamming!

Pretending to be on the verge of defeat when in reality he was on the verge of victory!

Owain's sword hacked into the muddy ground and his face glanced left, comical in its confusion as Medraut reared up and planted his boot on Owain's hip, shoving him over.

The yard fell silent as Owain, King of Rhos, sprawled in the mud, bested by a sixteen-year-old. It took but a split second of indecision before two of his warriors hurried forward to help him up.

"Treacherous whelp!" Owain roared. "That was a cowardly move!"

"Cowardly?" Medraut said. "I don't know how it is in the fine households of Venedotia, but at Cair Cunor we are taught to win."

"To feign weakness and then strike when your opponent is about to win is the pattern of a snake!" Owain went on. "And you do your tutors at Cair Cunor an insult! Treachery is not something they instil in the warriors of the Dragon Banner, I am sure. No, that poison was in you from birth!"

Medraut's face coloured. "What's that supposed to mean?"

Owain shrugged. "Should we expect anything less from the spawn of a witch and Venedotia's greatest traitor?"

Medraut looked ready to lunge at Owain but Guenhuifar had crossed the yard and placed herself between them, her right arm holding him back. "You speak to your own nephew, Owain," she told the big man.

"Nephew? That incestuous branch of our bloodline is so tangled I don't even know what he is.

Your son, perhaps, as the law has it. Well, teach him to show some manners when addressing royalty."

Owain had nothing more to say and turned away, leaving Medraut seething behind Guenhuifar's arm.

"That bastard …" he hissed.

"Hush!" Guenhuifar warned. "He might be your uncle and a boorish oaf at that, but he is still a king."

"He insulted my mother. His own sister!"

"That quarrel is over. You have no part in it, remember that."

But she knew she was lying to him. Her heart ached for him for he had no true sense of who he was or where he stood within his own family. He was of royal blood but had never known royalty. His life had been one of hardship until it was too late for him to be anything other than a commoner dressed in finery. *Just like Arthur.*

"Come with me," she said. "Guenhuifach will have dinner ready and you need to wash up."

They left the training yard and crossed the precinct to the steward's quarters. Guenhuifach came out to greet them, Amhar tottering beside her, clutching at her skirts. He was dressed warmly in a woollen garment with a hood and waddled like a little bear cub. Guenhuifar scooped him up in her arms.

"Have you been good for Auntie Guenhuifach?" she asked him, rubbing her nose against his pink cheek.

"He's an angel," said Guenhuifach. "He has a slight cough so I gave him some boiled fennel and honey."

"He must have picked it up on the voyage over. The straits were awfully rough."

"What's wrong, Medraut?" Guenhuifach seemed to instinctively pick up on the boy's mood.

"He quarrelled with Owain in the training yard," said Guenhuifar.

"I beat him and he couldn't take it!" said Medraut.

"You *beat* Owain?" Guenhuifach said.

"He's big and slow. It was easy."

"He's also a king and it does not do to insult him."

"He was the one who insulted me!"

"Owain is all bluster," said Guenhuifach. "I dread his coming to court every time for he always stirs up trouble. But let us put him from our minds. The pot is bubbling and Father will be back soon. Come now, Medraut, give your auntie a kiss and let's go in and warm ourselves."

As Guenhuifar watched Medraut obediently kiss her sister, she pondered the absurdity of Guenhuifach being his aunt for she was only four years older than him. But by law, that's who she was. The two of them had become great friends over the past three years and were exceedingly fond of each other.

They returned to Cair Cunor the following week for Guenhuifar was anxious for any word from the teulu. The winds were growing colder by the day and the peak of the Giant's Cairn was already dusted with snow.

When they dismounted on the parade ground, Cadyreith, the fortress's steward, hurried over to them. "My lady!" he cried. "There has been word!"

"From Arthur?" she asked, daring to hope that it might be true.

"Yes! He has reached an agreement with Cerdic. A border has been established and the teulu is coming home for winter!"

PART II

"The first battle was in the mouth of the river which is called Glein. The second and third and fourth and fifth on another river which is called Dubglas and is in the region Linnuis."
– The History of the Britons

492 A.D.
(Six years later)

Medraut

The air was chill and the wind biting as it cut across the precinct. The men, stripped to their waists, had been going through their spear work, practising their thrusts and parries until the sweat stood out on their torsos despite the cold.

Only a small detachment from the teulu had come with them to Cadwallon's Lys. Cei and the other commanders were wintering at Cair Cunor. Medraut had a bet going with Caurtam – his old tutor – that he could turn out a fitter, stronger and more efficient band of killers than he could and it was a bet he intended to win.

Six years. Six years had passed since he had joined the teulu. Six years since Arthur had brokered a peace treaty between Cerdic and established a border between the lands of the West Saeson and the kingdom of Dumnonia. Medraut could have screamed when they had returned from Ynys Mon that day to learn that the war he had so desperately hoped to join was over before he had even been accepted into the teulu. After all the training and hard work he had put in, it was like the gods were playing one big joke on him.

But another war was never far away. This one had taken its time in coming, however. Five years had passed in which he had worked his way up in the teulu; training himself to exhaustion, proving himself at every turn. Proving himself to his peers, to the captains – Cei, Beduir and Gualchmei – but proving himself to Arthur most of all. And at last, when the breeze of spring drifted through the mountain passes on the fifth year, it carried news from the east.

Years ago, King Edelsie of Lindis had thought to subjugate the North Angles – a Sais people who were forever raiding his borders – by marrying his daughter, Orwen, to their king, Athelbehrt. The marriage had resulted in a daughter but not before a hunting accident had put King Athelberht on his deathbed. While Athelberht lay with his groin skewered by a boar's tusk, Orwen fell sick and, before long, both died leaving an orphaned infant queen to rule the North Angles.

King Edelsie stepped in and proclaimed himself regent and ward of his granddaughter. But greed drove Edelsie's heart harder than love for his family and he sought to rule the North Angles indefinitely. As soon as his granddaughter was of age, he married her to a common man in his own following; effectively disinheriting her.

Not about to let a British king rule over them, the North Angles rallied behind a petty chieftain who promised to reclaim what had been stolen from them by British deceit. Wintra – the White Wolf as his people knew him – supported by his pagan priest, Scurwulf, drove King Edelsie out and took control of the lands south of the Afon Glen.

That had been almost twenty years ago and, ever since, the two kingdoms of Lindis and the North Angles sat side by side; a mutual desire to avoid obliteration the only thing preventing all-out war.

King Edelsie's granddaughter had given birth to a child of her own – Afloeg – who had been raised in humble surroundings, wholly ignorant to the fact that he was the heir to two kingdoms.

But secrets have a nasty habit of coming out and young Afloeg had grown to despise King Edelsie for many other things besides. When word reached him that Angle blood flowed in his veins and that he was the grandson of the old King Athelberht, he sided with the enemy who were all too keen to see King Edelsie overthrown at last.

No doubt hoping to use Afloeg as a puppet king on the throne of Lindis, Wintra supported Afloeg's insurrection. The other kings of Albion couldn't afford to let another British kingdom fall under the dominion of the Saeson so the mighty Teulu of the Red Dragon was called upon once more to drive back the combined forces of Wintra and Afloeg.

Medraut's first campaigning season had been nothing short of a thrill. Arthur had put him in charge of a troop and he had gloried in the slaughter of battle that turned the clear waters of the Afon Glen red. The season had ended with a decisive victory against the Angles but, though the cost was high, it had not bought a lasting peace. Come spring Afloeg and Wintra would stack the shield walls once more and Arthur would be pressed to ride east to defend Lindis from obliteration a second time.

"Good work today, lads," he told his men. "Get yourselves rubbed down in double quick time and I'll see to it that you receive a wine ration in hall tonight."

There were hearty gasps of appreciation at this. Most of the men were from his own troop and he was well liked. Firm but fair, he pushed them hard but always saw that they were rewarded for their efforts.

Once the last of them had disappeared into the armoury, he turned and crossed the precinct towards the steward's hall.

Candles flickered as he entered. It was sweltering inside and the hearth fire was piled high. The wicker door to old Gogfran's chamber stood ajar and Medraut could see Guenhuifach tending to him, her back to him as she sat on the edge of the bed feeding the old man broth mixed with one of her concoctions. The king's steward did not have many days left in him and Medraut would be surprised if he saw spring.

He knocked on the door to the quarters that had been given over to Arthur for his use.

"Come," said the voice within.

Medraut pushed the door open and entered the room. It was a low-ceilinged chamber beneath a storage loft but broad enough to accommodate a wide desk. It was littered with maps and parchments; all that pertained to the running of the teulu and the planning of the next campaign. Arthur reclined in his chair, sharing a private moment with Guenhuifar who sat beside a brazier that glowed with embers, a cup of something in her hand. Cabal lay nearby with his head on his paws.

"Sorry to disturb you," said Medraut.

"Oh, don't worry, Medraut," said Guenhuifar. "I can lend you your father once in a while, now that I've got him here all winter." She smiled at Arthur and rose, smoothing down the creases in her dress.

Medraut forced a smile. *My father!* Arthur was only six years older than him. *Six years was nothing!* Yet Guenhuifar had been the one who had plucked him from obscurity on the Isle of the Dead, taken him away from his grandmother's grasp and persuaded Arthur – his own uncle – to adopt him. Now he was burdened with a kindness he could never rid himself of. It had even been Guenhuifar who had given him his spear, the mark of manhood, in place of his dead mother. It would be laughable if it weren't so tragic.

"Will this take long?" Arthur asked him. "We shall be going to our meat in the Great Hall soon …"

"I just wanted a word," said Medraut.

"How go the exercises in the training yard?"

"Good. The men are excelling themselves."

"It's good to keep them occupied. Winter has a habit of boring men of war so that they seek out mischief to amuse themselves."

"I'll have no mischief from my men. They wouldn't dare."

"I know, Medraut. You have done well in training them. They like you."

"Have you thought any further on the matter of a fourth company?"

Before they had left Lindis for the winter, Arthur had mentioned the possibility of creating a fourth company with a new captain plucked from the ranks. The war had drawn more warriors to the teulu, bolstering its ranks considerably. The three existing captains – Cei, Beduir and Gualchmei – led fifty riders each and the marshy terrain of Lindis, scarred as it was by its many rivers, meant that larger groups of cavalry were less effective than smaller ones. Splitting the teulu over four companies instead of three made sense. But who then should lead the fourth?

"I have thought about it and I have much more thinking still to do," said Arthur. "I will let you know my decision as soon as I know what it is myself."

"Thank you, sir," said Medraut.

"Now, shall we head over to the Great Hall?"

Medraut bit down on his tongue as they left the steward's hall. He wanted to say much more to Arthur, to point out to him that he was respected in the teulu and to remind him of how he had led three troops in Gualchmei's company against the Sais wing and shattered it utterly at the great river battle last season. But he knew it would do no good. Arthur knew all of these things already. Why then did he delay? Why make him wait? Who better to lead the new company than his own son?

He did not see Guenhuifach at meat that evening and so went in search of her as the guard on the palisade was being changed. She had stopped living in the steward's hall in favour of her own accommodation beneath the western wall of the Lys. Her occupation required a little privacy for the sake of her clients and there was not enough storage space in the steward's hall for all her ingredients and potions.

Once they were confident that he had not been seen sneaking into her hut, they lay together on the wolfskin pelt that covered her pallet and made love. The walls were lined with shelves that held many glass jars and bottles containing Guenhuifach's potions, poultices and medicines. Powdered ingredients hung in pouches and the dried, shrivelled forms of various plants and animals twisted below the thatch.

The glow of the hearth fire bathed Guenhuifach's naked form in orange and made the shadow of her nipples waver across her creamy, goosepimpled skin. He adored her. He had adored her since he had first come to know her as the kind sister of the woman who had brought him out of the darkness and into the light. Guenhuifar may have been the one who saved him but it had been Guenhuifach's kindness that stood out in his memory amongst all the sceptical faces, half-veiled disgust and cruel words spoken by those who saw only his mother when they looked at him.

That initial kindness had developed into something more as the years went by. He had long known of his love for her but had been unsure that her smiles and warm embraces had been anything more than an older woman's love for a son she had never had. But, as he had emerged from adolescence a tall, strong man, he became aware that girls had begun to find him attractive. He wanted none of the tumbles with serving girls that the other young men of the teulu indulged in. He wanted only Guenhuifach and slowly, he began to understand that she wanted him too.

It had been hard for her at first and she had taken a lot of convincing. He knew as well as she did what people would say if they knew. They would see only perversion; a relationship between a youth and his aunt that bordered on incest. But there was a mere four years between them! What was four years between two adults who loved each other? That was what he had told her again and again to make her see that there was nothing wrong in what they were doing. So what if she was his aunt in the legal sense of the word? There was no blood shared and their lawful relationship was an artificial thing, a thing that rested entirely upon Arthur's marriage to Guenhuifar. She was no more his aunt that Guenhuifar was his mother. It was love that counted, not law.

She had come around to it eventually and they had carried on their relationship in secret, stealing moments such as these whenever Medraut accompanied Arthur to Ynys Mon on official business. But those meetings had become few and far between since war had broken out in Lindis.

As if reading his thoughts, Guenhuifach rolled onto her side and stroked his arm. "How many more times do we have before you ride away from me again?"

"As many as we like," he said, taking her hand in his and kissing it gently.

"You know that's not true," she said. "Every stolen moment is a risk we ought not to take."

"You worry too much. Nobody suspects."

"They will if you keep sneaking off to my hut. If somebody sees you, we will be ruined."

"If somebody sees me," he said with a grin, "I'll just tell them you are treating me for a dose of the clap from rutting with servant girls."

She slapped him playfully. "Be serious."

"I am serious! Who would see me coming here? Nobody notices if I slip away for an evening here and there. Not even Arthur."

It was true. His absence would not be noticed by those who generally disliked or at least distrusted him. He was liked well-enough by the men at Cair Cunor or around the campfire when on campaign for he was among fellow warriors who respected his skills in arms and leadership. But at the Pendraig's table with royalty – his own family even! – he felt like an unwanted guest. *Or an ugly reminder.*

He was convinced this was one of the reasons he and Guenhuifach were such a good fit. They were both feared, although for different reasons. Her for being a woman skilled in herblore and the birth mysteries, he for being his mother's son: a woman who had been feared much in the same way Guenhuifach was. They were a pair of outcasts finding solace in each other's arms and, as such, were free to hide from the world in its shadows.

"What of your men?" she asked him.

"They're getting drunk on the Pendraig's wine. Besides, what is it to them if I am absent from table? They probably think I'm off whoring as a good leader should. And they wouldn't be wrong."

"I'm warning you, Medraut ..." She tried to be stern but the smile forced its way through and she giggled, a tendril of her hair, fair as gold, dropping down over one side of her face. He loved to see her like this. Happy. Carefree. Utterly beautiful. He kissed her on the mouth and she sank beneath him on the wolf-skin pelt, letting him roll on top of her once more.

A hunt was arranged three days later and Cadwallon, Owain, Arthur and King Mor of Rumaniog, along with some of their keener retainers, saddled their horses and prepared to set out. The offer was extended, somewhat half-heartedly, to Medraut. As Arthur was going along Medraut thought he had better, if only to show his face and put Guenhuifach's worries to rest that he was not being seen out and about enough.

The ground was hard and the bare branches on the trees furry with frost as they rode out. With fur-lined cloaks billowing behind them and the breath of the horses steaming on the chill air, they plunged into the forests of Ynys Mon on the trail of a boar.

Medraut grimaced as he forced himself to ride behind the group. He could outride any of them but he knew that it would not be seemly to do so. It would be Cadwallon or one of the other kings who would make the kill. How could it be otherwise without causing offence? He didn't know how Arthur put up with them and their nonsense.

He hated winter and all the pointless activities men conjured up to keep themselves amused while they waited for the snows to melt. Even being close to Guenhuifach was not enough to keep him from feeling the ache of boredom. The king's Lys was no place for him. He craved real action – war and the company of his peers – not the company of kings and nobles: Cadwallon, Owain and all the rest of them who did nothing but sit about on their arses while men fought and died to keep them in comfort and safety! He wanted to ride away, back south to Cair Cunor or east where war awaited him! But he knew it was impossible. He had to wait out the winter here at Arthur's beck and call, hunting boar and training his men who were growing just as bored as he was.

The boar bolted from a thicket. Owain charged ahead, spear gripped overarm for the killing blow. He hurled. The spear went wide and thudded into the frozen ground while the boar crashed onwards into deeper undergrowth. Hindered by the dense briar, the horsemen reared up, curses on their lips at their lost prey.

"We need Cei here!" said Owain. "Now there's a man who can spear a boar!"

"Too bad you didn't bring him to winter with us, Arthur," said Cadwallon. "But I suppose Cair Cunor's stores need filling."

"If I know Cei," said Arthur, "There'll be more boars on Cair Cunor's tables this winter than there will be in the hills around it!"

They laughed at this. Medraut rolled his eyes.

"We should get that new lad of yours out on a hunt next winter," said Owain. "What's his name? Peredur?"

"Peredur?" Medraut spoke up. "I don't think he's much of a hunter. He grew up as wild and as unused to noble pursuits as I did."

The kings eyed him sidelong. "Well, if he's learnt to hunt half as well as he's learnt the art of war, then he's a better hunter than most," said Owain. "And besides, it's only fitting for the new captain to wet his spear-tip alongside us. Beduir and Gualchmei both skewered boars on royal hunts before they became captains as I recall."

"New captain?" said Medraut, turning in his saddle to look at Arthur.

Arthur gritted his teeth and looked embarrassed. "I didn't want you to find out this way, lad," he said, resting a hand on Medraut's shoulder. "I wanted to tell you myself."

"Peredur is to be the captain of the fourth company?" Medraut asked incredulously. "*Peredur*?"

"Aye. Don't take it hard, Medraut. I know you have it in you to lead, but it is not your time yet. Peredur has been with the teulu since Badon and has shown …"

"Save it!" snapped Medraut. "I don't care to hear your reasons!" He wheeled his mount and galloped off the way they had come.

He rode hard and fast through the snow, back towards Cadwallon's Lys, back towards Guenhuifach; the only person he wanted to be near, the only person he trusted not to betray him.

He thundered into the Lys's precinct and dismounted. A stable boy came to unsaddle the mare and rub her down and Medraut handed the reins over to him without a word. Then he made for Guenhuifach's hut, not caring who saw him.

"What's wrong?" she cried, her face showing alarm as he burst in through the hide apron. She had been mixing a poultice in a mortar and pestle and hurriedly set these aside to embrace him. That was Guenhuifach through and through. Always ready with a hug, no matter the bother. She had seen him like this before, angry, inconsolable. She always had a way of numbing his pain, of cooling the anger that boiled in his gut; an anger that even frightened him sometimes.

"The bastard has chosen Peredur!" was all he could say.

"As the captain of the new company?" she said, intuitively knowing what he spoke of.

"Aye. After all I have done for him, after all the effort I have put in to proving myself to be worthy!"

"Hush, Medraut! Arthur had his reasons, I am sure. What did he say?"

"Oh, he had his reasons! Reasons by the cartload. Almost as if he had prepared them in advance!"

"Well?"

"He said that I am not yet ready. That Peredur fought at Badon. Hah! If I had fought at Badon, you can bet that I would have slain twice as many Saeson as Peredur!"

"Don't compare yourself to him, Medraut. Arthur made his choice and you must accept it. He sees your potential, I know it. One day, he will make you a captain, you may be sure of it."

"A captain of what? There is no need of a fifth company. There may not even be a fourth company after the war in Lindis is over. This was my one chance to be a captain. And Peredur has taken it from me!"

"You can't blame Peredur …"

"I know, I know! But he's so bloody infuriating! He's long been Arthur's favourite. Why else would he let him marry that woman of his down south? Only captains can marry but Arthur made a special allowance for Peredur, almost as if he had him earmarked years ago! That Peredur can go riding off to see her in her fancy villa whenever he wants while we must carry on in secret as if our love was something immoral, something shameful! We should tell Arthur and Guenhuifar that we are lovers! What could they do?"

"Don't even think it!" said Guenhuifach. "It is true that our love is no immoral thing but it would be a thing of shame for all of us should Arthur and Guenhuifar learn of it! Think, Medraut! Use your senses! I am as good as your aunt in their eyes. They would never understand …"

"And so we must love each other in secret for the rest of our lives?"

"Perhaps. Will that never be enough for you?"

"No! How can it be enough for you?"

"It isn't. But what choice do we have?"

He placed his hands on either side of her head and kissed her lips. "One day there will be no need for us to hide, I promise you," he told her. "I'll find a way."

Arthur

The newly built fort stood on the bend of the Black River which cut south-eastwards towards the coast. From its spiked palisades the Britons could look across those dark, peat-stained waters to the woods of the southern part of Lindis which was now lost to them.

The Saeson had pressed forward as soon as the snows had melted and had reconquered all the ground Arthur and his teulu had pushed them out of the previous year. Everything between the River Glen and the Black River was theirs now, ruled over by Afloeg with Wintra and his North Angles looking on.

King Edelsie had been a fool, thought Arthur as he stripped off his armour and dressed in his saffron tunica and red cloak for dinner. As the easternmost British king he really should have known better. Hadn't the disastrous events following Vertigernus's actions a generation previously been warning enough to them all? The Saeson could never be trusted. The Night of the Long Knives, in which almost the entire Council of Britannia had been butchered by Hengest, was a tale spoken of with shame and deep melancholy across the island. It was a sore reminder that the Saeson could only be met by force of arms, not offers of marriage and union.

Cei entered the room and placed his helm upon the table. "Too bloody quiet south of the river," he said, almost as if it were a curse. "No lights at night, no movements. Quieter than a kingdom at peace and yet nobody knows anything. Or so they claim."

"Maybe they speak the truth," said Arthur. "The settlements closest to the southern bank are hardly likely to know of a Sais advance much earlier than us. If anything is happening, then it will be happening much further south. That is why I have employed spies in villages as far away as I could manage. Until they report back, we won't know anything."

"Do you trust them?"

Arthur nodded. "Not all are keen on having a man with Sais blood ruling over them. Especially not one who enjoys the support of the North Angles. This is largely Christian country and Scurwulf's sorceries are enough to kindle a flame of resistance in even the most jaded Briton's breast."

Scurwulf.

The name of King Wintra's pagan priest was spoken of with terror throughout Lindis. He was a holy man in the old way: a councillor, an advisor and a priest. As the mouthpiece of the Sais gods, his word was law and that law was followed to the letter ruthlessly by Wintra.

"Would it not be better to send scouts south of the river?" Cei asked, as Arthur passed him a cup of wine. "I'd sooner trust Cundelig's men than these spies you've paid off."

"No. Scouts are only good at spotting enemy movements, marshalling of warriors, that sort of thing. I want to know what Afloeg and Wintra's plans are *before* they start mustering their troops. Only those who live with the enemy can give me that sort of information. I'm afraid we're playing the waiting game now, Cei. The battle, when it comes, will be here, on the banks of the Black River."

He sat back in his chair and sipped his wine. He understood Cei's impatience although even Cei had been mellowed a little by age. The same could not be said for much of the rest of the teulu. Young upstarts like Medraut and his companions craved action, bloodshed and constant danger. They were so willing to hurl themselves into battle with no concept of life being anything more than blood and violence. Did the appreciation of the home hearth and the companionship of family come only with maturity? *Does a man need grey in his beard and the whisper of death in his ear to make him love instead of hate?*

It was on occasions like these that Arthur realised with a shudder that most of his warriors were younger than him. He had seen just twenty-seven winters and already he was one of the old-timers. He had a family, that was probably part of it. Another reason why it was wise to keep the warriors from getting married. *Let them chase after excitement instead of the marriage bed.* For Arthur's part, all he wanted to do was return home to Guenhuifar and his two sons.

Amhar was seven now and their youngest – Lacheu – was three. He missed them more than Guenhuifar even and longed to ruffle their tousled heads and pick them both up in massive bear hugs that made them squirm and squeal. He resented this war that kept him from them. He resented the Saeson and King Edelsie and everything that meant he had to remain here on the borders of civilisation while his sons were raised by tutors and weapons masters instead of their own father who could teach them more than any scribe or swordsman ever could.

"Any news from Medraut?" Cei asked him and Arthur realised that he had slipped into another of his melancholies and had forgotten that his friend and captain sat beside him.

"No, his company should return before dark. I only sent them as far as Banovallum. The Taifals can patrol the river east of there."

For many years King Edelsie had used the services of the Taifals who had settled at the foot of the Wolds years ago, recruiting them as his personal guard. The Taifals were the descendants of a warlike people from the coast of the Black Sea in distant Sarmatia. It had been the great Roman general, Stilicho, who had settled them in Britain during his military reorganisation of the island in response to renewed Pictish attacks. They had remained as an auxiliary cavalry unit under the command of the *Comes Britanniarum*. Ambrosius Aurelianus had been their last commander until the end of the Council of Britannia had disintegrated centralised control. Now Arthur, Albion's *Comes Britanniarum* in all but name, had reinstated the unit as an auxiliary in the defence of Lindis.

He had instructed them to refortify the old Roman fort of Banovallum and occupy it in order to guard Lindum from any boats approaching through the fens or up the Black River. The Taifals were fine riders just as their ancestors had been and Arthur was confident that no Sais army would try to cross the river to the east. When they did cross, he was sure they would converge on the part of the river closest to the walls of Lindum.

"Your son has good relations with the Taifals," said Cei.

Arthur smiled. He had never got used to considering Medraut his 'son' in any sense of the word. The lad had been nearly fully grown when Guenhuifar had convinced him that he needed adopting. Medraut had been some strange charitable obsession of hers. He had never understood it. Give the boy a home certainly, get him away from his demented grandmother and the shadow of his mother's crimes, by all means. But adopt him? He had agreed, mainly to make Guenhuifar happy but he had been too occupied with the war in the south to have much to do with the lad. He knew more about training and leading warriors than he did about raising sons. He knew nothing about how to be a father to a thirteen-year-old boy.

It had been different with Amhar and Lacheu, his true-born sons, whom he had known from the cradle. Medraut was uncommonly mature for his age, not yet a man but far too old for Arthur to have the first clue about being a father figure to. It had been left to Guenhuifar to take care of him and that probably hadn't helped. Medraut had known nothing but women in his life; lacking any sort of male role model which he sorely needed. All Arthur knew was that he was not it.

Arthur gave him a position in the teulu as was only right and he had been surprised at the lad's prowess. Guenhuifar had not neglected his studies in that regard or rather, Caurtam hadn't. Medraut was skilled, strong and courageous. In every conceivable respect he was the perfect warrior. Yet there was a sullenness to him, a hidden rage that only surfaced once in a blue moon but it was always there and it unnerved Arthur.

But Medraut was well-liked in the teulu and he led the men well. Arthur had given him a troop of nine warriors and Medraut had made it his own, instilling discipline and respect and ultimately, proving himself at the Battle on the River Glen the previous year.

"If I know those young rascals, they've returned already and are warming their bellies with some ale before reporting in," said Cei. "What say you we go down there and give them a start?"

"If Medraut has any sense he'll report directly to me," said Arthur. "Besides, I have this accursed banquet up at the palace this evening. King Edelsie wants me. He wants to flex his muscle and show his noblemen that trade routes will be protected for the foreseeable future."

Cei grinned as he rose and retrieved his helm. "When it comes to leadership, you're welcome to all the hobnobbing with nobility. I'm for the ale tent and then my bunk. I'll send Medraut up with a flea in his ear if I see him."

Medraut

As they entered the clearing, Medraut knew at once that somebody was hiding in the bushes on the other side. The group of Saeson they had pursued for the best part of an hour were small in number and it was entirely possible that they might be lying low rather than making for the river and risk being cut down.

The troop of ten riders drew up, spears poised. The rustling in the bushes died down.

"Shall we charge them?" asked Alan, the most senior of Medraut's men. "We'll run them through before they have a chance to bolt from their foxhole!"

"No," said Medraut, holding up a gloved hand to stay his men. "Come on out!" he shouted in the direction of the wavering bushes. "It's alright, the Saeson have passed!"

A man rose tentatively from the undergrowth and gazed at the mounted troop with a pale face and nervous, darting eyes. He wore shabby clothes of leather and rough-spun wool. Around his neck glinted the iron ring of a thrall.

"A slave …" said Medraut. "What are you doing this side of the river? Can you speak British?"

"Aye, lord!" said the thrall in the British dialect of the north-east. "I am no Sais!"

"Then you are a free man from this moment on for I'll leave no Briton in Sais shackles. What's your name and how came you to be a slave of the enemy?"

"My name is Bebro and I hail from the rich farmland of the Lindis Wolds. I was taken in one of the Sais raids three winters ago."

"And you have only just escaped?" Medraut asked.

"Aye, a man will resort to desperate measures when he learns that his homeland will soon be put to the torch. I've family in the Wold; a young laddie I've not seen these three years."

"What do you mean 'put to the torch'?" Medraut asked.

"Afloeg and Wintra are mounting an invasion," said Bebro. "They are planning to cross downriver and march on the settlements in the Wold, taking Banovallum by surprise."

"When is this invasion to take place?" Medraut asked.

Bebro shrugged. "They were all but ready to march before I escaped."

"Then they will be on the move," said Medraut. "Probably crossed the river already."

"We should ride back to Arthur so that the teulu can be mustered in time," said Alan.

"And leave the people of the Wolds to die while we flee west? No."

"We are but ten men!"

"But the Taifals are less than three leagues from here. We could warn them and organise a defence of the villages in the Wolds." He turned to one of his other riders. "Pasgen, ride hard for the fort and get word to Arthur that Afloeg is on the march. Tell him he must ride out and join us before the walls of Banovallum!"

"Yes sir!" said the warrior, with a salute.

Medraut turned to the thrall. "We shall see to it that your slave collar is removed when we reach the

Taifals. Ride with Morfran. If you can stand his ugly face, that is."

There was a low chuckle for Morfran was renowned for being ugly as sin. A face shaped like a boulder, patched with tufts of black hair that somewhat resembled eyebrows flashed a rotten-toothed grin at the thrall as he was helped up onto the saddle. Then the troop was off, riding hard towards the road that connected Lindum with Banovallum.

Arthur would no doubt disagree with his decision, Medraut reflected as they rode. But that was where he and Arthur differed. Medraut often found it hard to believe that the penteulu was the same Arthur who had stolen the Cauldron of Rebirth from the Morgens; who had rescued Ambrosius Aurelianus from the Sais-occupied town of Cair Badon; the Arthur who had won countless battles against Albion's enemies and whose name had become legend across the island. These were the tales Medraut had heard repeatedly ever since Guenhuifar had brought him to Cair Cunor. Arthur's name was spoken of as if he were a great hero of old like Bran or Caswallawn. But the fight seemed to have gone out of him at some point. Medraut had often seen him at the rear of the ranks, his face grim, his shoulders slumped like a man twice his age. It was almost as if the Arthur of legend had died and all that remained was his shadow, overseeing battles fought by younger men. The name lived on but the man had died long ago.

They had gone barely half a league along the road before the bushes atop the escarpment wavered with the passing of several figures. Medraut knew they had been tricked before the orders to dismount were shouted at them in guttural and heavily accented British.

Spearmen bearing the unmistakable round shields of the Saeson ran onto the road, blocking it with one of their dreaded shield walls. Men on horseback rode down from the escarpment on the other side, heavy swords and axes in their hands.

Medraut raised his fist in the air and the troop slid to a halt mere feet from the bristling shield wall. They were vastly outnumbered.

"Get off your horses if you want to live!" repeated the voice. It came from the mouth of a grey-bearded man who wore an iron helm. Pale and unblinking eyes peered through its two loopholes.

The thrall slid down from Morfran's saddle and scurried for safety behind the Sais lines. It was clear who had betrayed them. The scouting party they had followed that morning had been a ruse. The 'escaped thrall' left in their wake was merely bait for the trap. *And I fell for it*, Medraut thought bitterly.

"They have sent a messenger to Arthur," said the thrall to the Sais chief.

Medraut's men cursed and told the false thrall, in no uncertain terms, what they would do to him if they ever got their hands on him.

"You won't catch my man," said Medraut, his voice sour. "Sais scum on stolen horses are no match for a rider in the Teulu of the Red Dragon!"

If he had hoped to instil some sort of awe in his captors, he had been mistaken for the Sais chief shared a joke with his men in his own language at which they all laughed heartily. No riders were sent after Pasgen.

They were led south to the shores of the Black River where several shallow-bottomed boats were waiting for them. *This has been well-planned*, thought Medraut. They were bundled into the boats and then rowed across to the fens on the other side. Reeds towered over them as the boats navigated a path through the marsh, deep into enemy territory.

With much hauling and cursing, they were led out of the boats and then taken on foot across grassy plains to a village of thatched longhouses circled by a wooden palisade. All was of green-cut wood and fresh thatch. *This is a new village*, Medraut realised. A *Sais* village built on stolen land.

Villagers circled them as they were pushed forward. Faces jeered, leered and mouthed obscenities at them. Tawny beards foamed with wroth while flaxen-haired women screeched hate at them as they were ushered to the centre of the village. These were no Britons living under Sais rule. This was a settlement of Angles newly come to these shores. Afloeg's rule over the lands south of the Black River had clearly encouraged further migration of Wintra's countrymen, some from his kingdom, some surely from across the sea, seeking new homes on lands now considered conquered.

The prisoners were corralled into a wicker pen like livestock, their hands still bound. Three posts had been erected in the central plaza of the settlement and a gathering of sorts was converging. Medraut had the horrible feeling that a show was about to take place.

Heads turned almost in unison as a figure emerged from one of the longhouses. A hush settled over the crowd born either from great respect or great fear. The man who approached wore the long gown of a priest but there was no crucifix on him. It was a pale garment and Medraut was put in mind of the bards. His hair was long and jangled with ornaments of bone and bronze. His face was drawn but his eyes were as twin embers, burning with a terrible energy.

"Who's that?" asked Alan, his voice quavering.

"My guess is that it is Scurwulf," said Medraut.

Alan fell silent, his face pale.

Up ahead, Scurwulf wove his way between the posts. He spoke to the grey-bearded warrior who had captured them and an order was given. Three of the captured Britons were selected from the pen and dragged out. They were led over to the posts and their hands were untied and then re-fastened behind them, binding them to the stakes.

A rhythm was taken up on skin drums and old Scurwulf began to recite holy rites in the Angle tongue. Medraut could make out none of it but he had a fair idea that the mad priest was appealing to his gods. He had heard of the Sais deities. The thunder god, the one-eyed god of wisdom and others; pagan gods that demanded blood sacrifice.

Rope was brought forth and looped around the neck of one of the captives. The crossed ends were given to two men and, at a word from Scurwulf, the men began to pull.

"No!" Medraut cried. The thought that three of his comrades – men from his own troop – were to be sacrificed, *murdered*, before their eyes was too much for him.

Human sacrifice was all but unheard of these days. It was well-known that the druids had practised it but the obliteration of that order by the Romans and the consequent four centuries that had seen the gradual introduction of Christianity had put a stop to it. It was whispered that the Saeson sacrificed humans to their gods in more remote parts of their homelands across the North Sea but there had been no indication that such barbarity had been carried to Albion. This Scurwulf was evidently a priest of the very oldest and most savage kind.

There was nothing they could do. As they watched their companion grow purple in the face, the vein in his forehead bulging and his lips mouthing unknown prayers, Scurwulf produced a dagger from his robe. In three strides he was by the dying man's side and, with one swift jerk, he thrust the blade in between his ribs.

The drumming stopped. The prisoner gasped as the rope was loosened. Scurwulf drew out the dagger and the man slumped forward, his body held partially upright by the pole to which he was tied, blood dripping onto the hard-packed ground.

"You bastard!" Medraut yelled. He strained at his bonds but to no avail. Even if he could break free, even if he could hurdle the wicker walls that enclosed them, he would be cut down by the nearest spearman. All he could do was watch impotently as the rope was tightened around the throat of the next of his comrades with the knowledge that, once three dead men hung from the posts, three more would be plucked from the corral.

It all seemed like pointless butchery. It was clear that there was to be no attack on Banovallum and that they had been lured into a trap, but to what end? A diversion seemed likely. Medraut had sent a rider to Lindum. While they sat here waiting to be murdered one by one, Arthur was probably riding east with the entire teulu to counter an invasion that wasn't happening. And, as he did so, he would leave the portion of the Black River directly south of Lindum unguarded. If an invasion was to take place, then that was where it would happen. He had been such a fool! By the time Arthur got here they would all be dead and Lindum would be in Afloeg and Wintra's hands!

They watched, unable to look away as the next of their comrades was butchered and then the next. When it was over, the gate to the corral opened and rough hands reached for more victims for the mad priest's rites.

A bell began to ring in Medraut's ears, distant at first and he thought it was a sound only he could hear, something brought on by the gut-wrenching madness of the situation. But, as it grew in intensity, he noticed that others could hear it too. The guards wheeled away from their grisly business and glanced fearfully at the palisades.

There was a great commotion in the village. The rites temporarily forgotten, the gathering looked about, not knowing what to do. Scurwulf had a face like a thundercloud and, as warriors began to muster themselves, it became clear that his grand show was being put on hold.

The warriors headed towards the north gate. The crowd dispersed and vanished indoors. Scurwulf scampered off, holding up his robes as he ran. A gentle breeze swept across the plaza, sending billows of dust into the thatch of the longhouses.

"Sir," said Alan in a low whisper. "The gate to the corral …"

"Is untethered, yes I see it," Medraut replied.

"Shall we make a move?"

"Yes, but slowly. And keep your heads low!"

The ringing of the bell had thrown the village into enough of a panic that the guarding of a few prisoners had been dismissed as a matter of little concern. They had effectively been forgotten as all men with any fighting skill had marshalled at the north gate which was now opening.

Medraut shuffled towards the wicker gate and pushed it aside with his shoulder. Peering out, he looked about to make sure there was nobody in the vicinity. "Follow me close!" he hissed over his shoulder to his five remaining comrades.

He led them towards the shadows of the nearest longhouse and waited, his back to its planks until the last of his comrades had made it safely to cover. After peeking around the corner to check that the coast was clear, they were up and running the last of the distance towards the palisade. Alan gave Medraut a leg up and he swung himself over the sharpened timbers, wincing as they scraped his ribs. With him leaning down and Alan pushing up, between them they hauled the rest of the troop up and over the palisade to the other side. When there was just Alan left, Medraut reached down and gritted his teeth as

Alan grabbed hold of his bound hands and scrambled up to join him. Then, as one, they swung their legs over and dropped to the other side.

Arthur

Wine sloshed into Arthur's cup, filling it almost to the brim. The servant mopped the lip of the jug with a cloth and retreated as Arthur lifted the cup to his lips, gazing over its rim and across the food-strewn trestle table at his host.

King Edelsie was a man in his winter years and his grey hair, lined face and sagging belly were marks of pride for a king who had held on to his territory far longer than most managed to. He wore simple clothes of good quality material but little gold ornamentation. His finery was minimal compared to some of the kings Arthur had seen in the southern kingdoms. In all ways, Edelsie's appearance matched his surroundings.

The great dining room of the palace was a sombre reflection of past glories. Cracked and crumbling plaster and missing tiles in the vast mosaic floor spoke of Roman grandeur inherited by a people who lived in more meagre times. And with annual flooding and Sais wolves hammering on the doors of the kingdom, it was a wonder that Lindum had survived this long.

"I blame myself, naturally," King Edelsie said to his assembled guests. "I should have drowned that pup and his wretched mother along with him. It would have saved us all a lot of bother!"

Arthur gathered that he was talking of Afloeg and his mother – Edelsie's own granddaughter – who had been a babe in arms when the kingdom of the North Angles had found itself conveniently without a ruler.

There was a nervous clearing of throats and examining of plates as the assembled host tried to ignore the talk of infanticide. Edelsie appeared to recognise that he had misjudged his audience. "Well, what am I to do with this wretched spawn of my loins? Blood means little when it is watered down by Sais filth!"

If anybody present found it strange that Edelsie had not thought such a thing when he had married his daughter to King Athelberht all those years ago, they did not dare speak their piece now.

"Indeed," said one nobleman. "Does your highness intend to conquer the kingdom of the North Angles once the lands north of the Glen have been retaken?"

"By the holy cross, it is!" said Edelsie. "I'll not leave the beaten cur to lick its wounds on my doorstep. I'll drive it off into the hills for good, or in this case, back into the sea!"

"Very prudent of you," said another nobleman. "But what many of your loyal subjects wonder is if the illustrious Arthur and his mighty Venedotian teulu will march with us in such an enterprise."

"My job is to protect the kingdom of Lindis," said Arthur, feeling expectant eyes upon him once more. It was a look he was growing accustomed to. He had seen it in the eyes of the people of Dumnonia and now he saw it here. "Not to help its king expand his own borders; with all due respect."

"Defeating Afloeg and Wintra and their damnable alliance is only half the battle," said Edelsie. "Before the grass has grown over their graves a new chieftain will be leading the North Angles against my borders. You could ensure the eternal safety of Lindis by smashing them once and for all and giving me reign from here to southernmost borders of Wintra's kingdom."

"If such a thing can be achieved in the same season, then I shall do what I can to aid you. But, as I said, we are here to win back those lands your great-grandson and his Sais ally have stolen from you."

There was an audible disappointment at this for all knew that winning the war and conquering the North Angle lands was far too much to do in one season of campaigning.

There came the sound of hobnailed boots marching towards the doors of the dining room at a furious pace. A guard called out a warning and the one who approached bellowed a tart retort. The doors to the dining room were heaved open and a warrior strode in. He was in a muck sweat; his hair plastered across one side of his face, presumably by his helmet which he had removed and now carried under his arm.

Arthur recognised him as one of Medraut's troop. He rose slowly from his seat as the warrior saluted him, cut a short bow to King Edelsie and waited for permission to talk.

"Out with it, man!" said Arthur.

"The Saeson are planning to cross the border and fall upon Banovallum, sir!"

"When?"

"Perhaps tonight. If not, then very soon."

"How have you come by this information?"

"We encountered a runaway slave who had fled his Sais masters and crossed the Black River, hoping to find his way home. He told us that the Saeson are mustering and intend to launch a surprise attack on the Taifals. Medraut rode on to warn them."

"Damn him!" said Arthur, pounding the tabletop with his fist.

"Did he do wrong?" King Edelsie asked. "I should have thought it wise to warn the Taifals so that they can present some sort of defence of the river until you are able to get there."

"He leads a mere nine men," said Arthur. He glanced at the messenger. "Eight." He didn't know what had made him react with such anger. Medraut had done right but something made him fear for his adopted son who had so willingly charged in to danger against such odds. Even in the company of the Taifals they would surely be outnumbered at Banovallum. But that was Medraut all over. Head for danger and damn the consequences. Sometimes he could be as defiant as Cei only without the bluster. When Arthur admonished him and reminded him that his place in the teulu was as a warrior and not his son, Medraut would only seethe and accept the admonishment with thunder in his eyes.

Well, it couldn't be helped. He had done his duty this time although Arthur had a sick feeling in his gut for his safety. He would just have to hold out until the teulu could come to Banovallum's aid.

"You, lad," he said to Medraut's man. "What's your name?"

"Pasgen, sir,"

Arthur seized a chicken thigh from a silver platter and tossed to him. Pasgen caught it and grinned. "Get that down you and follow me. We must rouse those idlers down at the river and ride out as soon as we can."

They left King Edelsie alone in the dining room, gawping in their wake.

Rather than push their way through the crowded streets of the lower town, they took their horses from the forum stables and made for the east gate. Once free of the town, they galloped south towards the muddy riverbanks where the afternoon light glinted off the river like beaten bronze.

As well as building the temporary fort, Arthur had reinforced the northern bank with a series of palisades, submerged spikes and embankments that extended past the southern wall of Lindum for a mile on either side. Watchtowers gazed across the sluggish, dark waters of the river at the silent trees on the other side. They rode into the fort that stood on the high ground.

"Where is Cei?" Arthur demanded, as he dismounted Hengroen. "Somebody check the ale tent for Cei!"

Cei summarily appeared, looking a little rosy in the face. Arthur gritted his teeth. Cei had never been known to roll into his bunk early when there was an ale pot nearby.

"I hope you're not too much the worse for wear," said Arthur. "Because we ride out tonight!"

"Ride out?" asked Cei.

"Aye! Rouse the teulu! The Saeson intend to cross the river at Banovallum. Medraut is there now, organising the defence. He won't have long so we ride as soon as we are able!"

Cei cursed and strode off, bellowing orders. Arthur headed for his tent and called for his armour bearer to help him into his war gear. When he emerged, strapping on his plumed helmet, Gualchmei, Cundelig and a third man hurried over to him.

"You're not thinking of moving the teulu out now are you?" Gualchmei asked.

"I am, for Banovallum will soon be under siege. Why?"

"You should listen to this." Gualchmei indicated the third man.

Arthur recognised him as one of the Britons who lived south of the river whom he had hired to spy on enemy movements.

"What news?" Arthur asked the man.

"Movements," said the spy. "*Big* movements."

"Heading east?"

"No, north. Here!"

"Are you sure?"

"Afloeg musters the men himself, their ranks bolstered by Angles under Wintra's standard. Every village between the two rivers is sending its warriors."

"Afloeg and Wintra ride here together? You are sure of this?"

"They will be here before dawn!"

Arthur looked to the east where the waters of the Black River flowed away from them. Would Afloeg risk spreading his forces so thin by crossing the river at two different points? *Perhaps it's a trick. Perhaps Afloeg wants me to stay and defend Lindum while a secondary force sneaks across the river at Banovallum. Perhaps this spy has been taken in by a trick or maybe he has been bought by the enemy. Or, perhaps the attack at Banovallum is a ruse to get me to leave Lindum undefended.* Which information was he supposed to trust? What was he supposed to risk; Lindum or Banovallum? *The capital of Lindis or Medraut?*

He pounded his fist into his gloved hand in frustration. "Damn!"

Medraut

"We need to head north and find the river," said Medraut, as they entered the cover of the trees. "Whatever had our captors in an uproar has given us the diversion we need to warn the teulu that they are being tricked."

"We mustn't stray too far west until we've crossed the river," said Alan. "We don't want to come upon Afloeg's invasion force if it is indeed marching on Lindum."

"It will be," said Medraut. "And we've got to get our blasted hands free else we can't run for shit!"

They found a sharp stone and took turns placing the rope that bound their hands against a tree trunk while another struck at the cord with the stone. Soon all were free and rubbing their chafed wrists.

"Scurwulf will soon realise that we have escaped," said Medraut. "We will be hunted before long. Strip off your mail and other bits of armour. We must travel light."

They stripped down to their tunicas and hid their armour in some dense foliage. Then they took up a fast jog north with Medraut leading the way.

They plunged onwards. To the east they could hear the echoes of whatever battle was occupying the attention of the men who had captured them: swords clashing, men and horses screaming. To the west they could hear distant drums beating in the still evening air.

"That's Afloeg's warband alright," said Medraut. "They must be planning to cross the river and fall upon Lindum this night."

The urgency of their mission to warn the teulu not to leave the town undefended spurred them on to greater exertions. The blood pounding in their heads and their stomachs growling for they had not eaten since leaving the fort that morning, they hurried on, ducking under low branches and scrambling over mossy rocks.

The residual heat of the day made them sweat like hogs under the thick canopy of greenery. Their breathing was stifled as they ran and a deep thirst set in.

"I must have a drink of something," said Morfran, his wide, hairy brow glistening with sweat.

"Aye," said Sanddef, the one they called 'angel face' for he was as handsome as Morfran was ugly. "I'm about to drop dead with this heat."

"To think you lot made it into the teulu at all," growled Alan. "All the demons of hell march upon our comrades at Lindum and you two want to stop and wet your beaks! You don't hear my son complaining do you? And he several years younger than you?"

Sanddef and Morfran glanced sheepishly at Alan's son, Lonio, who showed considerable embarrassment at his father's words. He was only sixteen and bastard-born. That hadn't stopped his father from acknowledging him and encouraging him to join the teulu. As this was his first campaign, Arthur had put him in Medraut's troop where his proud father could keep an eye on him.

"Calm, Alan," said Medraut. "None of us have had a bite to eat or a drop to drink all day. We'll fall in our paces from exhaustion if we go on much longer.

Many tributaries of the Black River run through these parts. If we hear the sound of running water, we should be close enough to take a drink without losing too much time."

Morfran and Sandef's faces brightened at this while Alan brooded in silence. They took up the pace again, punctuated by short halts while they listened for the sound of water. Eventually, the chuckle of a brook could be heard in the stillness of the forest and they darted to the west, their hearts pounding and their dry mouths thirsting at the sound of running water.

Moss clung to the rocks of a small rivulet and the water bubbled white as it rushed over its stony bed. The companions gasped as they lay on their bellies and scooped up the chilly water in great handfuls and guzzled it down. They washed their faces and necks, grinning in relief despite their predicament.

"How far do you think we are from the Black River?" Alan asked Medraut.

"My guess is that we are no more than three leagues from the fens," said Medraut. "This brook flows north. We should be able to follow it to where it widens in to a tributary."

"Listen!" hissed Lonio, his young eyes wide and darting.

They listened. The jingle of harnesses and hoofbeats could be heard approaching. Then, a horse whinnied and a man called out to his comrades in the Sais tongue.

"Shit!" said Morfran.

"They must have been following our trail from the village," said Medraut. "Come on!"

They hurried north, following the stream at a distance and keeping to the most densely wooded areas.

The woods petered out and at last they came within view of the fens, their still waters reflecting the darkening sky. Night would fall within the hour.

Medraut came to a halt and glanced at the low-lying lands before them. "We must turn east," he said, glancing at a haze of treetops half a league from them.

"Why?" asked Sanddef. "We can practically see the Black River!"

"Across flat, open country, yes," said Medraut. "And those riders are almost upon us. They would cut us down in minutes if we tried to run across that distance. We have to try and lose them in the forest."

There were audible groans at having to abandon their current trajectory when the border and the relative safety it offered were so close. But there was nothing for it. Medraut was right. They couldn't outrun horses in open country.

"Come on, you dogs!" Alan bellowed. "You heard Medraut. Move your arses!"

The distance to the woods was short but Medraut hoped it would be short enough for them to cross in time. The riders could be heard coming through the trees behind them. They took off at a breakneck pace, their bodies already exhausted. The fear of being ridden down after they had come so far gave extra speed to their exhausted legs. Long grass whipped at them and clusters of heather threatened to trip them as they tried to cross as much country as possible.

"They've seen us!" cried Lonio from the rear of the party.

"Don't look back, Son!" said Alan. "Keep running! Keep pace with me, we're almost there!"

Medraut, his heart feeling as if it were about to burst, forced himself ahead of the group, knowing that these men looked to him to lead them to safety, and he did not want to let them down now. The treeline was so close, yet the sounds of harness and hoof and cries of encouragement from one enemy to another were coming up fast behind them.

They leapt into the shaded ferns of the forest and darted between tree trunks in a desperate attempt to get as deep into the woods as possible. They heard Sais curses behind them as their pursuers crashed into the undergrowth, horses slowing in the face of springy branches and tangled briar. It would take them some time to thread their way through the woods and that was all the time Medraut and his companions were going to get.

They curved around to the north again and pressed on through some of the densest undergrowth they had encountered yet.

"This'll stop the buggers," said Alan with a grin.

"Unless they abandon their horses and pursue us on foot," said Medraut. "Thank the gods they don't have dogs with them."

"I don't understand why they are so keen for our blood," said Sanddef.

"Apart from the fact that we are Britons and Arthur's men at that?" said Morfran.

"I mean, we escaped but why go to such trouble to catch us again? And with the attack on Lindum coming, why waste men chasing us? Surely our capture has served its purpose and the diversion has been pulled off?"

Medraut was silent. He agreed with Sanddef that it was odd for the Saeson to be so persistent in capturing a few runaways when all hell was about to break loose at Lindum. The pale face of Scurwulf haunted his thoughts. The false runaway who had led them into enemy hands had clearly been part of a plan to draw the teulu away from Lindum. But there was another reason for their capture that was almost too hideous to bear contemplating for long. *Blood*. A blood sacrifice to invoke the blessing of the Sais gods. He thought of the three men who had been murdered before their eyes. Rage boiled inside him and he swore that he would redden his blade with the blood of thirty Saeson to avenge them.

The woodland diminished and the lowlands of the fens could be seen once more, the distance to the river now considerably shorter.

"We seem to have lost them," said Alan, glancing back through the trees.

"Aye, they must have given up by now or lost our scent," said Medraut. "We're home free, lads! Come on!"

Refreshed after having walked for a while and with the scent of freedom in their nostrils, they ran the rest of the distance, cutting across empty scrubland to where the wide swathe of reeds denoted the fens.

Wading through the marshy shallows, they plunged into the peat-stained waters of the Black River and struck out for the opposite bank. After hauling themselves up onto the grassy northern bank, they did not stop to rest or even wring out their sodden clothes. The old military road that linked Lindum with Banovallum ran parallel to the river not far to the north of their position and they made for it with all haste.

Upon reaching the road they turned eastwards, hoping to come upon the teulu's heels before it was too late for them to turn back and save Lindum. They had not gone far when they heard the sound of hoofbeats coming down the road towards them.

"The Saeson must have crossed the river between us and the teulu's position," said Medraut. "Quick! Get off the road!"

They hurried into the bushes as the horsemen came into view, hooves thudding on the hard-packed road. As they thundered past, Medraut, from their refuge in the undergrowth, spotted the sigil they bore on their small round shields: a blue dragon on a white field, curling around a red boss to bite at a blue pearl.

"It's the Taifals!" he cried and hurried out onto the road, waving his arms and hailing the mounted warriors.

The Taifals had not forgotten the ways of their ancestors and still wore the conical helmets and knee-length scale armour shirts that had been handed down from father to son, preserved and repaired when needed. Their bowmen shot from the saddle using flat, Persian composite bows the like of which Gualchmei favoured while their heavy cavalry rode fine eastern horses armoured with mail coats.

They spotted him and wheeled about, drawing their horses in a narrow arc that reminded Medraut why these riders were so feared on the fields of battle. They rode at them, spears levelled, ready for the killing thrust. Medraut and his companions held their ground and fought back the urge to flee.

"You are no Saeson," said the leader whom Medraut recognised as Fritigernus, chieftain of the Taifals at Banovallum. "Indeed, I see the face of Medraut peering out of the darkness at me."

"Aye it is I, Fritigernus," said Medraut, stepping forward. "You have a good eye for faces."

"We Taifals are renowned for our sight but it comes easier when your prey wanders out onto the road."

"Prey?"

"We have been sent to find you by Arthur. He would have come himself but things are heating up over at Lindum."

"You mean the teulu hasn't marched for Banovallum? Did my rider not reach Arthur?"

"He did and Arthur knew then to prepare the defences south of Lindum for the worst."

"How did Arthur know it was a diversion?"

"His spies brought him news that all the villages south of the river were mustering their warriors and setting out towards Lindum."

"He has spies south of the river?" That was news to Medraut. The scouting units commanded by Cundelig stuck to the northern bank and western marches of Lindis. They never crossed the river for it was too dangerous.

"They are not men from the teulu," said Fritigernus. "Arthur has persuaded some villagers to inform on Sais movements. He most likely did not want it to be common knowledge to reduce the risk that they might be compromised. When he received news from one of your men that you had gone chasing the word of an escaped slave, he dispatched a rider to us to warn of a possible attack on Banovallum. When Arthur's man found that you never arrived at Banovallum, we assumed you had been captured and carried south of the river. Sais parties have been snatching scouts and small patrols all month. We knew of a Sais settlement not far from the river and so rode out to retrieve you."

Medraut coloured. "Then it was you lot who caused the disturbance north of the village we were taken to."

"Aye. We must have been spotted as we approached their village. Warriors appeared out of nowhere and blocked our path. I'm glad you were able to get out by other means."

"Your rescue attempt may have failed," said Medraut, "but it provided us with enough of a distraction that we were able to slip away. Thank you."

"Well, I'm glad we picked you up on the road. We had given up all hope, for time ran out and we are needed in the west. We must ride now and join Arthur below the walls of Lindum!"

"Have you horses you can spare us?"

Fritigernus nodded. "Spears too but you'll have to bear the shields of the Taifals."

"We would be honoured to," said Medraut, but in truth he burned with shame as well as anger at Arthur. How could he not have told them he had spies south of the river? What good was information on enemy movements if it was not shared with all the teulu? He was willing to bet that Peredur and the other captains knew about it. Instead he and his men had been allowed to blunder ignorantly into a trap. It was humiliating and it could have been avoided had Arthur only trusted him.

The Taifals gave them hard tack, dried meat and mare's milk which they wolfed down, ignoring the pangs of protest from their empty stomachs. The battle was undoubtedly underway already and they did not want to be too late in bringing whatever reinforcement they could. They rode on through the night, exhaustion banished for the time being by the lust for battle that swelled in their hearts.

By the time the walls of Lindum could be seen in the distance, it may as well have been daylight. The air above the water to their left blazed with fire arrows sent from the opposite bank towards the defences Arthur had constructed. Their trailing lights illuminated the hunkered heads of men in boats being rowed across the water, orange flame glinting from iron helms and shield rims.

"By Christ," said Fritigernus. "They must have drawn warriors from every village between here and the Afon Glen."

They spurred their horses in to a gallop and followed the reedy edge of the river to where the spiked palisades had been hammered into the peat. They passed behind the lines of warriors and made for the banner of the red dragon that could be seen atop a hillock, fluttering in the warm breeze off the river.

The figure of Arthur could be made out below it, his shoulders hunched beneath his red cloak.

"I am glad you made it, Medraut," said Arthur, as they rode over to him. He sat astride his horse, overseeing the shore battle as it unfolded below. The boats were unloading in the shallows and Sais warriors were wading through the reeds. Some stumbled and floundered in the water, their legs and abdomens pierced by the sharpened stakes that had been hammered in below the waterline. Arrows were loosed down upon them by Arthur's men standing behind the barricades.

"Why didn't you tell me you had knowledge of the enemy's movements south of the river?" Medraut demanded. "Had I known that they were planning an attack, I would have spotted that trap for what it was a mile off!"

"Trap?" asked Arthur.

"Aye, we were carried off by a Sais raiding party and taken deep within enemy territory. Scurwulf sacrificed three of my men in some bloody rite, the mad bastard! We escaped by the skin of our teeth and were pursued all the way to the river."

"I'm sorry, Medraut," said Arthur, genuine surprise in his eyes. "But I couldn't risk too many people knowing. If the enemy caught one whiff of me having spies in their villages, they would have called the whole thing off."

"You mean you didn't trust me!"

"Of course I trust you, Medraut. But the more people who knew then the greater the risk was for all of us."

Peredur galloped up the slope from the riverbank. "Sir! More boats are setting out from the southern bank. They are heading upstream to a point further west."

"Take your company and engage them as they make landfall," Arthur told him. "We will be able to hold the line here." He turned to Medraut and Fritigernus. "Ride with Peredur's company. Don't let a single Sais get within a spear's throw of the town's western walls."

Medraut stifled a curse and urged his mount away from Arthur to follow Peredur who had ridden off to marshal his company at the foot of the hillock.

The Taifals and Medraut's troop were to lead the vanguard and that was some small consolation to him. At least he would not be forced to ride behind Peredur. And it promised to be a hard fight of it. That suited him too. Despite his exhaustion, all he wanted to do right now was wet his blade in enemy blood for all they had suffered in the last twenty-four hours.

They galloped along the river's edge and could see the boats up ahead already making landfall. Men were wading through the shallows, axes, swords and spears in hand. Round shields were being unslung from their backs. If they were able to form a shield wall the vanguard would take considerable damage in charging them.

Fritigernus yelled out an unintelligible war cry in the tongue of his ancestors which was taken up by the other Taifals. Medraut just gritted his teeth, shifted his spear into an overhand grip and prepared for impact.

The Saeson had seen them and were hurriedly trying to get out of the reeds and present some sort of defence. They were too late. The vanguard slammed into them like a pickaxe, skewering men over the rims of their shields, trampling them under-hoof. Some turned back to the boats, confident that they would not be followed. They were right. The Britons dared not wet their fetlocks in the marshy ground at the river's edge for it would rob them of their mobility and make them sitting targets.

Instead, Fritigernus led the charge to the right, towards the trackway that led away from Lindum's western gate, wheeling around in one of his sharp turns. Medraut was no mean horseman but even he found it a tortuous struggle to follow the curve of the attack and not stray from the pack, even with the fine Arabian mare beneath him who had been trained in the Taifal way. Then, they charged back towards the last of the Saeson who had not fled back to the boats and made a bloody ruin of them.

That last bout of butchery signalled the end of the first Battle of the Black River. The fighting at the barricades had gone in Arthur's favour and what was left of Afloeg's war band limped back to the southern bank in their boats. When dawn broke, the river could have taken on a new name, for its dark, peaty water now flowed red.

Guenhuifar

The winds of winter brought with them the whisper of death. Venedotia lay in the grip of fear; a fear of something worse than the Saeson or the Gaels or the Picts. It was a creeping death that sneaked across the countryside and slithered in through people's doors, snuffing out life and leaving only death as evidence of its passing. The land had fallen into the grip of pestilence.

As Guenhuifar sat in Cair Cunor's praetorium listening to the report of the rider who had nearly killed his mare galloping east from the farmlands of Dunauding, she wondered how widespread the pestilence was in other parts of Albion. *Does Arthur now lead diseased men? Does the teulu find its ranks thinned not by Sais blades, but a more deadly and insidious enemy?*

"Are you saying that the entire village was wiped out by this sickness?" she asked the rider.

"Yes, my lady," said the man, his short cloak swept back over one shoulder and his hair ruffled by the wind of the ride. He was part of a troop that regularly patrolled the marches of the single commote that surrounded Cair Cunor, independently ruled by the penteulu. "We thought it odd that the harvest had only partially been gathered and there were no workers in the fields. We rode in to take a closer look and found the streets deserted but for a few feral dogs. There was an awful stink coming from every roundhouse and when we looked in, great clouds of flies were disturbed. The dead were everywhere."

The man's voice stammered with emotion as he recalled the horrific scenes he had only recently witnessed. Guenhuifar motioned a servant to bring him a cup of wine which he took gratefully. The crowded hall waited patiently as he took a few gulps and tried to steady his nerves.

"You are sure it was the pestilence?" Cadyreith, the steward, pressed him.

"Yes, sir. Nothing else could have wiped out an entire settlement. They had this awful rash all over their bodies, black and crusty. By the church we found mass graves, not properly filled in. They were stuffed with corpses, grey and stinking ..."

"What I fail to understand," interrupted Guenhuifar, eager to move the conversation down a more constructive avenue, "is why they did not send word to us. Or to King Efiaun at Din Emrys. Presumably he is aware that the pest has broken out in his kingdom?"

"Who knows what that man is aware of up in his mountain stronghold?" said Cadyreith. "It wouldn't surprise me if he is entirely ignorant of the fact that his people are dying."

"But how could the whole settlement just die out like that without calling for aid?"

"What aid could they expect to get from us, my lady? All our best healers are with your husband in Lindis. The village undoubtedly had their own and they all perished leaving their final patients to die in their beds, untended and alone. It was a small settlement. I have heard that pestilences can kill several families within ten days. They must have been overwhelmed and devoted their energies to tending the sick and burying the dead. Until it was too late."

Two figures darted in through the doors, their sharp laughter echoing within the sombre chamber. Guenhuifar glared at them and snapped her finger. The two boys – one seven and the other three – fell into a bashful silence. At a motion from their mother they scuttled over to her. Lacheu crawled up into her lap. Guenhuifar kissed him on the forehead while Amhar hovered at her side, watching the assembly with mild interest.

"The Pendraig must be informed," said Cadyreith.

"I would carry the message myself," said the rider, "but I fear that I am all but exhausted …"

"No, I shall send a rider of my own," said Guenhuifar. "You must rest here. You have done well. I will send my message tonight to tell the Pendraig to prepare for our arrival."

They all stared at her in silence.

"You are thinking of removing yourself from here to stay with your father at court?" Cadyreith asked. There was no trace of accusation in his voice but Guenhuifar could feel it nonetheless, just as she saw it in the eyes of the assembled men and women.

"I will not leave a single person within these fortress walls to face this pestilence alone," she said. "I shall remove us in our entirety to Ynys Mon until this pest has run its course. We will be safe enough upon the island and with the teulu gone we are few enough for the Pendraig's stores to feed for the foreseeable future."

"What if the Pendraig fears that *we* carry the pest?"

"We shall leave tomorrow morning. It will take us several days to reach the coast. That will be enough time for us to know if anyone in our ranks is a danger." She tried not to glance at the rider who had so recently walked amongst the dead. There would be enough people scrutinising his every move over the next few days.

The rider eventually put peoples' minds at ease for by the time they had crossed the mountains and reached the straits that separated Ynys Mon from the mainland, he had shown no signs of the pestilence.

But there were more worrying concerns as they made their way down to the muddy inlet from where the ferry operated. The small cluster of stables and houses that had built up around the ferry point was deserted. They poked about and found that it had been abandoned with everything of value taken as if the small group consisting of an innkeeper, a blacksmith and a few other caterers to travellers had simply upped sticks and moved away. There was no sign of the ferry either until, by squinting across the straits, they could see it moored on the other side beneath the shade of the overhanging trees.

"What the hell is going on?" Cadyreith said.

Guenhuifar did not answer. She had a horrible feeling in the pit of her stomach. Across those choppy waters lay her home and family. To be cut off from them with no explanation and the pestilence nagging at their heels was a new kind of fear for her.

"There is always the Lafan Sands ..." said Caurtam, scratching his big beard.

Guenhuifar shook her head. "I won't risk trying to cross on foot. Not with so many of us."

Lacheu sat side-saddle on the pommel of her saddle and she wrapped her wolfskin cloak around him tighter to keep off the chill of oncoming dusk. Amhar watched from the covered wagon behind her, his small, pale face gazing across the darkening waters at a safety that was suddenly denied him.

"Then we must procure a boat of our own," said Caurtam. "Let us try the fishing villages further along the coast."

"Good idea," said Guenhuifar. "Take some warriors with you and see what you can get. Explain to them that we are from Cair Cunor and must get across by the next low tide."

Caurtam rode off and returned after dark. They had made camp on the grassy knoll looking over the inlet. They huddled around small fires, wrapped in all the cloaks they had brought while they shared out the small amount of food they had carried in the wagons.

"We have a boat, my lady," said Caurtam. "But ..."

"What is it?" Guenhuifar asked.

"King Cadwallon has stopped all shipping to Ynys Mon. He has put the ferry out of commission and has halted all trading."

"But why?"

"He fears the pestilence. Several settlements on the Laign Peninsula have been affected. He took immediate precautions to prevent an outbreak on the island."

"While the rest of Venedotia can burn," said Guenhuifar, unable to keep the bitter sentiment unspoken. It wasn't Cadwallon's fault. He had done what any responsible ruler would have. "But what about us?" she said. "He must admit us once he knows that none of us have shown sign of the pest. We deliberately avoided all settlements on the way here and the villages you just spoke with were not affected, were they?"

"No, my lady."

"Then I must speak with him myself. Have the boat ready. I shall make the crossing as soon as the tide goes out."

In the pale light of morning they rowed across. They had barely made landfall when a contingent of warriors rode down to the bay to meet them. They bore the red dragon on their shields which denoted them as members of Cadwallon's household guard.

"No one may land here by order of the Pendraig!" they cried. "Turn your boat around and return to the mainland!"

"I am the Lady Guenhuifar!" Guenhuifar shouted in reply. "Wife of Venedotia's penteulu and daughter of the Pendraig's steward! I demand that you let us pass. We do not carry the pestilence!"

"Can't let anybody pass, my lady," said the leader of the troop.

Guenhuifar hitched up her skirts and strode up the embankment towards them. The warriors looked at each other nervously and even took a step back as if cowering from the pestilence itself.

"Listen to me," she said. "This island is my home. I have led my people from Cair Cunor across the mountains to safety. Not one of us has shown any signs of the pestilence and we have met no one on the trail. Let us in or you can explain to my father and the Pendraig himself why you let the family of Arthur perish on the shores of the mainland while you watched from across the water."

The warriors looked at each other and said nothing. Within a few moments the boat had been sent back across the straits to pick up the next group of refugees.

When Guenhuifar and her entourage rode in under the spiked palisade of Cadwallon's Lys she immediately detected the hostility and suspicion directed at them. This was a settlement cowering behind their walls, barricaded on their fortified island. Visitors were suddenly very unwelcome.

"Thank the Great Mother you came!" said her father as he made his way over to them. He kissed Guenhuifar on the cheek and then stooped down to hug Amhar and Lacheu. "I wanted to send for you as soon as we got word that pestilence was rife on the mainland but the Pendraig wouldn't risk it."

"For that he can't be blamed," said Guenhuifar.

"Sister!" cried Guenhuifach, running over to her. "Are any of you sick? Rashes? Aching backs?"

"Relax, Guenhuifach," said Guenhuifar. "We are all fine. I wouldn't risk coming here if I suspected that any of us were infected."

Guenhuifach looked relieved. "How are you, Sister? And have you heard from Arthur?"

"Not since I last sent word to the Pendraig. They won a great victory at some Black River but Afloeg and his North Angle allies keep regrouping and trying to cross the river at other points. It looks set to be a long season. Perhaps they will have to winter in Lindis."

"That may be just as well," said their father. "The pestilence seems to be moving from west to east. It probably came from Erin. We don't want our victorious heroes to come home to infection and death. Better that they remain in the east for now."

"Yes ..." said Guenhuifach.

"Are you familiar with this pest?" Guenhuifar asked her sister. "Would you recognise the signs?"

"Yes, I believe so," said Guenhuifach.

"Then I think it would be best if you check each and every one of us. It will help convince everybody that we are safe."

"Very well."

The checks took up the rest of the day and as the evening meal was being laid out in the Great Hall, Guenhuifach finished examining her last patient. Not one of them had a rash or any other signs of the ailment and once the news was shared it was as if the entire settlement breathed a collective sigh of relief. They were safe. But it weighed heavily on Guenhuifar's heart when she thought of what might happen to the rest of Venedotia who weren't so lucky to be admitted to the island.

As the days passed, the settlement fell into a false sense of security, complacent in their relative safety. Cadwallon did send riders to the mainland to ensure Venedotia's borders had not been invaded, but these men were thoroughly checked over and quarantined for ten days upon their return while their reports were conveyed to Cadwallon at his Lys.

The word was that the pestilence was sweeping its black hand across the countryside, wiping out small communities while leaving others devastated and mourning. The kings of Venedotia – the proud Dragons of the North – cowered in their forts, refusing all visitors and traders. But the pestilence was a thing unbound by laws and walls and, before long, to everybody's horror it found its way to Ynys Mon.

The first victim was a tanner who came to Guenhuifach with complaints of an aching back. Guenhuifach asked the man to remove his tunica so that she might apply an ointment and when he did so, she noticed the ruddy pimples that covered his lower abdomen.

When she brought news of this to Cadwallon, he ordered the construction of a shelter several miles from the Lys to which the man was banished until the disease had run its course. Guenhuifach was determined to continue treating the man despite the risk to her own health. This meant her own banishment too for nobody would trust a woman who had been in such close contact with the diseased.

Guenhuifar begged her sister to reconsider. "You are putting yourself at the gravest of risks tending to this man! In all eventuality he will not live so why allow yourself to be infected trying to save him?"

"I am a healer, Guenhuifar," Guenhuifach had said. "It is my duty to tend to the sick. We must pray that we might all live to see the end of this pestilence but we cannot turn on each other and let our fear make us monsters. I will tend to this man and, the Goddess willing, he will be the only one affected and

I will return to you in a month's time, as healthy as I ever was."

But the tanner was not to be the only one. Within three days, two more had the rash and were sent immediately to Guenhuifach. The damage had been done. Soon, there were too many sick to be sent to Guenhuifach's hospice in the woods and all knew it was futile in any case.

The sickness began with fever and back pains. Once the fever had died down, the rash emerged and after a few days it turned a crusty black and was excruciatingly painful. Bad cases resulted in death after the twelfth day.

None were spared. Most stayed within their homes, their bowels turned to water, coughing coagulated blood as their bodies ulcerated inside and out. Necessity alone drove people out of their homes. The dead, who were considerable in number, needed burying and blistered hands dug endless graves.

Cadwallon grew desperate. All his pains to isolate Ynys Mon from the plague which ravaged Venedotia had come to naught. None could tell him how the outbreak had occurred. Perhaps somebody had crossed at the Lafan Sands and slipped by the guards he had placed there? Perhaps a small boat had snuck into one of the coves on the north coast? It was pointless to concern themselves with that now. All energies must be focused on surviving the pestilence God or the Great Mother had seen fit to blight them with.

Cadwallon decided that the Morgens had to be consulted. The Nine Sisters of Ynys Mon had played little part in his reign since his coronation but they had been the advisors of the kings of old and were as knowledgeable about Modron's intents as anyone.

"Do you forget that they supported Meriaun in the civil war?" Guenhuifar said to Cadwallon the night he made his plan known to them.

"I have not," the Pendraig replied. "Nor have I forgotten their promise to me; that the evil that led them down that path has been cut out of their order. Anna is dead. The Morgens have not caused trouble these years I have ruled."

"The Christians won't like it," said Cadyreith, glancing briefly at Queen Meddyf.

"Indeed no," Meddyf replied. "Why we must resort to soothsayers and pagan priestesses is beyond me. I will be content to pray to the Lord God for deliverance."

"Whatever your feelings towards the Morgens may be," said Cadwallon, "they are renowned healers. It is for that reason I wish to consult them."

Cadwallon asked Guenhuifar to accompany him to the sacred lake near the western coast of the island. She shuddered at the thought. She had been there twice before; once with Arthur when they had attempted to steal the Cauldron of Rebirth and again when she had gone off on her own renegade quest to foil an assassin. Upon that second occasion, the Morgens had been somewhat helpful to her and Cadwallon clearly believed that she had developed something of a favourable acquaintance with the Nine.

Guenhuifar wasn't at all sure this was the case. She had a feeling that the Morgens helped people when it was in their own interests and those interests were as changeable as the wind. They listened only to the Goddess and Her voice was a fickle, vague thing known only to them.

She didn't feel at all up to travelling in any case. Her face was ravaged by spots, her whole body ached and the thought of riding a horse made her feel like she wanted to die. Besides, with Amhar and Lacheu wailing, their beautiful skin ruptured with spots, she was loathe to leave them if only for a day. But the Pendraig had requested her presence so she joined the small, miserable company that trotted out of the Lys on a bitter autumn morning and made their way slowly and painfully across the breadth of the island.

The strange villagers who lived to serve the Morgens showed no alarm as they arrived at the shores of the sacred lake. They did not cower from them, fearful of being contaminated as others might have. Guenhuifar wondered if they trusted their priestesses so much that they thought they were protected even from pestilence.

The Morgens emerged from their great roundhouse and at once Guenhuifar's heart sank. She didn't know why. The customs of the Morgens were a mystery but whenever they changed the colour of their gowns, you could be sure that something was afoot. After Cadwallon's coronation they had donned white, symbolic of a new era. When she had visited them three years later they had worn blood-red robes, symbolic of something else. Now they were dressed from head to toe in black, just as they had been thirteen years ago when Anna had used the Cauldron to try and bring Venedotia to its knees.

"Why are you dressed in black as if in mourning?" Cadwallon asked them. "We are not dead yet."

"Death is a phase just as night is," said one of the Morgens.

"Or winter," spoke another.

"Or the new moon," said a third.

"I don't have time for riddles," said Cadwallon. "We are dying. The pestilence has swept Venedotia leaving corpses in its wake. Tell us what can be done, I beg of you."

"What can be done?" One of them echoed. "What can be done about winter? What can be done about night? What can be done about—"

"I said I want no riddles!" he interjected angrily.

"I think they are trying to tell us that there is nothing that can be done," said Guenhuifar impatiently.

"The Lady is right," said the Morgen. "There is nothing to be done to change Modron's plans."

"Plans?" asked Cadwallon. "Are you telling me this is all part of the Great Mother's plan for us? Is this a punishment? Now you sound like the Christians! What have we done to deserve this?"

"Not a punishment. A necessary step. All great change in the land is marked by a *gormes* – a great oppression. Just as dawn emerges from night, spring from winter and the waxing crescent moon from darkness, so too must the land shed itself from a terrible suffering."

"Well what the hell does that mean?" Cadwallon demanded. His rage choked him and he doubled over as he coughed up a glob of blood. His attendants rushed to assist him.

"We can give you healing herbs and balms," the chief Morgen said.

"We have healers of our own," said Guenhuifar. "My sister tends to the sick, though she is sick herself."

"We are sure her skills are admirable, yet our order has been known as healers since time immemorial. We can ease the suffering but do not expect us to change Modron's will. We are but her servants."

There was little more to be said. They took bundles of herbs and jars of balm from the Morgens along with advice on how to apply them and departed. It had been useless. The Morgens spoke in riddles as always and yet it was hard not to agree with them that a great change was coming. The land and its people indeed suffered. *But to what end?*

As the days went by the death toll became devastating. Over half of all the young children in the settlement perished despite Guenhuifach's best efforts and the medicines given to them by the Morgens. Mercifully Amhar and Lacheu held on and Guenhuifar gave thanks to every god she could name.

Almost all of the elderly died including Guenhuifar's father. She and her sister wept bitterly by the side of his grave in the overcrowded cemetery. They wept for their father and for the very world they knew that seemed to be dying as the snows began to appear on the mountains across the straits. Come spring, what would be left of all they had built? What would be left of *them*?

The deepest feeling of despair was yet to come. Two weeks after the first outbreak, King Cadwallon, Pendraig of Venedotia, died. A crisis of succession was inevitable. Cadwallon's eldest son, Maelcon, had been handed over to the Church years ago after his disgraceful conduct in trying to have his own uncle assassinated. It had been Guenhuifar who had foiled that plot and unmasked the young prince's attempt to frame King Etern of Eternion for Owain's murder. Cadwallon's youngest son, Guidno, was only just a grown man, yet he screamed in his own torment while Queen Meddyf tended to his sores, her own pretty visage marred beyond recognition. If Guidno died then old envies would erupt once more as the other kings looked towards the vacant throne.

But such things could wait until the spring when the survivors of this deadly blight could fight it out amongst themselves. As it was, none would know of Cadwallon's death for some time, for trade and travel to Ynys Mon was still prohibited, however, redundantly.

It was agreed by all that the quarantine now served a different purpose. Rather than keeping out the pestilence, it now kept word from reaching the rest of the kingdom that it no longer had a king.

Arthur

News of the pestilence that was sweeping across Albion reached Lindis just as the fringes of the fens were beginning to grow a skim of ice in the mornings. Afloeg's Sais horde had been pacified for another winter and the thought of travelling home across a disease-ridden landscape was not so terrifying to Arthur as the thought of what he might find when they reached Venedotia. How badly had the pest ravaged their homeland? How many were dead? *Guenhuifar? Amhar and Lacheu?*

It was normal to demand haste from a warband at the end of a campaigning season when all that stood between a teulu and the journey home was the dismantling of camps, packing up of equipment and foraging enough victuals to last them, but Arthur was as a man possessed as he barked orders and worked his men through the night so as to be on their way as soon as possible.

King Edelsie wanted to hold a feast to celebrate their victories, small though they were. The Saeson had been pushed back, battle after battle, all along the Black River but nobody was under any illusion that they were beaten for good. Come spring they would return. And so too must the Teulu of the Red Dragon.

Arthur had no desire to waste time feasting and listening to speeches but he supposed he owed it to his men for one final celebration to mark the end of the season. And besides, he couldn't turn down King Edelsie. The old fool was desperate to ensure that they would return to safeguard his kingdom for him when the Saeson began looking north again.

It was a raucous, drunken affair as celebratory feasts always are and snow began to settle on the rooftops of Lindum as they toasted themselves within; both with drink and the warmth of great hearths where meat sizzled and spat. Arthur just wanted to leave, and on the following morning, with aching heads, the men roused themselves.

They found forts abandoned and many settlements little more than deserted gatherings of mouldy thatch. Whenever they did come across small populations, they avoided them, pressing onwards towards the mountains. It was only when they got to Deva that Arthur risked lodging the teulu within a town's walls.

They were told by their Powysian hosts that the pestilence had mercifully moved on although the cemeteries were full to bursting and the digging of mass graves had become a necessity. The population of the west had been ravaged and with so few people to gather the harvest, the granaries were barely full. That was hardly an issue, said Menw sombrely. Such a severely reduced population would not need full granaries this winter.

As they marched on through the moorlands of Rhos before cutting south-west towards Cair Cunor, Arthur began to dread what he might find upon arrival. The pestilence may have burned itself out and he was confident that none in the teulu had been infected, but had the damage already been done to their loved ones?

When he saw no guards atop Cair Cunor's palisade he nearly slid off Hengroen's back to lie weeping on the road. There wasn't a sign of life about the place. Menw placed a hand on his shoulder to steady him.

"There are no banners either," the old bard said. "In all probability your wife has moved the household to a safer location."

Arthur steeled himself with this hope as they entered the fortress and saw to the billeting of the warriors. As they poked about in the deserted buildings his spirits rose for it was clear that there had been no death here, only an orderly retreat.

"Guenhuifar got them out before the plague reached them," he said, tears of relief brimming in his eyes.

"Aye, she's a smart lass," Cei agreed. "She'll have done right by them."

They found old Deacon Arminius in his lodging by the church. His face was pock-marked and he looked frail but he was alive. The cemetery was covered with freshly-turned earth and the poor man's hands were calloused from the digging of graves. He was the only person left in the vicinity. He told them that Guenhuifar had moved the entire household to Ynys Mon while he had stayed to minister to the folk in the nearby settlements.

"I ride north tomorrow," Arthur told Cei. "See to the settling of the teulu. Make ready for winter."

"You ride north alone?" asked Medraut. "Let me come!"

"No!" said Arthur a little more harshly than he meant to. "There may be pockets of pestilence in the countryside and we don't know how badly Ynys Mon was affected. I won't risk more lives than I have to."

"Then let me go instead," Medraut persisted. "Why risk your own life?"

"Because it's my family!" Arthur snapped. "Help Cei prepare the fortress for our homecoming. Guenhuifar and I may choose to winter here. If any of our people are left alive that is."

He rode out as soon as it was light and made good time in reaching the coast. He found the ferry out of order and assumed that Cadwallon had quarantined the island to save it from the pestilence. His hopes soared at this for it meant that his family were surely safe.

He made for the Lafan Sands and waited impatiently for the tide to go out. Then, leading Hengroen by the bridle, he crossed to the island.

He was overjoyed to take Guenhuifar in his arms and he hugged his two boys so tightly they began to squirm for air. His heart broke to see their pock-marked faces. They had been relatively lucky compared to some poor folk who would be disfigured until the end of their days but it was a sore reminder of what they had been through and what they had all lost.

Arthur was stunned at the news that Cadwallon had died. He was equally astonished that Venedotia had been without a high-king for some time without even knowing it.

"I wanted to keep the news from reaching the other kingdoms until our position was a little more secure," Meddyf explained. "We have lost so very much and with you and the teulu gone, we are as a flickering candle caught in a draught. Once word of my husband's death is out, Venedotia's enemies will begin to circle us like wolves. The Picts won't forget old hurts and the Gaels won't let a chance to recover their lost territories pass them by."

"Picts and Gaels can gnash their teeth all they want," said Arthur. "The teulu sits at Cair Cunor and if any of the buggers dare overstep their bounds, I'll make sure the Red Dragon scorches their arses for them so they'll think twice in future."

Meddyf smiled although it was clearly an effort for her. "It's not just Venedotia's enemies that have me worried. It's Cadwallon's own kin."

"The other kings?"

"Yes. The old grievances have never fully healed. I fear that some may try to take advantage of Cadwallon's death and seize a power they have no right to."

"But Cadwallon has heirs! Grown men at that!"

"Maelcon was Cadwallon's pick for the throne but he is lost to us in the cloisters of Illtud's abbey."

"There is Guidno."

"He is too young."

"He's seventeen!"

"Yes, but his spirit is younger than his years. And he is so sickly. It is a miracle that he survived the pestilence. It left him ravaged and, although God saw fit to spare him, he is still very weak and gets tired so quickly. He is not ready for the responsibilities of being a king, and the Pendraig at that."

Arthur had to agree with her. Guidno had always been a sensitive, insecure child. He might make for an indecisive king but kingship was a skill to be learned, surely? And truly, what other choice did they have? Maelcon was out of the picture as Meddyf had said, and that was just as well to Arthur's mind. If ever there was a child more unsuited to be a king then it was the petty, vindictive Maelcon.

"At any rate," she continued, "thank God you brought the teulu back to winter in Venedotia. I've been at my wits' end! What if the other kings don't support Guidno? It will be civil war again …"

"No it won't," Arthur assured her. "Guidno is Cadwallon's son. They *must* support his claim."

"Do you trust them?"

Arthur was silent. In truth he did not. As Meddyf had said, old hurts had not been forgotten. "Perhaps he should have a regent. To guide him through the early part of his reign."

Meddyf looked at him keenly. "Arthur … you?"

"No, not me!"

"But you are the penteulu! Who better to safeguard our young king? All Venedotia looks to you for you have led our warriors through so much and to such great victories. And you are the boy's uncle, after all."

"It is precisely *because* I lead the teulu that I must not be regent," said Arthur. "The other kings would see it as a military coup. Who could refuse me with five-hundred warriors at my back? No, it must be somebody else. Owain perhaps?"

"Yes!" said Meddyf. "Owain rules a small kingdom but with your support he would be strong enough to keep the other kings at bay if they attempt anything."

"Would that not amount to the same thing as Arthur being regent?" Guenhuifar said.

"More or less," Arthur replied. "But Owain would be an easier choice for the other kings to swallow. He is the late Pendraig's full brother and a natural regent for Guidno."

"Good," said Meddyf. "I will send for him before I make it known that Cadwallon has died."

"Are you telling me Owain doesn't know his own brother is dead?"

"I had to keep things together until the pestilence passed," said Meddyf. "Cadwallon ensured that nobody came or went from the island. I have upheld his ruling. But now people are beginning to wonder, I am sure. The time has come. We must make our plans."

Owain arrived in a matter of days along with his queen, Elen, and their household. By that time, Arthur had called certain members of his own following to Ynys Mon and among them was Menw who arrived a day ahead of Owain.

"The Great Mother is cruel sometimes," Menw said upon learning how few had survived the pestilence.

"We went to the Morgens," said Guenhuifar. "But aside from some medicines my sister could have mixed up herself, all we got was riddles out of them."

"Did you expect anything more from them?" said the bard. "They interpret the signs as they see them but they have no power other than that."

"They said the pestilence was a sign of great change."

Menw sniffed. "Seeing as how we are now without a king, our settlements and villages are devastated and winter is about to set in, I'd say that was anything but a riddle."

Owain was distraught upon hearing of his brother's death and insisted on visiting Cadwallon's grave immediately. It stood a little to the north-west of the Lys in a cemetery set aside for the pagans. It was a small cemetery in comparison to the plot of Christian graves that surrounded the church. The recent devastation of the pestilence made the area a gloomy scene that stank of freshly-turned earth and shallow graves.

"I owe my very kingdom to him," said Owain, wrapped in his bear-skin cloak as they stood by the graveside. "Father wouldn't hear of it but Cadwallon understood how important it was to me. So he made me a king. Could a man ask for a better brother?"

"He gave you your kingdom because he saw that you were fit to rule it," said Meddyf. "Now, say you will rule Venedotia as regent until Guidno is old enough to be crowned Pendraig."

Owain turned his reddened eyes to look at her and then at Arthur. "Aye," he said. "I'll do it. The young lad is the heir to the eight kingdoms and the gods help anyone who tries to deprive him of that."

PART III

"…The second Gwenhwyfach struck upon Gwenhwyfar: and for that cause there took place afterwards the Action of the Battle of Camlan…"
- Three Harmful Blows of the Island of Britain. The Triads of the Island of Britain.

Medraut

Medraut sat astride his horse watching the farmers leading the bulls into the byres for slaughtering and thought back to his youth on the Isle of the Dead. He had been in charge of the goats and it had been his job to preserve the meat for their winter larders. Those days were hazy in his memory even though he had been nearly fully-grown when he had left his grandmother. He wondered if she was still alive. Probably not. The winters were harsh on the western coast; nothing but hail and bitter winds.

As yet another winter sank its teeth into the land, Medraut found himself not resenting it as much as he had other winters. The campaign in Lindis had sated his lust for excitement for the time being though the gods knew he might develop a craving for it once more before the endlessly long nights and dull days were over.

He was close to Guenhuifach; that was probably it. And now that she had moved out of the Lys's precinct he was able to visit her more or less on a whim. The makeshift infirmary she had set up to deal with victims of the pestilence in its early days had proved to be a convenient arrangement for everybody. There was more bed space for those who required observation as well as ample storage room for all her herbs and plants. The isolated place of healing became a permanent infirmary for everybody's ailments.

He had helped her enlarge the infirmary and they had spent many gloriously frosty days thatching a roof on a larger storage hut and extending the wattle walls of the bed area. When they were done they would eat in her small bothy and make love as the snow began to fall in the night air outside. Nobody saw anything inappropriate in two unmarried members of the opposite sex spending so much time together alone in the woods. She was his aunt after all. It would be perverse to suggest anything might be going on between them.

He turned his horse and followed the track that led back towards the Lys. It was late and he wanted to drop in on Guenhuifach and surprise her before the evening meal in the Great Hall. He often took the opportunity to ride out and leave court life behind him for a brief spell. It felt good to breathe the cold winter air and let the silence of the pines envelop him. It was so crowded up at the Lys now that all the other kings had arrived to pledge their support to Guidno.

As he approached the point on the road where the narrow footpath led off into the trees in the direction of Guenhuifach's infirmary he spotted a figure walking with his back to him. He wore the robe of a monk with the hood up.

"Can I give you a ride, Father?" Medraut asked, trotting up alongside the man. The snow was deep and the hem of the monk's robe was sodden. Besides, he was a slight figure and would be a light burden for his mare to carry the short distance to the Lys.

As the monk turned his head, Medraut saw that his light frame was due to his youth. He could not have been much more than twenty. Little more than a *novitiate* in the clergy.

"That is kind of you, sir," the monk replied. "But as a servant of God, I am bound to my oath of humility. I have walked this far. I can walk the rest of the way unaided although I would be glad of the company if you could spare it."

"What brings you to Cadwallon's Lys?" Medraut asked, as they continued side by side. "We have some Christians but most of Cunedag's kin are followers of the old path."

"Yes, the pagan streak is still strong in the descendants of Cunedag," said the monk. "But I come not to preach nor to condemn. I have been sent by my order to oversee the pledging of the Dragons of the North to their new king."

Medraut glanced sidelong at the monk. "I had no idea the Christian Church took such an interest in the affairs of pagan kings."

"The Church is interested in all corners of Albion and what occurs in them. The pledging ceremony will be overseen by members of pagan orders, am I right?"

"Yes, old Menw will be presiding over the ceremony as he does over most things in these parts."

"Then is it not only right that a representative of the Christian faith be present? After all, Venedotia's kings may be pagan but its people are predominantly followers of Christ."

"I suppose so," said Medraut. In truth, religion had played little part in his life since he had left his grandmother's small sect as a youth. He supposed he was as superstitious as the next warrior and keen to stay in the favour of the gods as much as his life depended upon it. But the differences between the old gods and the new Roman god and his prophet held little interest for him.

"Tell me, warrior," said the monk. "What do you think of your new king and his regent?"

Medraut shrugged. "The king is little more than a boy. Of him only time will tell." He had a fair few things he could say about Owain of Rhos but, as none of them were pleasant, he refrained from telling them to a stranger. "I serve the banner of the Red Dragon, not whoever sits upon the throne of Venedotia."

"It will be Owain who will sit upon Venedotia's throne for the time being," said the monk. "Figuratively speaking, of course. Not a popular man in many parts of Venedotia."

"Oh?"

"He was never a king under the old Pendraigs. Cadwallon showed unbecoming favour in giving him Rhos and creating another king for the all the others to bicker with."

"The Church doesn't approve of Cadwallon's decision?"

"The more kings there are the more fighting there is. This is just simple fact."

They travelled the rest of the way in silence. The gates to the Lys stood open as there were so many visitors. The guards atop the palisade glanced down at Medraut and his clerical companion with curiosity.

Medraut left the man to find his way about and went to stable his horse. He was starving and the smells of roasted meat and fresh bread from the Great Hall made his stomach rumble all the louder. He realised that he had forgotten to visit Guenhuifach, so preoccupied he had been with the monk and promised himself that he would take a ride later and spend the night with her in her bothy. He could make it back before dawn and avoid detection. He had done it before.

He washed up and made his way over to the Great Hall. It was bursting at the seams with eight rulers and their households. It was a wonder that Queen Meddyf had stocked enough food and fodder for them all considering how short-handed they were these days but she had somehow managed it.

The seven kings that had come to pledge fealty to young Guidno and his regent sat at trestle tables at the head of the hall; Owain, Mor and Efiaun on one side, Usai of Caradocion, Cadwaldr of Meriauned, Condruin of Docmaeling and Cungen of Eternion on the other, each with their queens. Guidno was seated in the middle, sandwiched between his mother and Owain. He sipped his broth slowly and occasionally looked about at the assembly with nervous eyes.

Medraut made his way towards the benches beneath the gaze of the kings. Alan motioned him with a jerk of the head and made sure there was space for him among the warriors. He sat down and meat was passed to him while a serving girl poured him some mead. The banter was jovial and he allowed himself to slip into the warm company of his companions.

Both Alan and his son, Lonio, had accompanied Arthur's party to Ynys Mon. Medraut had requested it. With the rest of the teulu wintering at Cair Cunor, he was keen to have some of his own troop with them. Arthur had granted this although a little begrudgingly it seemed. Medraut and his troop had become something akin to heroes in the teulu as the tale of their capture by Scurwulf and their daring escape, not to mention their conduct at the first Battle of the Black River, did the rounds. His name was rising fast through the teulu and he felt that Arthur showed a touch of jealousy.

Medraut glanced up at the high tables and was glad he was not noble enough to sit in that frosty atmosphere. Seven kings who didn't particularly like much less trust one another were being forced to eat and make small talk together along with their queens who despised each other equally by the looks on their sour faces. Arthur and Guenhuifar sat at the end of one of the tables and looked like they wanted to retire to bed as soon as it was polite to do so.

It was getting late when a figure entered the hall and drew everybody's attention away from their plates and cups. Heads turned and necks craned as conversation dipped to a low murmur. Medraut turned around to follow Alan's gaze. It was the monk he had met on the road and he was striding towards the kings, his hood raised about his ears.

"What's this?" spoke Owain from the high tables. "Are we to be preached at while we sup? And do you not think to lower your hood when entering the company of kings? Where are your manners, monk?"

"My apologies, King Owain mab Enniaun," said the monk. "But years tucked away in a cloister have made me forget the customs of royal company." He reached up and pulled his hood down to reveal his tonsured head.

A stillness descended as many in the hall – those at the high tables especially – peered at the man's face as if remembering somebody long forgotten. A loud gasp escaped the lips of Queen Meddyf and she clasped a hand to her mouth. Her face had gone a deathly pale.

"Hello, Mother," said the monk.

"Maelcon!" said Owain. "What nonsense is this appearing before us like a shade at Samhain? Why did you not send word of your coming?"

"I thought to surprise you, dear Uncle," said Maelcon. "And it looks to have done the trick, for by your faces you all forgot about me long ago."

"That's not true," said Meddyf. "I wrote. Many times, as did your father. I visited you even."

"Yes you visited me at Abbot Illtud's school. Once. And you did not stay long."

"It was upsetting for me," said Meddyf. "I missed you so and knew it would be many years before I would see you again."

"Was it not your idea, Mother, that I should take my vows and become a servant of God?"

"It was all I could do to keep you close to me. Your father was talking of sending you far away, of marrying you into a distant family."

"I fear I am not the marrying sort, as Queen Tarren can no doubt attest." His eyes glanced to King Cungen of Eternion and his queen. "I am glad to see that a suitable replacement was found." Maelcon had been betrothed to the Princess Tarren as part of her father's terms in supporting Cadwallon during the civil war. Maelcon's attempt to squirm out of that marriage had taken the form of an attempt on Owain's life resulting in his subsequent exile to the Church. Before old King Etern had died, he had married his daughter to Cungen, the nephew of King

Ridfet of Powys, bringing a long-standing feud to an end. Cungen glanced uneasily at Maelcon. As the only king at the high table who was not descended from Cunedag, he no doubt already felt out of place among the wild Venedotian kings.

"Nevertheless, here I am," Maelcon continued. "Come to pay my respects at my father's grave, however ashamed he was of me."

"Is that the only reason you are here?" asked Owain. He and his queen, Elen, glared at him with utter loathing in their eyes. Elen still bore the scar from the hired knife Maelcon had sent to murder Owain.

"As a matter of fact, I am on Church business," said Maelcon. "Bishop Dubricius has sent me to witness the pledging ritual."

"Why would the illustrious Bishop of Erging care about our pledging ceremony?"

"Erging is just his seat. Bishop Dubricius is the most highly-respected of all the bishops in Albion. His influence extends across the west. He chose me to witness as I am kin to the Pendraigs."

"Bishop Dubricius spoke to you himself?" Meddyf asked. Being a Christian, a note of pride slipped into her voice at her son's acquaintance with such a high-ranking figure in the clergy.

"Oh yes. The bishop is good friends with Abbott Illtud and regularly visits the school. He is most interested in seeing that its students do the work of God in all corners of Albion."

"And your father's untimely death had nothing to do with your prodigal return?" asked Owain, unable to keep the sneer from his voice. "You wouldn't be thinking of pressing a claim to his throne, of course."

"Nothing could be further from my mind," said Maelcon. "I am well aware that my dear brother has been chosen to be Venedotia's king and I wouldn't dream of interfering. I have followed a different path and am content to be God's servant in other ways."

"Oh, never mind all this about crowns and kings!" spoke Meddyf suddenly. "My son has come home to me!" She rose from the table and swept down to embrace him.

There was an uncomfortable stirring in the Great Hall. Everybody remembered why Maelcon had been sent away. Those who had known him as a youth had little pleasant to say about him. It came hard to accept that he had changed, even now that he was a man and wore a monk's habit. Old prejudices died hard and none knew that better than Medraut.

For his part he was uncertain of the young monk he had escorted to the Lys. He hadn't known Maelcon before so had little opinion of his past crimes. Nevertheless, he had lied to him and he was pretty sure that was something frowned upon by Christians. But then, Maelcon had wanted to surprise his family and avoid being announced upon arrival. Surely that warranted a small lie? As for his intentions, he seemed genuine enough. But one could never tell with royalty. They learned tricks of the tongue from the cradle.

Arthur

"Not interested in the crown, my foot!" Owain seethed. "He pops up before the grass has grown over his father's grave and with the pledging ceremony mere days away! A little too convenient, don't you think?"

Arthur, King Mor and King Efiaun looked at him uncertainly. The feast was over and most people had retired to their beds, including Maelcon who had been given his own quarters near the Great Hall. They sat at one of the high tables as the servants cleared up the remnants of the meal. Arthur's head was groggy with tiredness and drink but Owain had called an informal council to discuss the sudden return of Cadwallon's eldest son.

"It hardly matters even if he were interested," said King Mor. "Guidno has been chosen and Maelcon is just a monk. He has no teulu to back his claim."

"But the Christians may support him," said Arthur. "And they are of considerable number in Venedotia."

"But *Guidno* is a Christian," said Mor. "Meddyf convinced Cadwallon to allow both boys to be baptised despite his own faith."

"Guidno is young and sickly," said Arthur. "If he should die then the crown would pass to somebody else, some other family member. A pagan, most likely. Having finally got one of their own in line for the throne, the Christians won't want to risk losing it. It may be preferable to support Maelcon rather than Guidno. It's a case of backing the fastest horse."

"What matter is this?" said Owain with an irritated sigh. "The *people* don't choose their king."

Owain was technically right but his view on the world had always been rather simplistic, and a day later a letter arrived from the south which proved that point. The first Arthur knew of it was when he walked into the Great Hall to the sound of Owain's booming voice.

"What makes this bishop think he can meddle in our affairs?" Owain roared, the scroll unfurled in his hand, its wax seal dangling.

"He is looked to as a figure of authority by every Christian in the west," said Meddyf.

Owain rounded on her. "Surely you aren't in agreement with Dubricius that Maelcon should be king instead of Guidno?"

Meddyf fixed a hard stare upon Owain which she probably intended to mask her opinion on the matter but Arthur could see the conflict in her face. "Asking a mother to choose between two of her children is a hard thing," she said. "Not to mention futile."

"You mean to say that it makes no difference which of your sons wears the crown," said Owain. "Well let me tell you, Meddyf, it makes a good deal of difference. You and Cadwallon both agreed that Maelcon is lacking in morals. He tried to have me killed and nearly started a civil war just so he could get out of marrying Princess Tarren!"

"That was many years ago," said Meddyf. "He is a man of God now …"

"I'll believe that when I see it with my own eyes. Are you sure you are not allowing your religious faith to stand in the way of your good judgement? Guidno is also a Christian, remember, and a far more moral boy than his brother. You have already made the right decision, Meddyf. Maelcon's sudden return is irrelevant as is this bishop's support for him. Do not let whatever love you still have for him suggest otherwise."

And as if this statement marked the end of the conversation, Owain got up and left the hall. Arthur watched him leave. Owain, he decided, was more than making himself at home as regent and in his late brother's household no less. Telling the queen her own mind? Meddyf had always been a pillar of strength in her husband's court, wise as she was determined. But since Cadwallon had died she seemed to be in a state of uncertainty, always second-guessing herself. It was a version of their queen he was entirely unused to.

"Surely you are not having second thoughts about putting Guidno on the throne, my lady?" Guenhuifar asked the queen after most of the courtiers had dispersed following Owain's departure.

"I don't know," said Meddyf. "I just don't know anymore. Had you asked me a week ago, I would have told you that Guidno was the only choice to succeed his father. But now that Maelcon has returned ... Guidno is so very young after all and had Maelcon stayed here instead of being sent to Abbot Illtud's school, he would have been the natural choice."

"But it was you yourself who sent him to Abbot Illtud," said Guenhuifar.

"Yes. To teach him discipline, to make a good Christian of him, but most of all to remove him from

Court. He earned himself many enemies through his trickery and none greater than his own father. I feared he would be lost to me forever if Cadwallon had had his way. Now that he is here carrying the blessing of Bishop Dubricius, all is changed."

Guenhuifar glanced at Arthur, her expression worried.

"It may be too late to have second thoughts, my lady," said Arthur. "The other kings are here to pledge their support to Guidno. They do not love Maelcon as you do."

"I know, Arthur," she said. "But I know they are wrong in their judgement of him. He has changed, I can feel it."

But the conflict Meddyf felt for her eldest son did little to change events that had already been set in motion. The next day the seven kings pledged their loyalty to young Guidno in the Great Hall.

"Where is Medraut?" Guenhuifar asked, as they filed into the cavernous space to take their places before the dais. "He should be here!"

"He'll stumble in late as usual," said Arthur, dressed in his finest tunica and cloak.

"As long as he doesn't make a scene. I don't know what he gets up to these days but he's never around when I want him."

"Here he comes."

"Ah! Medraut!" said Guenhuifar, turning to face the youth as he threaded his way through the throngs towards them. "And you've found Guenhuifach too! Good. The ceremony is about to start. Come, stand with me, both of you."

Arthur took the banner of the red dragon from his standard bearer and mounted the dais to stand behind the throne, his presence a symbol of Venedotia's might.

Menw officiated which was something of a courtesy on Meddyf's part. Guidno was to be a Christian king and, by extension, Venedotia would become a Christian kingdom. But old traditions died hard and so Menw performed a stripped-down version of the ceremony that accommodated both faiths while Maelcon stood to one side, a silent yet vigilant representative of the Church.

As Arthur watched the seven kings came forward to kneel at the boy's feet and kiss the Pendraig's sword which was held outwards by Owain, he pondered the unspoken symbolism in the whole scene. Owain, holding a sword that was too heavy for a sickly boy to wield; Menw, the muted remnant of the kingdom's pagan past on one side; and Maelcon, the representative of the growing Christian faith on the other; Meddyf, standing at the boy's shoulder, whispering encouragement into his ear; the young king-to-be, impotent on his throne at the centre of the whole ceremony, little more than a pawn of his elders.

And what then did Arthur represent? His loyalty was to the Pendraig of course and yet things were far more complicated now than they had been under Cadwallon. Now there were many voices, many minds beneath one crown; the young king, the regent, the Queen Mother, the pagan past and the Christian future. *May all the gods forbid that these factions should come into conflict with one another,* he thought as the last king's lips touched the sword and the hall erupted into applause.

"I'm worried about Medraut," said Guenhuifar to Arthur the following day. They were walking in the marketplace, their furs wrapped tightly around their upper bodies, holding hands beneath the folds, enjoying each other's warmth.

"What on earth for?" Arthur asked.

"We barely see him. He doesn't even take meat in the Great Hall most nights. What does he find to do with himself?"

Arthur laughed. "Is that what troubles you? I tell you he's found a woman."

"A woman?"

Arthur laughed again at her confused expression. "He's a red-blooded male, Guenhuifar. And a warrior at that. Such men quickly grow bored during long winters and seek sport and warmth wherever they can."

"Oh, do they now?" she asked, one eyebrow raised.

He nudged her playfully. "You must understand this. He's a handsome lad in the fullness of youth. He'll be ploughing some rich field as we speak."

Guenhuifar tutted.

"Don't be so disapproving," he told her. "We aren't his true parents, after all. I can no more admonish him for his frolics than I can any man in the teulu."

"As long as he doesn't marry the girl, isn't that right?" Guenhuifar said, her voice still rank with disapproval.

"Such has it always been," said Arthur. "I didn't make the rules."

"But you uphold them."

"Aye, because they make good sense. How many warriors could I count on come spring if every other one of them would rather stay at home and take care of a wife and babes than go to war?"

"So it's better they leave poor girls on their own with swollen bellies and their reputations ruined?"

Arthur sighed. "What my men do when we're not on campaign is their business. I don't approve of it but I can't stop it. All I can do is my job. And part of that is making sure we don't have other commitments keeping the men back from their duty. By refusing to let them marry, the number of those commitments is curbed. Oh, some of them still father little bastards here and there but few will acknowledge them and let themselves be tied down by marriage vows."

"Well, I just hope Medraut isn't stupid enough to get the poor girl with child."

"These are the only two scamps we must concern ourselves with!" said Arthur, as Amhar and Lacheu came waddling over to them, wrapped up in their winter clothes, faces red with the chill. Arthur scooped Lacheu up and tickled his ear with his beard bristles.

"There's an awful row going on in the Hall," said Amhar.

"Why, what's up?" Arthur asked.

"A letter came from some bishop to the queen. Uncle Owain is roaring at everyone!"

Arthur and Guenhuifar shared a look and Arthur set Lacheu down and made for the Great Hall. Guenhuifar took the two boys by their hands and followed in his wake.

They found the hall crowded and up at the far end they could see Owain and Meddyf in heated debate. Owain was bellowing as he often was these days.

"And you invited him?" he raged at Meddyf.

Meddyf faced him down with more resolve in her eyes than Arthur had seen in them for a long while. It was as if the old Meddyf had returned at last, indecision banished from her face. "You may be the regent, Owain, but this is still *my* household," she said coldly. "I invite whomever I choose."

"But this man means to undo everything we have achieved! He will pour honey in your ear in an attempt to curry your favour."

"Do you know so much of a man you have never met? And do you think so little of my will that you fear it will be changed by sweet words spoken by a stranger?"

"Come, Meddyf, you know the man's intentions! I am worried that he will try to rend the fragile agreement we have extracted from all the other kings."

"He is coming to spend the Advent Fast with us and to instruct myself and Guidno on certain matters of our faith. We are to have a Christian king, after all. A good relationship with Bishop Dubricius will undoubtedly be of great help in the future."

"Bishop Dubricius is coming here?" Arthur asked, moving to the front.

"If you can believe it," said Owain. "Our young king's mother has invited him personally. You must see that this is dangerous, Arthur, just as I do."

Meddyf looked to Arthur expectantly. He knew he could always speak his mind in front of his sister-in-law but Owain's manners were beginning to grate on him of late. "As the Lady Meddyf says, she can keep her own council on whom she invites," he said.

Owain threw his hands up in the air. "Then don't say I didn't warn you! I don't trust this bishop. No more than I could throw the bastard!"

Guenhuifar

The bishop's arrival was met with jubilation from the Christian majority and curiosity laced with suspicion by those who still followed the old ways. Nevertheless, members of both faiths turned out to see Dubricius and his entourage ride in through the gates, the hooves of their horses making deep impressions in the newly fallen snow. Meddyf and her two sons greeted the bishop in front of the Great Hall, framed by its massive doors.

"God's blessings be upon you, my lady," said the bishop after dismounting. He bowed to Guidno. "And to your royal highness. I trust you are well?"

Guidno nodded. "Yes, thank you, your Grace."

"It is good to see you again, your Grace," said Maelcon.

Bishop Dubricius smiled and clasped Maelcon by the arms affectionately. "And you, my boy. It pleases me to see you back in your family home, bringing all you have learnt at Illtud's school to this corner of Albion."

The collection of priests and deacons who huddled behind him, their breaths steaming in the air, were introduced to the family before the whole gaggle went into the warmth of the Great Hall.

As a rule, the Christians fasted in the days leading up to the commemoration of the birth of Christ. It was a sombre time of reflection and prayer which kept most of them within their homes. The pagans carried on as usual but the Lys had a still, quiet atmosphere and mealtimes were underpopulated affairs. Of Meddyf and her sons, Guenhuifar saw little for they spent most of their time with the bishop.

"I tell you he is twisting Meddyf's mind," Owain kept saying.

Guenhuifar said nothing. With all the Christians squirreled away at their prayers and all the pagans wondering what was going on behind closed doors, the settlement seemed more divided than ever. Something had to be done she decided, or the damage all this suspicion and mistrust was wreaking would be irreparable. She had always had a good relationship with Meddyf and felt sure that an honest conversation between the two of them would put to rest much of the ill feeling in the settlement.

She found Meddyf instructing the servants on the stocking of food in preparation for the midwinter feast which was a festival shared by Christian and pagan alike. Guenhuifar looked at the great wheels of cheese and racks of salted meat and wondered how Meddyf could stomach to be among it all with an empty belly. The fasting of advent was well into its second week now.

"My lady, might we have a word?" she asked.

"Certainly, Guenhuifar. We have seen too little of each other of late. We must make use of your time here before spring draws you back to Cair Cunor."

Guenhuifar smiled and took a deep breath. She felt it was best to get straight to the point. "There are grumblings that Bishop Dubricius is exerting too much influence on you."

Meddyf sighed. "I know, Guenhuifar. It is only natural that they should feel anxious with such a powerful figure of the clergy with us. The pagans have ruled Venedotia for generations. They fear the Church's involvement in our affairs but I assure you that their fears are unfounded. Look to the other kingdoms in Albion! Do they suffer as a result of their conversion to the Christian faith? Bishop Dubricius seeks only to bring us into the fold and under the protection of the Lord God."

"With respect, my lady, it is not the Church the people fear. They have gladly accepted a Christian king in the form of Guidno but they fear that Bishop Dubricius may intend to back Maelcon instead."

Meddyf's face took on a harder look. "You do not like my eldest son, I know that, Guenhuifar. After all, you were the one who foiled his plot to bring about a civil war. I sent him to Abbot Illtud's school in good faith for he had been very wicked. But I know that he has repented. His time with Abbot Illtud has taught him many things and regret for his past behaviour most of all. He is changed, Guenhuifar, I only wish that you could see it as I do. You must give him a chance. The *kingdom* must give him a chance."

Oh, gods ... thought Guenhuifar. *She actually means to support Maelcon. It's all true! Owain's fears are true!*

"In time, they will learn," Meddyf continued. "The other kings and the commoners too; they will learn that Maelcon is a kind and generous man as well as a wise and just ruler. It will take a while of course, I know that, but perhaps through your example they might learn to accept him. If you could give him a chance first?"

She wants me to openly voice my support of him! "My lady, I fear it is not that simple. The other kings have already pledged their support to Guidno. And then there is Owain. He is regent and will not step down in favour of Maelcon."

"Owain is regent, true," said Meddyf. "But how strong is he? Rhos is a small kingdom with few warriors."

Guenhuifar stared at Meddyf, not sure if she had heard her right.

Meddyf held her gaze without wavering. "The simple fact of the matter is that whoever has the support of your husband is Venedotia's true ruler."

She left Guenhuifar alone in the storeroom. Guenhuifar gazed after her, speechless. She understood the barely concealed implication in Meddyf's words and felt a chill to her very bones.

The birth of the Christ fell upon the same day as the midwinter solstice and the day was marked by the festivities of two faiths. While the Christians attended a midnight vigil in the church, Menw led a group of bards in training to gather mistletoe from the oak trees, just as the druids had done of old. Traditionally the king would choose the finest tree to be felled and burnt in the hearth, kindled with the charred remains of last year's log so that the gods would favour the household in the year to come. Meddyf instructed Owain to do the honours as Guidno was busy at his prayers with Bishop Dubricius.

With the massive oak log crackling in the hearth and the doorways and pillars of the hall decorated with mistletoe and evergreens, Christian and pagan alike filed into the Great Hall for the midwinter feast. The fast of Advent over and their prayers fulfilled, the Christians were ravenous and ate shoulder to shoulder with their pagan brothers and sisters. The scene was one of joy and optimism during the darkest days of winter and Guenhuifar was pleasantly reminded of happier and less divisive times.

Guidno sat at the head table, flanked by his mother and Bishop Dubricius. Ordinarily the seat to the right of the young king-in-waiting was occupied by Owain but the regent had grudgingly ceded this honour to the visiting bishop after much grumbling.

Partway through the feast there seemed to be an urging on the parts of Meddyf and Dubricius that Guidno should stand and raise his glass in a toast to the assembled feasters. His face pale, the nervous youth awkwardly got to his feet.

There was a hushing from various parts of the hall for everybody to be quiet. A respectful silence fell over the crowd.

"Friends ..." said Guidno in a voice that was barely audible. His mother motioned him to speak louder and he dutifully did so. "Friends! We are gathered here to mark the longest night and the shortest day, the middle of winter and the birth of our Lord and Saviour. Let us raise our cups to the return of the sun from shadow and the birth of Jesus Christ!"

It had been well-rehearsed, and entirely without Owain's input, apparently. Was this how it was to be?

The regent sitting to one side; while a southern bishop and the Queen Mother steered the young king through his duties?

There was a palpable silence as mead and wine were swallowed. Before cups had left lips, Guidno broke into another speech just as rehearsed as the first.

"I was honoured to become your king, even though I required a regent to rule in my stead. It is because of that regent that I speak to you all tonight. You deserve a king now, not a king tomorrow or in several years' time. I am indebted to you all for your trust in me but it was a trust misplaced when you already had a worthy king to rule you. I hereby abdicate my position in favour of my dear brother, Maelcon."

The stunned silence was long enough for Guidno to slump back into his chair and fumble for his wine glass from which he drank deeply. Everybody else remained standing.

And then the uproar poured forth.

It was mostly from the pagan quarter, scattered as it was throughout the hall. Some Christians voiced their anger also, having no love for Maelcon. Owain hammered his fist down on the table and then jabbed an accusatory finger at Bishop Dubricius.

"That man overreaches himself!" he bellowed.

"*That man*," said Meddyf, rising from her seat in a sudden energetic burst, "had nothing to do with Guidno's decision!"

"Come now, Meddyf!" said Owain. "He has been whispering in to the lad's ears since he got here and yours too! You can't expect us to believe that he hasn't deliberately stirred up a hornet's nest here!"

"Believe what you want, Owain, just know that I only agreed for Guidno to become king when I thought my eldest son had given his life to the Church."

"A career he quickly abandoned once he received word that his father's throne was vacant!"

Maelcon rose alongside his mother and the two of them faced Owain. Guidno remained seated looking like he wanted to be anywhere but there in the centre of all this turmoil.

"I have accepted this honour with much regret and great humility," said Maelcon. "I never wanted to be king and was prepared to spend the rest of my life doing God's work. But, after arriving here and seeing how my family had torn itself apart and seeing my mother's desperation and my little brother's fear, I knew that God had chosen me to intervene. By speaking to Bishop Dubricius, I learned that it was God's will that I should sit on my father's throne."

"Oh, yes, I'm sure Bishop Dubricius is in regular conversation with the Almighty about such matters," Owain sneered.

There was more outrage at this and this time it was from the Christians. Even those who despised Maelcon took offence at the disrespect dealt to the bishop.

Guenhuifar could see things were getting out of hand. More insults might lead to violence and then it would be Christian against pagan, Maelcon's supporters against Guidno's. The peace of midwinter was coming dangerously close to being broken.

"My lady," said Arthur, rising from his seat. "How can you ask the other Venedotian kings to support Maelcon when they have already pledged themselves to Guidno?"

"That pledge was a nominal oath," said Meddyf. "It is not binding while Guidno remains uncrowned and certainly not after he has decided to abdicate. We shall recall the Dragons of the North to pledge their support to Maelcon upon his coronation in the spring."

"Do you see them giving this oath willingly?"

Meddyf regarded Arthur. "To not swear their fealty would make them traitors," she said coolly.

"And then it would be war," said Arthur. "Again."

"Yes. We must pray that it does not come to that."

There was little further to be said. The decision had been made and until the minds of the other kings were known, it was unclear where the night's events would lead the kingdom. To war or to peace? To a bright future or to ruin?

Owain departed with his usual decorum and many others took this opportunity to excuse themselves too. Many remained and it was clear where loyalties now lay. Guenhuifar looked at Arthur, seeing the indecision in his face. After some hesitation he rose and they followed the departing group outside.

"Meddyf's gone mad if she thinks the other kings will roll over and change their allegiance to that toad on her whim!" said Owain, once they had stepped out of the hall. The night air was chill and the torches flickered, illuminating the backs of those who were returning to their homes.

"She may have more support than you think, Owain," said Arthur. "Everybody knows Guidno will be an ineffectual king. They might be willing to overlook Maelcon's faults in favour of a stronger ruler. Then there is King Cungen to consider."

"What about him?"

"He's a Christian and will probably support Dubricius's endorsement of Maelcon. And he has the backing of his uncle. We may be faced with the involvement of Powys …"

"Gods, is there not enough meddling already with bishops popping up and kicking over the chamber pot! If Powys sticks its oar in to Venedotian business it will be war like the bad old days."

"Aye," said Arthur. "What should we do?"

"Do? What can we do but resist Meddyf and that blasted bishop and hope the other kings stand with us? I shall return to Din Arth tomorrow. I'll be damned if I'll stay here now that lunacy reigns. While Maelcon remains uncrowned, I am still regent whether Meddyf and Dubricius want it or not. As far as I'm concerned, Din Arth shall be Venedotia's seat from now on."

"That would be a very provocative thing to claim," warned Menw.

"I'm surprised at you, Menw," said Owain. "Surely I at least have you on my side?"

"Sides?" said the bard, his lined face showing worry. "There may yet come a time for sides but I hope it is not now. Perhaps in the meantime, it would be best to not let hot heads do the thinking.

Venedotia is in a very precarious position. It is, in effect, without a ruler."

"The Hounds of Annun it isn't! *I* rule Venedotia!"

"Your claim as regent is in dispute," said Menw patiently. "There is no denying that. Many support you but many do not. And, with no definite ruler on the throne, there is no clear-cut solution. It's a rather unprecedented situation."

"Well, as long as I have the support of the Teulu of the Red Dragon, I feel my position is a sight more legitimate than Maelcon's. What say you, Arthur? I do have your support, don't I?"

Guenhuifar saw the turmoil in Arthur's eyes as he sought an answer. He glanced at Menw. "If our wise bard with all his knowledge of Albion's legal systems can give no clear answer due to the uniqueness of the situation, then I can only put my support behind a leader I know to be the more moral and honourable of the two. Aye, Owain. You have my support. But I cannot guarantee the support of the entire teulu."

"What is that supposed to mean?" Owain demanded, fire in his eyes.

"The teulu is made up of warriors from every kingdom in Venedotia. Some are Christians, some pagans. Some no doubt approve of Maelcon or at least are devoted to his mother while others would prefer to see you remain as regent. Until questioned, I have no idea how many of my warriors will support you."

"Well question them, damn them!" spoke Owain, full of wroth. "And remind them that their loyalty is to their penteulu; wherever his loyalties lie, so too do theirs!"

Once they had retired to their quarters, Guenhuifar rubbed some of the tension out of Arthur's shoulders while the candle flickered beneath the hide-covered window.

"Gods, what am I to do, Guenhuifar?" he asked her. "There are too many bloody arses trying to sit on one throne!"

"Are you sure it is wise to support Owain? You near as much pledged yourself to him today."

"I know! I had to give him some sort of answer for he's already trying to drum up supporters. Compared to Maelcon he is by far the better man but he means to push Venedotia in to another civil war!"

"Will he really be so stubborn?" she asked him.

He gave her a look. "Stubborn? Owain practically invented the word."

"But it was you and Meddyf who made him regent in place of Guidno. Surely he must stand down if Guidno is no longer to be king?"

"He will do whatever he can to ensure that his power is not threatened. He fears Maelcon. He knows that he might find himself stripped of his kingdom if Maelcon becomes Pendraig."

"This is madness!" sighed Guenhuifar in exasperation. "Why can men not stop fighting over crowns and thrones? Will it never end?"

Her worries were to be overshadowed several days later when the court was thrown into yet more outrage and this time it cut much closer to home.

Bishop Dubricius had departed for his villa in the south with promises to return in the spring to crown Maelcon. He left one of his deacons – a man called Velius – to oversee the building of a new church west of the Lys. This rapid laying of stone was a testament to the benefits the clergy were to receive with Maelcon on the throne.

It happened just as they were all heading into the Great Hall for their evening meal. Deacon Velius appeared as he always did, seeking warmth and a hot meal after a day inspecting the construction of the church. He approached Guenhuifar and Arthur as they were sitting down at the tables, his face severe.

"My lord, my lady, I must have a word."

"What can we do for you, Deacon?" asked Arthur. Neither he nor Guenhuifar were accustomed to members of the clergy wanting anything from them.

"It is about your son. And your ladyship's sister."

"Medraut and Guenhuifach?" Arthur asked, and as soon as he had spoken their names together, Guenhuifar's heart was gripped by a dreadful chill. Events of the last few weeks seemed to take on a new light. *Medraut and Guenhuifach.* They had spent much time together building the infirmary in the woods. Ever since it had been finished, Medraut had constantly been missing, turning up late for meals, being so secretive. And Guenhuifach was, well, *Guenhuifach*, always keeping to herself, living the life of a hermit out in the woods. Medraut had taken a lover, Arthur had said. *Gods no, it couldn't be true ...*

"There was an accident at the church site yesterday," the deacon explained. "One of the workers had his finger crushed by a hunk of masonry. I sent him to the Lady Guenhuifach to get it seen to and he returned with a tale that was appalling to my ears. The Lady Guenhuifach and the man she calls her nephew – your son – were enjoying each other's company in a manner that no two members in the same family should. I understand that he is not a blood relation and I understand that you are not followers of the word of Christ but surely, even pagans would find shame in such carryings on in their own household! I dread to think what the bishop will say when he hears of this."

Arthur rose from his seat, his face rigid. "You overreach your station in telling us where our shame should lie, Deacon."

Guenhuifar rose also and moved away from the table for she had just seen Medraut and Guenhuifach enter the hall. *Together.*

"Tell me it isn't true," she said, as she swept towards them.

They gazed at her with childish innocence, surely feigned.

"Tell you what isn't true, Guenhuifar?" asked Medraut.

"Tell me that the deacon lies, that his worker lies. Tell me he did not find you both together. *As lovers.*"

The word seemed to draw attention to itself and a silence settled over the hall as people turned their heads, sure that some quarrel was brewing.

"Sister, I don't know what that man has been saying to you," said Guenhuifach, her eyes darting to the deacon who stood at Arthur's side, an expectant look on his face, "but he has no doubt twisted the truth."

"And what *is* the truth?" Guenhuifar demanded.

"None of his damned business," said Medraut, glaring at the deacon.

"Oh, gods!" cried Guenhuifar, looking from one to the other. The hall was silent now. All were gazing at them, eyes goggling, mouths open. "Your own nephew, Guenhuifach! How could you?"

"How *could* I?" Guenhuifach retorted, her face colouring. "He is no more my nephew than he is your son!"

"It's immoral!"

"That morality is an artificial thing forced on us by you! You were the one who adopted Medraut, not me! I loved him from the moment I set eyes upon him!"

"Love for a child, surely! And now that love has become a twisted, perverted thing …"

"He was no child when you brought him to us! He was a man grown. Oh, it was no romantic love in the beginning, I'll grant you, but it was a love nonetheless. And yes, it did change but not into something perverted. No more than your love for Arthur or anybody's love for the one person they want to spend their lives with."

"It's impossible," spoke Arthur from the rear of the hall, his voice cold and hollow, filled with the necessity of duty and no more than that. "Medraut is a warrior in my teulu. He cannot take a woman, not officially. And besides, there could be no marriage for even if he were not my warrior, he is my legal son and would require my blessing to marry you."

"A blessing you would never give me. Am I right?" said Medraut.

Arthur was silent.

"Medraut, you must see ..." Guenhuifar began.

"See?" snapped her sister. "All we see is that your love came first and so ours must be denied! You have stolen this from us! You were the older sister so you received Father's blessing and were able to marry the man of your choice. Now I must go without mine because you have adopted the one man I would ever consider being with!"

Guenhuifar felt a stab of hurt at the mention of their father. That loss was still too fresh and she felt anger at her sister for bringing him into this. "Father would never have given you his blessing to marry a boy I love as a son. Your actions would have shamed him!"

The slap came sudden and with an explosive force. Guenhuifar reeled backwards, her cheek stinging from the blow. Guenhuifach stood there, arm hovering, shaking in mid-air, its energy spent. Her eyes looked disbelieving at what she had done.

Chairs and benches scraped as people rose nervously, not knowing what to do.

Arthur strode forward to Guenhuifar's side looking like he wanted to throttle her sister. She held out her arm to restrain him. Medraut stood tense by Guenhuifach, his eyes daring Arthur to place one finger on her.

Tears started in Guenhuifar's eyes and she refused to blink, forcing the lump in her throat down. She would not weep, nor would she allow her resolve to break in front of the entire hall. Instead, she turned from them, one hand involuntarily raised to her smarting cheek as she hurried towards the doors.

Medraut

The scandal that had so rocked the court seemed to go on indefinitely, eliciting wagging tongues and titillated smiles wherever Medraut looked. He raged inwardly at them all. Who were they to judge him? He felt a fresh hatred for them that had been borne that night in the Great Hall. It had been the first time he had shouted at Arthur and it had given him a power, a release of all that he had held back countless times in the past. It was a power he did not intend to give up.

His and Guenhuifar's conduct that night had taken them past the point of no return. Not only had two members of the penteulu's household engaged themselves in an immoral affair, but Guenhuifach had slapped the penteulu's wife in front of the whole hall. They may be sisters but what was Guenhuifach to the Lady Guenhuifar of Cair Cunor? An unmarried healer woman with no lands or titles could not strike a noblewoman. It was an outrage and there were many calling for her to be publicly whipped for her insolence.

As for Medraut, his shame was no less; a boy carrying on with his own aunt? Unthinkable! There had always been something *wrong* about him in the eyes of just about everybody else. After all, what can one expect? The son of *you-know-who* and raised by a witch ... All the wagging tongues, suspicions and presumptions succeeded in doing was making Medraut more convinced that Guenhuifach was the only person he loved or trusted.

But he and Guenhuifach were to be kept separate; she at her infirmary well away from the Lys and he within the Lys's palisade where a close eye could be kept on him. A more permanent arrangement was hastily urged by Meddyf who no doubt wanted to convince her precious Bishop Dubricius that Venedotia's seat was not a hotbed of pagan lust and immodesty. There was talk of having Guenhuifach baptised and sent packing to a nunnery but that idea had been mercifully put down and by Guenhuifar no less. Angry as she was with her sister, she had no wish to lose her to Christian seclusion. Instead, it was Medraut who was to be sent away. Arthur decided that he would accompany Owain to Din Arth and remain there for the foreseeable future.

"Does he mean to strike you from the teulu?" Alan asked him, as they watched the wagon train being loaded up at the foot of the palisade. It was a clear day. The skies were the colour of azure without a cloud to be seen but the wind was chill and the frozen trees outside the Lys were as white skeletons against the blue.

"I should think so," said Medraut. "Why else send me to Din Arth? Why not send me to Cair Cunor where I can await his return in the spring? He means to wash his hands of me and pass me on to his bloody half-brother." A black gloom had cloaked his heart. The thought of becoming Owain's man was as sour ale in his gut and made him want to retch.

Alan sighed. "I'm sorry, sir. If I could go with you I would but I doubt Arthur will let me."

"Thank you for your loyalty, Alan," said Medraut.

"The other lads would say the same. You would have made a fine captain. It's a sore shame we will never ride in your company."

Medraut thanked him again but could not bring himself to feel any happiness at his friend's kind words. His rage at everybody burned like a brand thrust into his flesh. Since Guenhuifar had plucked him from obscurity and introduced him to his family, he had gathered scraps of things to him like blankets against the cold: love, friends, acceptance. Now he had lost it all: his position in the teulu, his companions but most of all, Guenhuifach. All of these things were gone like wood smoke on the wind. And it was all because Arthur and Guenhuifar insisted on treating them like children. They were only six years his senior! Arthur should never have adopted him. It had been a burden disguised as a kindness and he would forever be in his shadow, forever in the ridiculous position where he was unable to marry whom he liked without his uncle's blessing.

Later that day, Maelcon approached him as he was crossing the precinct. "Might we have a word?"

"Of, course, my lord." They walked towards the Great Hall. Medraut was surprised to be approached by the king-to-be. They had not spoken since that day on the road when he had accompanied him to court. He was still dressed in his monk's habit and looked very humble for a man who was due to rule eight kingdoms.

"I am sorry that things turned out as they did for you and Guenhuifach," said Maelcon, "for I see that you are both very much in love."

Medraut was taken aback. What care did the future Pendraig have for the affairs of lowly warriors?

"It seems a cruel twist of fate that you are denied the woman you love merely because her sister and her husband adopted you."

"What is the Church's mind on such things?" Medraut asked him.

"Seeing as there is no blood relation between the two of you, the matter is purely a legal one. Nothing immoral has taken place, no matter what spiteful tongues are saying about it."

"Your mother seems to think Bishop Dubricius will take exception to the matter."

"My mother is queen no longer. Her opinion is of little import. I know the good bishop in ways she does not."

"If it is not a moral matter then the issue of legality still remains. Arthur will not permit me to marry, both because I am his legal son and because I am a warrior in the teulu – at least for the moment – and it is against the rules."

"Legal matters are like knots," said Maelcon with a small smile. "Sometimes they can be untangled, sometimes a simple slice of the knife will do but there is always a resolution. It all depends on who wields the knife, as it were."

"Namely you, my lord," said Medraut. "Once you are crowned Pendraig, that is." He was no fool. He could see that Maelcon was offering to do some sort of favour. *But what does he want in return?*

"You are quite correct," said Maelcon. "Once I am king I will have considerable leverage on all matters and people; even your uncle."

"But it isn't just Arthur," said Medraut. "Everybody has condemned us. They see us as immoral."

"Who would dare suggest that you are immoral if the Pendraig himself has blessed your union? I could even command you to marry Guenhuifach if I so chose it."

They had entered the Great Hall through a side door and now stood in the colonnaded aisle. There was nobody else in the hall and Medraut realised that Maelcon had taken him to a place of privacy.

"Why would you help me?" Medraut asked him. "What's in it for you?"

Maelcon smiled. "You are a canny man, Medraut, and far wiser than Arthur gives you credit. No, I do not wish to help you out of some sentimental desire to see two love birds united. I am offering to help you because I need something in return."

"And that is?"

"You are to journey with Owain to Din Arth soon. You will be close to him."

"What of it?"

"Owain is a dangerous man. He still believes himself to be regent even though my brother, God bless him, has relinquished the throne."

"You wish me to spy on him."

Medraut smiled. "Owain has always seen himself as a grander man than he really is. That was why he persuaded my father to make him king of Rhos. Do you think he would have ever been content with just that? Ever since my mother made him regent he has seen a chance to rule all of Venedotia. It is a power he does not intend to give up."

"Surely you don't think he would stand in your way to the throne?"

"I know he will, Medraut. My uncle's ambitions know no bounds. Mark my words, if we do nothing we will be calling Owain Pendraig before next winter."

Medraut frowned. "What *can* we do?"

"There is but one solution to this problem." Maelcon let his sentence hang in the air until realisation dawned on Medraut.

"You can't mean …?"

"Yes, I am afraid so. And the sooner the better. This cannot be allowed to fester and corrupt more people than it has already. Remember that Arthur is a friend to Owain and has made his feelings of me known already. If Arthur were to side with Owain against me then I might find myself fighting against my own teulu, or at least those who choose to follow Arthur. And to follow him would be to follow him to the grave."

"There are some who would not," said Medraut, and he was surprised at himself. His anger at Arthur had done the speaking in that moment but he could not truly say that he regretted his words. It was the truth. He remembered Alan's words of loyalty to him that morning. *And others would surely follow suit. Lonio, Sanddef, Morfran …*

Maelcon placed his hand on Medraut's shoulder. "That is good to hear. I know I can count on loyal men such as yourself in the hard days to come. But we must rescue the rest of the teulu from Owain. We must rescue *Arthur*."

Medraut bit his lip, knowing what Maelcon was asking him. "Is there no other way?"

Maelcon shook his head. "He is already too strong. Too popular. If I am to be king and if you are to marry Guenhuifach, Owain must die. Everything depends on it."

The rivers still had their skim of ice around the edges, crusting in the bends like sleep in the eyes of the land after its winter slumber. Instead of following the coast path, they had cut south-east through the picturesque landscape of frozen waterfalls and frost-bitten hills towards the fording point of the Afon Conui.

They had ridden in silence for the most part. Medraut hung at the back, wary of the warrior Owain had ordered to keep pace with him to make sure he didn't bolt for the wilderness. He didn't know why they bothered. The scene back at the Lys that morning had surely been enough to convince Owain that he had accepted his fate with grim determination.

He had desperately wanted to say goodbye to Guenhuifach before they left for Din Arth. *He* knew now that the time would come – once he had fulfilled his promise to Maelcon – when he would return to her and they would be finally free to love each other. But *she* didn't know that and he had no way of getting word to her. He feared that once he was gone she would be so consumed with grief that she might do something stupid like Branwen in the old tales.

But as it happened he had been able to convince her after all. She had appeared at the Lys just as they were preparing to set out and had all but flung herself in front of their horses.

"Why don't you just kill us both and be done with it!" she had cried. "Why torment us by separating us as if we were errant children?"

"Guenhuifach!" Guenhuifar had gasped, as Arthur sent two men to restrain her sister.

They began to drag her away and Medraut could not bear it. "Stop!" he cried, sliding down from his horse.

Owain and Arthur tensed, ready to foil any spontaneous escape the two lovers might attempt but Medraut held his hands up to them to show that he meant no mischief. "I just want to talk to her," he said.

They were allowed to embrace. Everybody probably thought that Medraut could calm the hysterical Guenhuifach, say his goodbyes and they could be on their way.

"Listen to me, Guenhuifach," Medraut had said softly into her ear. "We will be together again. And soon. It's been arranged."

She drew away from him and regarded him curiously through teary eyes.

"I can't explain now. You must trust me. We have an ally. But for the sake of all the gods, don't speak a word of it to a soul! I will return to you, Guenhuifach, I promise. But for now, let them think they have won."

Guenhuifach did him proud and slipped from his arms to kneel weeping as Owain's man came to take him back to his horse.

That sight of her, feigned though it may have been, had haunted Medraut the whole journey and made him even more determined not to fail in his task. *Soon, my love*, he thought. *Soon we will be free.*

It had taken them all day to cross the straits and wind their way through the rocky valleys. Night was falling and the Afon Conui was still a good distance off so a camp was made and they ate mutton around the fire, washed down with mead for extra warmth.

Those lucky enough to have tents clambered into them, their breaths steaming on the night air. The rest of the party bedded down around the campfire, cloaks wrapped tightly around them. Medraut positioned himself so that he had a good view of the entrance to Owain and Elen's tent.

As the snores began to sound around him, Medraut tried to stop his teeth chattering and wondered if it was the cold or the awful thing he had set his mind to. It wasn't the fear of being caught that made him so uneasy. There were few enough guards with the company and he could easily fight his way to freedom if the plan went sour. And he was confident that Maelcon would protect him should any accusations head his way. It was the primal gut-feeling of the whole thing. It was wrong, so wrong, he knew that. Yet, as Maelcon had told him, it was the only way to avoid the considerable bloodshed and destruction that was sure to consume Venedotia if it was not done.

And it was the only way he could be with Guenhuifach.

It was a selfish justification, but a powerful one nonetheless. It was a strange notion; to strike the first blow to ensure peace, but there it was.

The others were asleep now, he could hear them and he had to fight to keep his eyes open to avoid drifting off into slumber himself. He was so tired and it was so bitingly cold.

What if Owain failed to emerge from his tent? He would be forced to think of something else, and by that time they would be at Din Arth with guards all around not to mention all the handmaids, servants and stable boys that would make his task considerably more difficult.

The tent flap rippled and Medraut was sure it was just the breeze, toying with his nerves. But no, a hand fumbled its way out followed by Owain's bulky form, still cloaked in his bearskin mantle.

Does the bastard sleep in that thing?

Owain shook himself against the cold and ambled off towards the river, untying his breeches as he went. It was just as Medraut had hoped. Owain had been guzzling mead that night and, with the river bubbling and burbling nearby, a man's bladder required only so much coaxing.

As Owain's close-shaved head disappeared behind the tent, Medraut rose as silently as he could, hoping none of the others sharing the warmth of the campfire were awake to see him leave. He would have to take that chance.

Stealing quickly across the camp, he wove between the tents and made his way down to the riverbank.

Owain stood, his feet placed apart, steam billowing from his yawning mouth and the stream of piss that melted a hole through the icy crust of the river's edge.

Medraut's mouth was dry. He trembled all over and he tried to steel himself, summoning every ounce of courage and resolve. He would only have one chance at this. If he bungled it …

He stooped down and plucked a heavy river stone from its frozen depression. He weighed it in his hand as he approached Owain from behind. It was a good size. Heavy enough for the job.

He stood right behind Owain and held his breath so no wisp of warmth would give him away. He drew his hand back, the rock raised high.

Owain turned his head, only a fraction and Medraut would forever wonder what had given him away. It was of no consequence for the rock connected with the back of Owain's skull a fraction of a second later. He did not cry out but a small 'uuunnggh!' of surprise escaped his lips.

The sound was a sickening crunch. Blood started immediately, drenching the tawny bristles that covered the back of his head. He sank to his knees upon the ice which immediately crumbled, toppling him headfirst into the river.

Medraut tossed the stone into the water where the flow would wash away all traces of blood. Owain gurgled and spluttered, face down in the icy river. Blood pooled around him, flowing away in dark tendrils. Where it had stained the ice it showed pink, even in the moonlight. His arms worked, scrabbling at the riverbed, pushing, scraping.

He's trying to rise!

The job was not finished and, without a second thought, Medraut jumped forward to land on the stricken man, his knees in the small of his back.

Using both hands, he pushed Owain's head down, the scalp slippery with blood beneath his palms. Owain struggled, knowing that somebody was on top of him. He bucked and rolled and Medraut clung on with his knees as if he were breaking a stubborn colt.

He kept pressing down for what seemed like an age. Owain's thrashings grew weaker and eventually, mercifully, they subsided altogether.

Medraut got up off him and the body remained submerged, the great bearskin cloak sodden, weighing the dead man down. He washed the blood from his hands with scoopfuls of ice and tried to stop shivering. It was done.

The silence of the dark hills seemed laced with judgement and all that could be heard was the chuckling of the stream. Medraut looked to the starry sky as the tears froze on his cheeks.

Arthur

Slipped. The word was so careless. Flippant. Almost comical. *Slipped and fell*, they said. Apparently Owain had gone to take a piss in the river by moonlight and put a foot wrong which sent him tumbling into the freezing waters where he cracked his head open on a stone.

And Arthur didn't believe a word of it.

It was all far too convenient. Owain had represented the only real threat to Maelcon's ascension to the throne. It stank of conspiracy. He didn't think Bishop Dubricius was behind it but he did not put murder past Maelcon. *After all, the boy tried to murder Owain once before …*

But no accusations could be made. There were no witnesses and no suspects. It was possible an assassin had followed Owain from Ynys Mon and waited until dark to make his move but it was much more likely to Arthur's mind that the killer had been somebody in Owain's own following, some traitorous swine disguised as a servant.

It was said that all who had accompanied Owain to Rhos had been examined at length in the lofty hall of Din Arth but none of them knew anything. The elusive killer might as well have been a phantom.

There was to be a funeral of course but the icy atmosphere Owain had left behind him meant that it was to be held at Din Arth. Then there was the matter of his successor. Rhos was in a very precarious position. Owain's eldest son, Cunlas, was a mere child and would be even more ineffectual than his cousin,

Guidno. Once more, a regent would have to be appointed.

Arthur looked up at the guards on the palisade. Wrapped in their furs they looked like bundles of rags propped up by their spears. A light sleet was falling and the ground was slushy. He made his way to the Steward's Hall where Guenhuifar would be instructing the servants in the packing up of their belongings for the journey to Din Arth. After the funeral they would head south to Cair Cunor and await spring with hearts full of hope for a change in the wind for Venedotia.

As he passed the entrance to the Great Hall he spotted Guidno playing a game of chess with one of the guards in the antechamber. He was a deft hand at the game by all accounts and, as he moved one of his little bronze figures to take one of his opponent's silver ones, he grinned from ear to ear. It was the first time that Arthur could remember seeing the young lad smile. He supposed all the smiles in the world were his now that the unwelcome weight of his father's crown had been removed from his head and placed on his older brother's.

The hall of Guenhuifar's father felt desolate and empty since old Gogfran had died. Arthur thought back to the day when he, Cei, Menw and the others had carried a wounded Gualchmei to its door, begging for shelter from the Gaels. He had seen that hall rise to a noble household at the centre of a bustling court full of promise. Now both hall and court were a shell once more; a dead leaf of autumn drifting on changeable winds.

He found Guenhuifar in their bedchamber with a couple of handmaids. They were filling a chest with clothes and jewellery. She looked flustered. Her hair was tied back but one fiery tendril kept slipping loose and dangling in front of her left eye. She tucked it behind her ear irritably.

"Maelcon is preparing his own household to leave," he told her, "for Din Arth."

She glanced up at him, the stress of packing forgotten for a moment only to be replaced by concern. "You don't think he intends to travel with us do you? Oh, I couldn't bear that, Arthur!"

"No, we shall be well away before the royal household fully musters itself. Maelcon has gathered quite a following of servants and sycophants for a man who came here alone in a monk's habit."

Guenhuifar looked a little relieved at this. "I just want to get out of here, Arthur. I can't stand it, what with my sister not speaking to me and Maelcon strutting about as if he were already crowned when we all know that he …" she stopped herself just in time. Her unspoken words may be tantamount to treason once Maelcon had the crown of Venedotia on his head.

"Have you seen Guenhuifach?"

She shook her head. "She is hiding from the world in her infirmary. I intend to visit her before we leave but I haven't had the time with so much to organise."

Arthur glanced around at the packed chests and the stripped furnishings. "We don't have to take everything with us. This is still your family home."

"I would very much like to never set foot in it again," Guenhuifar said bitterly. It feels like a bed in the lion's den. Besides, Maelcon will be choosing his own steward sooner or later. He'll probably want to give this hall to whatever dribbling fawner he picks."

"He can't do that. This is your home."

Guenhuifar sighed and stepped into his embrace. "We both know that our king-to-be is very good at getting what he wants."

Arthur said nothing and held her close.

They were received at Din Arth with a mixture of desperate optimism and melancholy gratitude. Arthur had been a friend as well as a brother to Owain yet, as penteulu, he represented the military might of Maelcon's new rule.

Queen Elen gave them the same chamber that Arthur had previously learnt was the very chamber his mother had occupied during her brief stay, when he had been a babe in arms and her the abandoned lover of a king. It gave him a strange feeling to be in that very chamber after so much had happened in the intervening years.

In the Great Hall that night, Arthur spotted Medraut lurking in the shadows. He approached him with a horn of mead. Medraut considered the offering and took it almost begrudgingly.

"It's good to see you again, Medraut," Arthur said. "I am sorry for what happened on the road. It can't have been pleasant."

Medraut said nothing.

"You were there that night," Arthur continued. "Did you see anything? Do you suspect anybody who might have—"

"I have already gone over all this with Owain's steward with Queen Elen looking on," Medraut said peevishly. "I'm a stranger here. I know nothing about the people I travelled with save Owain and now he's dead."

"All right, I'm sorry," said Arthur. "Of course you have. I just want to find out who the killer is. He was my brother, after all." *And your uncle*, he nearly added. "Anyway, I want you to come back to Cair Cunor with me and Guenhuifar. There is little point in you remaining here. It was only ever a temporary solution."

"To Cair Cunor?" Medraut echoed.

"Yes. You are still my warrior as well as my son."

"Am I? It's hard to remember sometimes."

He did not specify which and Arthur did not ask.

The arrival of Maelcon and his followers two days later was met with much grumbling. Queen Elen did her best to play hostess to the man who was soon to be her king but all could see that it was a struggle to accommodate one whom many thought had murdered her husband. She even gave over her own chamber to Maelcon's disposal and Arthur knew that must have stung, but really, what choice did she have? Rhos's very sovereignty hung on its ability to stay in Maelcon's good graces.

King Mor and King Efiaun arrived and Arthur was glad to see them for they had been strong allies in previous years. They were the only kings to attend the funeral. Owain may have been well-liked by his own people but he had fostered a prickly relationship with the other rulers. The poor attendance only made Rhos's situation appear even more tenuous.

Owain's funeral was a sombre affair with much weeping on the part of his household. Bannermen from the Conui valley came to pay their respects and they were led by Afall, Meddyf's brother. Their father, old Maeldaf, had died several years previously and the valley bannermen looked to Afall with the same confidence and loyalty as they had looked to his father. They had also been fiercely loyal to Owain after he had ridden to their defence in the civil war, and now that their new king was regarded by many as Owain's murderer, the proceedings were given a fresh layer of tension.

Arthur watched Afall's face as the funeral rites were performed over Owain's body. Afall's eyes were fixed on his young nephew as Menw's words were all but snatched away by the wind. Owain had been a staunch pagan but he was one of the last. Menw's services would not be called upon for many more funerals as, one by one, Christian kings rose up to inherit pagan kingdoms. Maelcon stood alongside his mother and their attendants on one side of the great pyre while Queen Elen and Cunlas, the young son and heir of the deceased, faced them on the other with most of the other guests behind them. The new ruler of the eight kingdoms and his party were significantly outnumbered at the graveside but there was no doubt as to who held the upper hand.

The wind whistled across the moors and threatened to extinguish the torches that were intended to light the great pyre. It would be a considerably bad omen for Owain's shade if that were to happen. Little Cunlas visibly wept as the final words were said over his father's body; his thick head of tawny curls bowed in sorrow. At a nod from Menw, the attendants came forward with the torches and kindled the fire.

The feasting lasted for several days and was far longer and more drunken than Arthur felt was strictly necessary. But he could hardly blame them as he watched the sots crashing about between the benches, fighting, wenching and doing their damnedest to blot out reality for a few days. The worst offenders had loved Owain dearly and clearly strived to honour a man known for his own raucous behaviour. And all knew that a return to sobriety meant a return to the cold world of winter politics and the many unanswered questions about the future of Rhos.

Maelcon watched the debauchery with mild interest and great patience. He was biding his time, sipping his wine slowly and undoubtedly making his plans.

Eventually the feasting came to an end as everybody knew it had to. The stores were exhausted and most of the furniture broken and the revellers utterly spent. Only then did Maelcon call his council.

The hall was cleared of debris and slumbering wrecks. The servants were ordered to scrub it clean, lay down fresh rushes and hang the Pendraig's banner behind the dais at the head of the hall. Now was the time for talk.

Arthur arrived to find Maelcon already seated at the high table with Mor and Efiaun taking their seats.

"This is to be an unofficial council," Maelcon began. "My first real council will be held once I am crowned in the spring."

"Speaking of which, my lord," said Mor, "has a date been decided on for that much-anticipated event?"

"Two days after Pascha," said Maelcon. "Bishop Dubricius will crown me before the rulers of the other kingdoms. And that brings me to the first point on my agenda. Rhos is without its king. One will have to be chosen."

"Surely Owain is to be succeeded by his eldest son, Cunlas?" said Efiaun.

"That would be the most prudent way forward," said Maelcon. "But Cunlas is only thirteen. He will need a regent."

Several pairs of eyes turned to Arthur. Maelcon noticed this and smiled. "I appreciate the notion, my lords, but Arthur is a military man, not a king and I need Venedotia's penteulu ready to strike down our enemies at a moment's notice. He will be absent from court too often to provide much of a guiding hand for Rhos's young king-in-waiting."

"Then who, my lord?" asked Mor.

"Me," answered Maelcon. "I am his cousin, after all. And I have given serious thought to moving Venedotia's royal seat back to Cair Dugannu. From there I can be close enough to Din Arth to give the young Cunlas my undivided attention."

"You think to abandon your father's Lys? Efiaun said.

"My father's stronghold on Ynys Mon was an adequate base for his campaigns against the Gaels but those dark days are over and we must look to Venedotia's place in Albion's ever-changing political landscape. For too long has our family isolated itself on that windswept isle while our southern borders lie neglected. Cair Dugannu was my childhood home and from its vantage point I intend to play a much stronger role in the ruling of the eight kingdoms than my father ever did."

There was a noticeable moment of discomfort among the assembled council members as each struggled for something to say.

"Has the idea of your being Cunlas's regent been discussed with Queen Elen?" Arthur said. "Has she given her consent?"

"Consent?" asked Maelcon. "I was not aware that the Pendraig required a widow's consent in matters of state. She will accept my decision and my protection. It is, after all, in her best interests."

Once the council had adjourned, Maelcon asked Arthur to remain behind for a private word. "They look up to you, Arthur," the young prince said. "You have brought Venedotia fame and honour far from its borders. I hope now that you will be as loyal and valiant within its borders for, make no mistake, dark days are ahead."

"My loyalty is, as ever, to the dragon standard and to Venedotia," Arthur replied. "And as for dark days ahead, do you know something we do not?"

"I face opposition; that is no secret. Perhaps my allegiance to the Church and to God has made me enemies among the followers of the old path. Mor and Efiaun I know are pagans. What about you, Arthur?"

"My mind is open on the subject of religion," said Arthur. "Like you, my mother was a Christian and my father a pagan. I pay all gods the appropriate respect out of a desire to hedge my bets."

"I see. Perhaps, once you have seen what I can achieve with God on my side, you will reconsider your position and place your 'bet' on your mother's faith."

"Perhaps."

"But in order to achieve great things in God's name I shall need you, Arthur. That is why I want you with me at Cair Dugannu."

"Cair Dugannu? We are leaving for Cair Cunor in two days' time. I have not seen my commanders since we wintered."

"Your commanders will have things under control, I am sure. People tell me that no penteulu in all Albion inspires such loyalty in their men. I need the hero of Badon by my side in these treacherous times."

"Surely you don't expect a threat to your life?"

Maelcon shrugged. "Who knows what men will do to preserve their own interests? I represent a change for Venedotia, make no mistake. And yes, Arthur, I do fear for my life and for Venedotia's future. We have rocky days ahead but we shall emerge victorious, so long as you are with me."

He left Arthur then, and retired to his chambers. Arthur felt stunned. He trusted Maelcon no more than any of the other council members yet the boy had a way with words, it had to be admitted. After only a brief conversation, Arthur was left with a creeping shame for ever having entertained the notion that Maelcon had murdered Owain. And yet, deep within him, that suspicion remained, festering and threatening to rise. But what could he do about it? He had as good as pledged his loyalty to Maelcon once more, not three minutes past. The prince had an uncanny way of making even the staunchest opposer act as a friend if only in his presence. He would follow Maelcon to Cair Dugannu. What choice did he have?

He found Mor and Efiaun waiting for him outside.

"The boy must be stopped," said Mor in a hushed tone. "Else he will start laying claim to all our kingdoms, one by one."

"Let's not exaggerate things," Arthur cautioned. "He sees an opportunity in Owain's death. It sits as ill with me as it does with you but there it is; an opportunity he wishes to exploit, no more than that."

"He seeks to build his powerbase," said Mor. "With the backing of the Church, he already has most of the people on his side. They have been waiting for a Christian ruler for many years now. We are the remnants of the old way of things. And now, he has set his eyes on Rhos and one of the mightiest forts in Venedotia. We must be cautious of his ambitions, Arthur."

"Elen will not take this lightly," said Efiaun. "What of Meddyf? Does she condone her son's decision? She and Elen were friends as I recall."

"Meddyf's power, I fear, is dissipated," said Arthur. "Between Bishop Dubricius's manipulations and Maelcon's ruthless ambition, she has been effectively side-lined. Her thoughts on the matter are irrelevant."

"But ours aren't," said Mor. "Maelcon can be stopped if we work together. Not all the other kings will support him, I am sure of it. If we could get word to them …"

"Stop!" said Arthur. "I beg you not to pursue this conversation in my presence."

"Come now, Arthur! You of all people surely do not fear a stripling of a lad, or the backing of his precious Church."

"Fear? I fear for my own honour. I am pledged to him in ways far stronger than you are. I am Venedotia's penteulu and as such, am answerable directly to him. And he already fears rebellion. That is why he has asked me to remain with him at Cair Dugannu."

"He's asked you to what?" Guenhuifar exclaimed later that evening.

She was packing once more. Now that the funeral feast was over, she was eager to continue their journey to Cair Cunor.

"I am to help him in the organisation of things at Cair Dugannu. There will be much to do and I believe he fears dissent. It is a precaution, nothing more."

"You are the most renowned warrior in Venedotia, husband, but you are just one man. What protection can you offer him when the entire teulu is at Cair Cunor?"

Arthur had no answer to that. The request had struck him as odd too but he was honour-bound to do his duty. If the Pendraig wished him to handfeed him olives and honey he would have to obey. "You are to continue to Cair Cunor with Medraut. See that he is settled back in and given plenty to occupy his mind. He still grieves for your sister. Tell Cei to have the teulu on standby. We don't know how the coming weeks are going to go. I will come to you as soon as I am able."

"Arthur, he is separating you from the teulu, you do see that, don't you?"

The thought had occurred to Arthur but, as with all things Maelcon said and did, his true intentions were masked. "I have no choice, Guenhuifar. I am the penteulu. I *must* heed his demands."

"Your loyalty is to Venedotia, to its people. What if Maelcon is the worst thing for both? Will you willingly defend a tyrant?"

"Tyrant? Now you sound like Mor and Efiaun. They were all for including me in some hair-brained rebellion earlier today. Maelcon is young. He hasn't even been crowned yet. None of us know what sort of a king he will be. All this suspicion and ill-feeling may be unfounded."

"Arthur, he murdered Owain!"

Arthur felt anger bubbling within him. "What would you have me do, Guenhuifar? Betray the Pendraig? Cast to the flames all my years of loyalty to Venedotia and to the dragon standard and make us traitors? Would you have another civil war?"

"Want? I want none of these things." She approached him and placed a hand on his bearded check. "All I want is for you to do what you know is right."

Guenhuifar departed the next day. As the wains were being loaded and the small column of warriors and attendants marshalled in Din Arth's courtyard, Arthur made his way down from the Great Hall. He spotted Medraut heading towards the training yard with a pair of wooden foils over his shoulder. He was stripped to the waist, the chill morning air apparently about to be banished by several energetic rounds between the posts.

"Why aren't you getting ready to march south with the others?" Arthur asked him.

Medraut turned his sullen eyes upon Arthur. "I'm not going to Cair Cunor. Maelcon has asked me to journey with him to Cair Dugannu. I am to be the captain of his personal guard."

"I wasn't made aware of this. Nor did I give my consent."

"The order came from the Pendraig. I'm sure he doesn't require your consent."

Arthur knew he wasn't going to get anywhere with Medraut and so left him to continue on his way to the training yard. He headed back to the Great Hall in search of Maelcon.

"My lord, I have just learned that you have removed my son from the teulu and placed him in your service."

"Yes, young Medraut surely deserves some recognition for his heroic exploits in Lindis," said

Maelcon. "He told me of his frustrations at not being promoted to the rank of commander within the teulu; your own son at that. For shame, Arthur!"

The comment was accompanied by a jovial wink but it rankled all the same with Arthur. He was in no mood for jests.

"You could have broached the subject with me, my lord."

"I assumed you would have no objection. After all, was your rakish son not banished to Din Arth after carrying on with his own aunt? I would have thought you'd like me to take him off your hands. And I must say that most fathers would be proud to see their son serve in the Pendraig's household guard. I apologise if I stepped on your toes, Arthur, but you see, I have grown rather fond of your son. Do you know I met him on my way into my father's Lys at the start of winter? It was Medraut who first welcomed me. We have had a few good chats."

"No," said Arthur. "I did not know that."

"Well, I hope it's all right, me taking him from you. And his companions. I've heard they serve him as loyally as Cei or Beduir serve you. It would be a shame to separate them. That kind of devotion in men to their captain cannot be bought."

Arthur had nothing further to say. If Maelcon wanted men from the teulu to serve in his own household, there was little he could do about it. In fact, there was little he could do about anything Maelcon set his mind to, other than nod and agree as a dutiful servant should. This thought preyed on his mind as he bade farewell to Guenhuifar and his sons later that day and watched the small train of wagons head south, away from him.

Arthur had visited Cair Dugannu a couple of times in the past few years but he could never shake the haunting memories of the night he, Cei, Guenhuifar and the others had retaken it from the Gaels. It was that daring mission that had brought the civil war to a close and heaped fame and honour upon their names. But for him that night could only be a nightmare. The men they had butchered in their sleep; the weight of Diugurnach's severed head in his hand as he held the grisly trophy up to intimidate his followers into surrendering; Anna and her cauldron up in the royal apartment: *Medraut's mother.*

Medraut showed no emotion as they rode in through the east gate. The fortress, straddling two hills was occupied only by a small garrison who hastened to form some sort of reception party for the new Pendraig. Many of the buildings had not been inhabited in years and they showed it. Thatch had mouldered and fences were furry with green moss. If this was to become Maelcon's new seat, then there was much work to be done.

Arthur found himself at a loose end over the next few days. Medraut, Alan and Lonio were no longer his men and, as such, he had very little to do with them. They spent much of their time training new recruits and selecting the best for induction into the king's guard.

People began to trickle in from near and far, word having spread that Cair Dugannu was to become a royal seat once more. As more warriors were selected, more food and craftsmen were needed and the surrounding settlements hustled to deliver. Houses and outbuildings were repaired, the granaries filled and smoke began to emerge from forges and hearths long left cold. Within a few days the fortress had begun to resemble its old self once more.

It was the arrival of the party from Ynys Mon that completed the transition from partially abandoned outpost to royal seat. Maelcon had ordered the rest of his household along with all people of use to him to depart his father's Lys and cross the straits for their new home. Meddyf arrived with her handmaidens and was given her old chambers on the north face of the fortress.

With them came Guenhuifach.

Many eyes watched Medraut cross the muddy courtyard to take her into his arms. They held the embrace for several moments. Nobody said anything. Nobody dared. Medraut had taken his place in this new world Maelcon was forging and it was a place of high status. Many warriors who guarded the palisades had been trained by him and, as captain of the Pendraig's guard, he held a position of considerable authority.

That night in the Great Hall, Medraut declared his and Guenhuifach's betrothal. Arthur slammed his wine cup down as the hall erupted into applause. Later he took Medraut by the arm and pulled him to one side.

"Just what the hell do you think you're playing at?" he demanded.

Medraut shook himself free of his grip. "I assume you are referring to my marriage plans."

"You can't marry Guenhuifach. She's your bloody aunt!"

"We've been over this, Arthur," Medraut said. A fire burned in his eyes, born of more than the mead he had drunk. "She is only my aunt because you adopted me. There is no shared blood and therefore no sin."

"Sin? Since when do you care about the laws of the Christian Church?"

"Since now. And I am going to be paying much closer attention to them in the future for we are to be baptised before our marriage. It will be Bishop Dubricius who marries us. Maelcon has spoken to him."

Arthur blinked. *Medraut, a Christian?* The notion was less surprising than the realisation of how close Medraut was getting to the Pendraig and his spiritual advisors. *Close enough for strings to be pulled and favours granted.* His mind drifted to a mountain pass; moonlight turning an icy river to silver. Blood streaking the snow. Owain face down in the freezing water.

Stop.

It was a path he did not want to walk down for its destination was too awful to be true. It *couldn't* be true.

"We are to be married and there is nothing you can do to stop it," Medraut went on. "Unless you want to defy the future Pendraig."

"This will break Guenhuifar's heart," said Arthur.

There was a brief moment of regret in the boy's eyes at these words but he quickly masked it with his usual bravado. "She must learn to live with her decisions. As must we all."

Maelcon called a council the following day and Arthur found himself sitting at a table in the Great Hall along with Medraut, whose presence at the table he found questionable. What purpose did a captain of a king's household guard have at a king's council?

The young prince arrived wearing his customary monk's robe. Arthur wondered if he would start dressing like royalty once he was crowned or if he would carry on this faux-humility for his entire reign. His tonsured head had at least started to vanish under a short mat of hair so it didn't look like a monk was ruling the eight kingdoms.

"We have made great progress, my lords, in fortifying my new royal seat here at Cair Dugannu. Medraut has bolstered our garrison with expertly trained troops and our palisades are as strong and high as ever. We are in a prime position to strike at our enemies, just as we were under Cunedag and Enniaun Yrth, not cowering on some island as my father did."

If anybody else felt discomfort at these words, Arthur did not notice. He seemed to be the only person at the table who wasn't nodding and smiling in agreement with Venedotia's new master.

"The time has come for us to strike at our enemies before they have a chance to strike at us," Maelcon continued.

"And who exactly are our enemies?" Arthur asked.

Maelcon smiled. "It is no secret that I face opposition from within the eight kingdoms. You have all heard, no doubt, King Mor and King Efiaun voice their opinions of me."

"Opinions are one thing," said Arthur, suddenly not liking where this discussion was headed. "Enemies are made of more than words."

"On the contrary, Arthur," said Maelcon. "If the seven kings do not accept me as their Pendraig, then that refusal will only fester into outright treason. And I do not have to remind you that Rumaniog lies between here and Cair Cunor. If King Mor turns against me, we will be cut off from the teulu."

"But we can be sure of Eternion's support," said Medraut. "King Cungen has voiced his approval of you."

"And yet he would have to cross Rumaniog to reach me. Communications between us would be vulnerable to disruption by King Mor's agents. You must understand, lords, that I cannot have a hostile territory isolating me from my allies. That is why we must strike Mor before he can put whatever treachery he has in mind into practise."

"What do you mean 'strike Mor'?" Arthur asked.

"A complete invasion of his kingdom," said Maelcon. "Oust him from his royal seat and absorb Rumaniog into Rhos."

There was a silence at the table. Even Maelcon's strongest supporters were rendered momentarily speechless by such a drastic and ruthless plan.

"Mor has been a loyal supporter of the dragon banner for years!" exclaimed Arthur. "He was the first to heed the call to arms during the civil war. His support helped us win that war. He is no traitor!"

"He is your friend, I know, Arthur. But you must see that his loyalty to the dragon standard has waned. His loyalty to me is non-existent by all accounts. This will be hard for you but you must see that immediate action is prudent else we get dragged into another civil war. Nobody wants that, surely? As my penteulu, it is time for you to show your loyalty to me, Arthur. You must ride to Cair Cunor on the morrow and marshal the teulu. I will send a messenger with orders to strike at Rumaniog's southern borders while I simultaneously march in from the north. We will catch Mor between us and, God willing, without too much bloodshed."

Arthur could barely believe his ears. He had always been loyal to the Pendraig, indeed his very presence here at Maelcon's side was testament to his loyalty however much he found it disagreeable. But now he was being asked to invade a peaceful kingdom, a kingdom ruled by one of the Dragons of the North. A kingdom ruled by his friend. It was sheer madness. Mor was no more plotting rebellion than he was. But Maelcon had seemingly infected all of his followers with his paranoid delusions.

But he needs the teulu to carry out his orders. He remembered Meddyf's words to Guenhuifar in his presence several months ago; 'Whoever has the support of your husband, is Venedotia's true ruler.' It was not a thought he had ever liked to dwell upon but the simple truth of it was brought kicking and screaming to the forefront of his mind. Whoever had his and the teulu's support, could rule Venedotia. And he had just been made aware that almost anybody was a preferable ruler than Maelcon.

He rose from his seat. "No."

Surprised heads turned to face him.

"No?" Maelcon repeated. There was a half-smile on his face that told Arthur something. It told him that this had all been a test of his loyalty. Perhaps Maelcon wasn't really serious about invading Rumaniog and had just wanted to see what his response would be. Well, Arthur had given it. He had said no and declared himself an insubordinate. Very well. If that was how Maelcon wanted it. He would not serve a madman who toyed with people like this. And he would not attack an ally.

"This plan is madness," he said. "Mor is a loyal subject and to attack him without provocation would be a monstrous act. I will not do it."

"Then perhaps the time has come for me to appoint a new penteulu," said Maelcon.

"Do as you will. I release myself of your service but know this; I will not be alone in my opinion. If you proceed down this unjust path, you will find the teulu to be greatly reduced, no matter who you appoint to lead it."

And with that he turned and left the table, his footsteps echoing in the lofty hall. As he pushed his way through the doors, he felt a hand grab his arm.

Fearing assault, he spun around, his own hand reaching for the dagger at his belt. It was Medraut.

"Don't be a fool, Arthur," said Medraut. "You can't turn your back on the Pendraig."

"He is not yet the Pendraig," Arthur replied. "And whether or not he becomes the Pendraig at all is largely dependent on the support he enjoys so you might want to consider that now, while there is still time."

"I am confident in my support of him."

"Well, what he has just asked me to do has caused me to gravely question mine."

"So, what are you going to do, join Mor in his revolt against Maelcon?"

"Mor's so-called revolt is a fever dream of a mad tyrant! He isn't Maelcon's enemy but if we invade Rumaniog, he will be and few other kings besides! Maelcon means to throw us into another civil war, can't you see that?"

"Maelcon is a wise ruler. His reign could usher in a new era for Venedotia, one that sees it become stronger than it has ever been before! If only people will take a chance on his dream!"

"Are you sure your opinion of him is not influenced by his support for you and Guenhuifach? A favour can be as good as a fishing line to reel in a catch. Before long you may find yourself asked to do something you find questionable and be powerless to refuse."

There was a look in Medraut's eyes that Arthur couldn't not quite decipher. Was it guilt? Shame?

"We must all do things we find unpleasant if we are to bring about a brighter future," said Medraut, his eyes looking at the ground. "Small sacrifices in the greater scheme of things."

And there it was. *Maelcon already has him on his line and he is slowly but surely reeling him in. What did he make you do, lad? By all the gods, say it wasn't that!*

"Is there anything you want to tell me, Medraut? Something on your mind? I know we haven't seen eye to eye of late but I am still your father and if you are in any trouble I will do what I can to save you."

Medraut said nothing.

Gods, are those tears welling in his eyes? "I am going to leave here," Arthur told him. "Come with me."

Medraut shook his head and looked up at him. If there had been any trace of tears in those eyes they had quickly vanished to be replaced by the usual defiance. "You must do what you deem right, *Father*. I have already made my bed."

He turned away and strode back into the Great Hall leaving Arthur alone in the windy courtyard of the northern hill.

Night fell over the coast like a mantle of velvet. The sky was clogged with clouds and there was precious little moonlight to see the hills and treetops nearby. Points of torchlight from the sentries were the only sources of light and it felt as if the fortress was alone in a black void.

A footstep creaked on the wooden gallery that ran along the inside of the northern palisade. The door to Arthur's chamber was pushed gently open and a shadow filled the doorframe. Light from the torches on the gallery made the figure a silhouette, its face a black oval.

It stepped into the room, silent as death, and approached the bed. What little light there was caught the long blade the figure held in its hand. It stood over the bed and raised the implement high. It paused, knife held up. It reached out with its other hand and whipped the blanket off the bed revealing an empty mattress.

Arthur stepped out of the shadow of the open door and slipped his arm around the assassin's throat, gripping him tightly. As his body tensed with fright, Arthur slipped his own dagger up under the ribs, just above the right kidney.

A sharp gasp escaped the assassin's lips and Arthur withdrew the dagger and then brought it up to the throat, drawing it quickly across, severing the windpipe.

As the assassin sank noiselessly to the floorboards, Arthur saw that it was a man he did not recognise. Blood bubbled and foamed in the man's mouth and at the gash in his throat as he choked and bled to death.

Thank the gods it wasn't Medraut.

If Cabal had been sharing his bedchamber, the assassin wouldn't have even made it to the bedside before having his throat torn out. But when Arthur was not on campaign, he always kennelled the dog for it was not considered seemly for a noble to share his bed with an animal. Another reason why Arthur preferred the warrior's life of canvas tents and close company to the draughty loneliness of nobility.

He hadn't been sure that Maelcon would try to have him murdered that night but the thought had crossed his mind. Maelcon was hardly going to allow him to leave his service and return to the teulu at Cair Cunor after his public defiance of him. It paid to be cautious, so he had decided to sleep in the chair he had placed behind the door, just in case. Now he knew. Now he knew the nature of the monster he had to escape from, had to save Venedotia from. And he was glad. His mind had not been so sure of anything for months.

He had to leave, before the assassin's failure became known. He wiped his blade on the dying man's tunica and sheathed it. He had to travel light and so he took only the essentials. He buckled *Caledbulc* around his waist and threw a riding cloak over his shoulders. Then, he left the dying man in his chamber and stepped out onto the gallery.

The courtyard on the northern hill was deserted. Wisps of smoke drifted from the torches on the palisades and the shadows were long and thin. Arthur descended to ground level and made his way towards the kennels. He found the kennel boy asleep and even the whining of the hounds at his approach did not wake him. He released Cabal and they left together, heading towards the gate that led down from the northern hill. It was open, as it always was during peacetime, but Arthur knew the eastern gate would not be.

The stables were down in the dip between the two hills and Arthur kept close to the rock and out of sight from the palisades as he headed down the path towards them. He found Hengroen nibbling at the hay feeder and the white stallion nickered softly as he sensed his master's familiar presence. Arthur saddled him as quickly and as quietly as he could and then led him by the bridle out in to the night.

A single guard stood atop the gate, facing outwards, the light from the nearby torch glinting off his helm. He probably was unaware that Maelcon had tried to have Arthur murdered and would open the gate if Arthur ordered him to but he didn't want to take the chance. If the guard was forewarned, then he would raise hell.

Arthur crept into the shadows of the buildings and plucked up a pebble from the mud. With a careful aim he hurled it at the guard, hoping to bounce it off the back of his helm and gain his attention. As it happened, his aim was poor that night and the pebble fell short, striking the back of the palisade by his left foot. But it had the desired effect and caused the guard to glance down and then back into the fortress.

It didn't seem to bother him too much for he soon lost interest and resumed his vigil of the surrounding countryside. Arthur picked up a second pebble and hurled it higher and harder. This time it struck the guard in the small of the back and he yelped in pain. He spun around and made for the ladder, muttering foul curses to himself. As he approached the shadows of the buildings, Arthur heard him say; "Little bastards! Don't know what your parents are thinking letting you be up and about at this hour! If I catch you, I'll have the hides off you!"

Arthur led Cabal into a space between buildings and they hid in the shadows of the overhanging thatch. As the guard passed by, he whistled. The guard spun around and strode towards him. "I've got you now!" the guard hissed.

When he was near enough, Arthur lurched out of the shadows and grabbed the guard by the throat. Ripping the helm off his head, he slammed the unfortunate warrior headfirst into a thick pillar that supported the overhang. He slumped to the ground, unconscious. Cabal whined softly and regarded Arthur with a cocked head.

After concealing the slumbering guard within the shadowed overhang, Arthur hurried up to the gate and began unbolting the great double doors.

"Hold it!" said a voice from the darkness and Arthur turned to see two young warriors approaching him from the buildings. One of them levelled his spear at him. The man recognised Arthur and his face showed a sudden concern and deep suspicion. "Lord Arthur, sir," he said. "Why are you opening the eastern gate at the dead of night? And where is the guard?"

"The guard got taken suddenly ill and ran off to empty his bowels," Arthur lied. "I am taking the night air."

"Outside the fortress?" the warrior asked. "And is that your pale horse I see loitering in the shadows? Looks to me like you're leaving us."

"You overstep your mark, warrior," said Arthur. "Return to your post and we shall say no more about it."

"No, I don't think so," said the warrior. "You see, we serve Medraut, not you. And I heard about the row in the king's council this afternoon. The talk is that you think to defy Maelcon, our new Pendraig. And here we find you sneaking out under cover of darkness with the guard mysteriously vanished. I'm afraid we're going to have to accompany you to the Great Hall to await examination. *Sir.*"

"Don't do this, lads," said Arthur, his hand dropping to *Caledbulc's* hilt.

"I shall do my duty," said the warrior.

Arthur drew his sword and the warrior lunged. Dodging the thrust, Arthur hewed through the elm shaft and booted the man in the belly, doubling him over. The second warrior followed up the attack and Cabal went for him.

He yelped in pain as the hound's jaws closed on his thigh and beat at Cabal's head with his spear butt.

Arthur brought *Caledbulc* about in a sideways sweep, slashing through leather and cloth and opening the first guard's belly so that his intestines bulged outwards. He fell with a cry. Arthur turned his attention to the other warrior. He barked an order and Cabal released him. The guard took his moment to turn tail and flee at a fast limp.

"Stay …" Arthur told Cabal. Then, he cursed. He couldn't let the wounded guard rouse the entire fortress or they would be ridden down before daybreak. He plucked up the spear the guard had dropped and twirled it into an overhead grip. With a leap and a lunge, he hurled it at his retreating target. It flew through the air and embedded itself in the young warrior's back, the force of it hurling him forwards. He fell headlong, the spear wobbling in his back.

Arthur gritted his teeth. He had wanted to get away without bloodshed but now the first two casualties in the war to come had fallen. He dragged them both into the shadows of the stables and then jogged back to the palisade to retrieve Hengroen and be on his way.

Once beyond the fortress walls, he mounted Hengroen and kicked him into a gallop, following the sweeping curve of the hill as he turned south to follow the Conui valley, Cabal keeping pace with him.

His mind roiled like a tempest. To return to Cair Cunor and the teulu after he had defied Maelcon and left two dead men in his wake, would be as good as declaring war on the Pendraig. But there were no other options left open to him. Maelcon had pushed him in to this.

Most of the teulu would follow him but some, *many*, would rather not be called traitors and might leave the teulu to support Maelcon. There was no telling who would have the larger following.

He rode through the night and for much of the next day, stopping only to water and rest Hengroen and Cabal. As the familiar walls of Cair Cunor came in to sight by the evening light of the next day, the three of them were utterly exhausted.

There was much confusion and concern as he rode in through the fort's gates and he was greatly comforted to be surrounded by his friends and family once more. Guenhuifar ran down from the principia to greet him, Amhar and Lacheu running along in her wake. Cei was summoned and he came hurrying down the central range.

"What's happened?" Guenhuifar asked, as Arthur drew his sons close to him and hugged them tight.

"Venedotia has fallen into the hands of a tyrant. I barely escaped with my life."

"He tried to have you killed?" Cei asked. "Then Mor and Efiaun were right …"

"Yes. Muster the teulu. Send word to Mor and Efiaun and tell them to do the same. War is coming."

"War?" Guenhuifar exclaimed. "What of Medraut?"

Arthur pulled her to him and held her tightly. "Maelcon has poisoned his mind against us. We've lost him, Guenhuifar. He is no longer our son."

PART IV

"...and the third: the three-fold dividing by Arthur of his men with Medrawd at Camlann."
- Three Unfortunate Counsels of the Island of Britain. The Triads of the Island of Britain

Medraut

The wedding of Medraut and Guenhuifach took place in Cair Dugannu's Great Hall with all the honours and attention to the occasion afforded. As promised, Bishop Dubricius arrived to preside over both baptism and wedding.

Being a man who had paid as little attention to religion as he could get away with, Medraut had no objection to going along with whatever was required of him but Guenhuifach showed more reserve.

"I look to the gods for guidance and instruction in my healing practices," she said. "The old path has been my path all my life as it has been for many of us on Ynys Mon."

"Nobody is asking you to turn your back on the old gods," said Medraut. "What's one more?"

"You don't understand. Men like Dubricius see the old gods as false or worse; companions of their great enemy, Satan. If we are to be baptised, we will be asked to renounce the old gods."

"Play the game, Guenhuifach," said Medraut. "Maelcon has populated his court with Christians to keep old Dubricius happy and ensure the support of the Church. He's doing what he can to ensure the best for Venedotia. So must we. It's just for appearances."

Guenhuifach did not look pleased but Medraut convinced her that the only way they could get married was with Maelcon's blessing and that came with a price. And so, upon the morning of their wedding, a great plank tub was carried into the hall and placed before the dais. Many pails of water were needed to even half fill it and when Medraut clambered in, stripped to his underclothes in front of the assembled court, the icy water just reached to his middle.

The bishop spoke words in Latin as he anointed Medraut with oil and Medraut responded as he had rehearsed by confirming that he renounced the devil and all his works and confessed his faith in the Trinity. Then, a silver bowl was produced with which the bishop scooped up water and poured it over Medraut's head, leaving him shivering and stifling a curse.

He was allowed to towel himself off while Guenhuifach stepped into the baptismal tub and the process began anew. As he watched her standing there, her white shift billowing about her waist in the water, her golden, unbraided hair falling loose on either side of her neck to cover each breast, he was reminded of how beautiful she was. His love for her swelled with the knowledge, that as she renounced the old ways and confirmed her faith in the Christian religion, she was aching inside with the feeling of treachery. He knew that feeling all too well and he loved her for doing what was needed for the greater good.

Their faith officially confirmed, they were led to the dais and stood side by side, their dripping hair forming puddles on the flagged floor as the wedding ceremony began. When it was over they were allowed to retire to their chambers and dress in more appropriate clothing while the hall was prepared for the wedding feast.

It was a grand affair and Maelcon seemed to have spared no expense, celebrating the guests as if it were a royal occasion. Part way through the feast, he rose and called for silence.

"Companions, I want you all to join me in honouring one of my most loyal supporters in his marriage to such a rare beauty."

Benches and chairs scraped against the flags as the entire hall rose and lifted cups, horns and goblets to drink the health of the newlyweds.

"My lord, I am deeply flattered ..." said Medraut, colouring at the attention.

"Now is not the time for humble meekness, Medraut," said Maelcon. "Tonight is not just a celebration of your marriage." He turned his face to the rest of the hall. "Tonight I have an announcement to make that will begin to set things right in Venedotia. As you know, the great Arthur has deserted my side and thus abandoned his duty as my penteulu. I have decided to name a new penteulu; a man who will carry the banner of the red dragon to new victories and that person is Medraut!"

The hall erupted into applause and Medraut felt his legs go weak. He glanced to Guenhuifach for support but received only a pale gaze that mirrored his own. *Penteulu of Venedotia? Replace Arthur?* It was everything he had ever hoped for and yet everything he feared rolled into one. He desperately thought for something to say but Maelcon was not finished.

"We have been left vulnerable since Arthur fled leaving two dead guards in his wake."

There was a low grumble at this. Arthur's betrayal had stung them all deeply.

"He undoubtedly sits at Cair Cunor plotting with my other enemies. Medraut here has remained loyal when his own uncle and adoptive father betrayed the dragon banner. His victories against the Saeson in Lindis are renowned and that is why I know he is the man to lead our teulu and our kingdom to greatness in the years to come! Drink now, to Medraut and to Venedotia's bright future!"

The air was ecstatic and wine and mead were poured down throats hoarse from jubilant cries. Medraut sat down and fumbled for his own wine cup. Things were moving too fast. In a matter of weeks he had gone from a lowly patrol captain to the highest military rank in Venedotia, perhaps all Albion.

Why then, am I filled with dread?

Guenhuifach sensed his trepidation and placed her hand in his. He looked at her and smiled. *At least I have you, my love. At least we are together at last.*

The following day Maelcon called Medraut to a private audience.

"We must move swiftly," he told him. "I don't know how Arthur will react when he learns that you are the new penteulu but have no doubt; the news *will* reach him soon."

"You don't think he'd pose a threat, my lord?" Medraut asked.

Maelcon shrugged. "You know him better than I. If Mor and Efiaun throw their support behind him then we may very well be facing a rebellion from Cair Cunor. The teulu is there at the moment and even those among them who are my supporters may feel too afraid to flee north and take their places under your command. We must draw them out of that fortress. Once they are in the open, we shall see Arthur's warband dissipate around him."

"Draw them out? How?"

"By attacking Rumaniog. It was my original plan but after Arthur threw it back in my face and turned traitor, I have been unable to follow through with it. I have called for support from those kings loyal to me; men from Docmaeling and the Laigin Peninsula. It will take them some days to get here but until they do, we must make ready for war."

The following days passed as a blur in Medraut's mind. There was so much to do, so much to organise and initially he felt as if he were floundering, not having the first clue where to start. He was used to leading a patrol of nine men – men that he knew and had trained with for years – but building a teulu from the ground up? This had never been a plan of his.

Fortunately, Maelcon did his part to ensure a steady flow of new recruits and it fell to Medraut to train them and organise them; a task much more suited to his skills. Politics had always been a mysterious art far beyond his ken and there was a great deal of political wrangling in the raising of a teulu from nothing.

The new warriors mostly came from the commotes of the Laigin Peninsula, the lords of which had bristled for years under the rule of Efiaun. Cadwallon had punished their part in supporting Meriaun in the civil war by stripping them of their independence and giving them over to Dunauding's control. Now they were eager to support a new Pendraig who might restore to them their previous status as independent commotes. There was a deep grudge, Medraut realised, that had festered in Venedotia since before he had been born. A grudge created by their fathers and uncles. The coming war was the only thing that could cleanse it. The old order must be swept aside so that Maelcon's rule could be the final cure that would put old hatreds to bed and ensure peace for generations.

Warriors from the coastal settlements and the mountain villages trickled in through Cair Dugannu's gates to bolster the growing teulu, along with men from Docmailing who crossed Rhos's eastern marches. Medraut soon found himself in charge of more men than he knew what to do with.

He appointed Alan as his first captain. He wished Sanddef and Morfran were with him for they too would make fine leaders of companies. He knew that their loyalty to him would come through once Arthur led what was left of his teulu out in to the open and they were given the opportunity to desert him. Just as Maelcon predicted. He looked forward to that day with an eagerness as keen as his sword's edge.

Finally, after many days of hard training overseen by Medraut and Alan and much resourcing of manpower, horses and fodder, Maelcon's teulu began to resemble a fighting unit that could defend and protect borders, smash enemies and hold fortresses. It was smaller than Arthur's teulu, there was no doubt about it, but Medraut sensed a youthful hunger and keenness for battle that had been lacking in Arthur's teulu in recent years. These were men with much to lose but so much to gain. They wanted the bright future Maelcon promised them as much as Medraut did and he knew that this would give them the victory wherever they went.

The day for their embarkation arrived and Bishop Dubricius blessed them before they set out. "God goes with you, brave warriors!" he said. "Never forget that you are on the side of right – the side of Christ – and our pagan enemies surely cower before bringers of the light!"

There was a cheer from hundreds of throats as they rode forth, their morale boosted considerably by the bishop's words. They were not just marching for Maelcon and Venedotia. They were on a holy mission. God was with them!

The gateway to Rumaniog was the Conui Valley and the bannermen who held it owed fealty to Meddyf's brother, Afall, who had succeeded Maeldaf as lord of the valley several years ago. He ruled from the old hill fort on the western bank of the Conui and guarded the river with a falcon's eye. It was to be hoped that Afall would join with the teulu, seeing as he was Maelcon's uncle but these hopes were to be disappointed as Lonio led the vanguard back to the main column in tatters.

"We were set upon without warning!" Lonio gasped, his mail coat and the sides of his mount splashed with blood.

"By Afall's men?" Medraut exclaimed. "Has he gone mad? He attacks his own nephew's teulu!"

"Perhaps he thought you were common reivers," said Alan. "Did you state your business?"

"Didn't get a chance! They charged us from the valley slope and surrounded us before we knew what was happening. Three of my men were skewered in their saddles. I had to cut a retreat, we were outnumbered!"

"Calm, Lonio," said Medraut. "You did right to return to us. I do not want to lose my vanguard this early in the campaign. It is to my mind that your father is right and your identity and intentions were mistaken. I wish to send an envoy to Afall. He is no doubt on his guard in these troubled times."

"They are camped not five miles upriver," said Lonio. "At least a hundred mounted men with tents and attendants. We could smash through them with ease ..."

"I know you mourn for the men you lost, Lonio. We will honour our three fallen brothers and do what we can to ensure no more are slain needlessly."

But there had been no mistake. The envoy Medraut sent upriver came back tied to his horse and without his head. It was an appalling display of treachery for a member of the Pendraig's family and Medraut was determined to see it was answered for.

They formed up and Medraut split the teulu into two companies, one led by Alan and the other by himself. Afall's forces were concealed behind the valley wall as the river curved around to the west and Medraut sent Alan's company ahead to feign an attack and draw their attention. They would then retreat, drawing Afall's men down the valley where Medraut's company would be waiting to charge them from the high ground.

As Alan and his men set off, Medraut led his company up the steep valley side, weaving their way through the trees to a prime vantage point. There they would wait until the return of Alan's company could be seen on the valley floor.

It was a long wait for men who were impatient to strike the first blow in the first battle of Maelcon's war. Medraut watched the scudding clouds overhead, casting shadows on the sweeping green of the valley.

A scout came galloping along the rise in great haste. "Sir!" he cried, sliding off his foaming mount. "The plan has failed. The enemy has tricked us!"

"How so?" Medraut demanded.

"When we rounded the bend in the river we found Afall's men had struck camp and retreated further upriver. Bowmen concealed by the trees loosed arrows upon us. Alan shouted the retreat but the men lost control and rode up the slope to cut down the bowmen …"

"Riding straight into Afall's trap," Medraut finished, nodding his head grimly. "Damn them all! Can't they listen to their captain?"

"What do we do?" the scout asked.

"We ride on and do what we can to save them." He turned to his company. "Follow my lead exactly! We must ride along the ridge and come upon the enemy on an equal footing. We dare not lose the high ground. Keep the ranks narrow!"

It was a dangerous scheme but Medraut had learned during the battles in Lindis that the more dangerous the scheme, the less prepared the enemy were and the more ultimate the victory if it succeeded. And besides, this was his first battle as penteulu. He'd be damned if he'd lose it to a valley chieftain like Afall.

The valley side grew unbearably steep as the river curved and they were forced to dismount and lead their horses by their bridles. Small stones and slabs of damp earth were dislodged by their passage and clattered away from them down the slope.

As they rounded the bend, the ground mercifully levelled out somewhat although it grew densely wooded. They mounted up and, further along the slope, Medraut could see Alan's small company being engulfed by the enemy who held the high ground while bowmen snuck around to loose their shafts into their flanks.

"We have the advantage of surprise and an equal footing!" Medraut said to his company. "Let's not waste it!" He lifted his spear high as a rallying gesture and then kicked his mount into a gallop.

He rode straight towards the enemy's left flank and could hear the thundering hooves of his companions keeping pace with him on either side. He pushed his mount on, keen to be the first of them to spill blood. That would bolster their courage.

They slammed in to the enemy host like a slap of a wave against a small craft with all the power to capsize it. There was a cheer from Alan's beleaguered company as the enemy staggered and slipped and slithered on the grassy slope, turning this way and that as Medraut's counterattack cut through them.

It was a devastating blow for a host who, seconds earlier, had thought themselves the victors of a successful ambush. Now the tables had turned and men tumbled from their saddles, run through by red-tipped spears. Horses lost their footing and rolled, kicking up clods of earth and crushing their riders.

"Venedotia!" bellowed Medraut, as the charge emerged from the other side of the decimated host, exhilarated at their success and, with the scent of blood in their nostrils, keen for more.

A small group of bowmen were retreating uphill, away from the slaughter, seeking a higher point of refuge from which they could continue their abrasive assault. Medraut pointed a bloody spear at them. "Don't let them get any higher," he said, and a squad broke off from the company to cut down the scampering foe. "The rest of you with me!"

Medraut led a second charge and this time it was a harder fight. The enemy had done their best to regroup and face the new threat head on. They slammed together and Medraut's spear shaft splintered in his hand. He reached for his sword and began cutting and hacking at those around him, working himself deep into the enemy ranks.

Alan had finally barked some discipline in to his men and they had regrouped further along the slope, their retreat made possible by Medraut's attack. Now they were climbing to higher ground with the intention of falling upon the enemy's rear.

Medraut saw them before the enemy did and bellowed for his men to keep the enemy's attention focused on them. When Alan led his company into the fray, it was as good as over for Afall's men.

They knew they were beaten and those who still lived did the smart thing and begged for quarter. They were hauled down from their horses and corralled together while Medraut saw to his wounded and assessed their losses.

It came as a surprise that Afall himself was one of the prisoners. Medraut had never set eyes upon the man but the way the captured men huddled around him and glanced at him with worried, darting eyes, made Medraut suspicious. When asked, Afall did not try to hide his identity. His virulent opposition to his nephew and to Medraut's invasion of his lands gave him a boldness that defied any sense of self-preservation.

"What shall we do with him?" Alan asked. "Send him north with an escort? Maelcon will surely like to see him."

"Maelcon will be joining us shortly," said Medraut. "He intends to play a leading part in the invasion of Rumaniog. We will keep Afall with us and use him as our key to taking his own stronghold."

Afall's fort was a small settlement on a high shoulder of the valley ringed by a spiked palisade. Horns bellowed at their approach and Medraut ordered his men to spread out as much as the narrow incline allowed and to have shields ready as a precaution against a volley of missiles from the fort.

"I will approach the gate with Afall," he told Alan, indicating the prisoner who sat astride his horse with his hands bound behind his back. "See if we can't get them to open up."

"Sir, that's very dangerous," said Alan. "What if one of the buggers takes a shot at you?"

"Then I hope one of you will shoot back," said Medraut. "Right into the back of Afall." He winked at the prisoner to ensure his point had got across. By Afall's pale face, it had.

Medraut took the reins of Afall's horse and together they trotted towards the gate, well in to bow range. Medraut thought he could hear the creak of a dozen bows as they approached but it might have been the wind in the nearby treetops.

Helmed heads could be seen atop the gate, turning this way and that as the defenders glanced uncertainly at each other.

"Stay your hands!" Medraut called up to them. "Unless you want to see an arrow in the back of your Lord Afall!"

"Who are you?" a voice called down.

Medraut sighed. "I am Medraut, penteulu of Venedotia and you are rebels and traitors. Open this gate immediately or face sterner justice."

There was the sound of low conversation atop the gate. Medraut glanced at Afall. "Care to have a word with your men? I won't wait about all day."

Afall spoke to him through gritted teeth. The day's events had seen him pushed to the very edge of what he was prepared to endure. "I am Maelcon's bloody uncle! You have marched in to my lands and butchered my men. Now you think to steal my own home from me?"

"Perhaps things may have gone better for you if you hadn't launched an unprovoked attack on my vanguard," said Medraut.

"My nephew is a monster and a murderer," said Afall. "You shame your family by doing his dirty work for him."

"I have no family," said Medraut. "Save this teulu. And we support Venedotia's rightful Pendraig."

There was no more time for discussion as the men atop the palisade had seemingly made up their minds and the gate slowly creaked open.

They faced no resistance, not once the gate was wide and Medraut's teulu began making its way into the main compound. A mere skeleton garrison guarded the place, most of Afall's men having ridden out to battle.

Medraut lost no time in making himself at home. Horses were stabled, fodder foraged, prisoners secured and men billeted. The teulu was hungry and Afall's plentiful stores yielded meat, mead and wine. Afall remained under guard in his own Great Hall along with his wife, son and daughter. The daughter in particular was exceedingly beautiful but she eyed Medraut with a cold hatred that seemed most out of place on so fair a face.

Word was sent north that the lord of the Conui Valley had fallen and, within two days, Maelcon and his entourage arrived. Medraut wondered if Meddyf would come to see her errant brother but, for whatever reason, she had remained at Cair Dugannu. "Probably disowned the bastard," said Alan, as they watched Maelcon approach Afall down the length of the hall.

"My dear uncle, what have you made me do?" Maelcon said. He wore simple war gear more befitting a man in the teulu than a king. The only thing on him approaching ostentation was crimson mantle trimmed with fur that was swept rakishly over one shoulder.

"What any man who honours your father's memory would have done," said Afall.

"I fail to see how standing against me, attacking my men and diverting precious attention away from our primary concern is at all honouring my father."

"Your father chose Guidno to succeed him."

"And yet God had a different plan for Venedotia."

"I doubt God's plan involved the murder of your uncle Owain."

There was a deathly silence in the hall. Medraut felt a dark pit open deep within him; a pit he had tried so hard to cover during the last few weeks. Although many had cast suspicious eyes upon Maelcon following Owain's rather convenient accident, nobody – *nobody* – had directly accused him of murdering his uncle.

"I am sorry you feel that way," said Maelcon. "You are wrong of course. But I can see how the lies of my enemies have turned my own family against me. It breaks my heart to say this, for I know it will break my mother's heart more, but you, Uncle, have proven yourself to be a traitor. I hereby condemn you to die so that others may learn from your mistake."

There was a sudden gasp from the assembly. Afall's daughter gave out a cry of anguish that spoke for many in the hall. Medraut glanced at Maelcon, feeling that he knew what was coming next.

"Medraut," said Maelcon. "See to the execution please."

Medraut hesitated. *How many of his uncles does he want me to kill?* He said nothing and did nothing as if he was frozen to the spot. Maelcon glanced at him expectantly.

Alan, seemingly sensing his conflict, stepped up and spoke softly so that only Medraut could hear him. "I will deal the stroke, if it please you, sir. It would not be seemly for the penteulu to do common executioner's work."

A common executioner ... Medraut thought. *Am I anything but?*

"Thank you, Alan. See that it is done quickly."

Alan motioned to two of his men and they approached Afall,

"You can't do this!" the traitor cried. "I am your uncle!"

"Yes," said Maelcon. "And that is what pains me the most. But I must be firm. My subjects must be shown that treason will not be tolerated. Even by my own kin."

The wailing of Afall's daughter echoed in the hall as Alan's men seized the prisoner and dragged him towards the doors. She made to run forward but, at a glance from Maelcon, two of his household guards rushed to halt her. They held her weeping in their mailed arms as Afall was hauled outside to his place of execution.

"I feel we should give my uncle the courtesy of witnessing his execution," said Maelcon. "We must not shy away from justice, however hard it is to bear. Come, let us follow them out."

It was a sombre, stunned crowd that filed out of the Great Hall in Maelcon's wake. Afall was already kneeling in the mud, his head bowed forward. One warrior stood guard while the other worked up a keen edge on his spatha with a whetstone.

A deacon who lived in the fort was hustled forward to administer the last rites. As he read them he kept glancing at Maelcon, hoping, praying perhaps, that execution would be called off and all would be revealed as a tasteless joke or an elaborate threat. But no such confirmation was forthcoming from Maelcon who watched the proceedings with an impassive face. The rites completed, the deacon scurried out of sight and the executioner began rotating his arms, loosening himself up for the job at hand.

Afall had his eyes closed and his lips mumbled soundless prayers. Alan's man placed the cold edge of the blade against the nape of his neck, quickly crossed himself, and then swung.

It took only two blows to sever the head; a sure sign of a man who knew his work. Afall's body slumped forward while his head rolled across the mud towards the queasy crowd.

The only sound was the wailing of Afall's daughter who had been restrained within the Great Hall.

The feast that night was elaborate and bountiful enough to mask at least a little of the day's unpleasantness. Medraut had done his best to acquire as much food and drink from the valley bannermen as he could in anticipation of Maelcon's arrival. Mead and wine flowed with enough abundance to make even the followers of the late Afall forget their woes, just a little.

Afall's head had been mounted on a spear in the main compound. Maelcon had ordered the release of the captured warriors and they had been paraded past the head of their lord as they entered the Great Hall. They sat uneasily at the benches, occasionally glancing fearfully in the direction of their king.

"Dark days are ahead," said Maelcon from his seat at the head of the hall, "and we must not let ourselves become bogged down in petty vengeances and tit-for-tat retributions. My uncle, who so grievously betrayed me, is dead. You who sit before me no doubt had no choice but to follow his orders. You are free of your obligations to him as of now and you have a second chance to prove your loyalties to your new Pendraig. Drink now and come forth to pledge your allegiance to me and your faith in a brighter future for Venedotia!"

The entire hall rose and drank to Maelcon and then, one by one, the bannermen of the Conui Valley came forward to kiss Maelcon's sword.

When all was done, Maelcon took up his address once more. "Lords and ladies, I have a further announcement to make. In but a few weeks I will be crowned Pendraig of Venedotia. In order to rule the eight kingdoms, I shall require a queen at my side. I have decided to marry and my betrothed shall be crowned alongside me. With the aim of healing hurts and drawing the men of the Conui Valley back to the dragon standard, I have chosen Guallen, daughter of Afall, as my bride.

There was a stirring in the hall that bordered on uproar. Guallen, who had been made to dress and adorn herself appropriately despite her grief, had sat in silence at the high table, watching the proceedings with disinterest. Now she knew a fate worse than death; to be forced into marrying the killer of her father. Her face drained of all blood and she positively cringed from Maelcon in terror.

A knife hilt began to hammer on a tabletop and more and more warriors took up the applause until the entire hall rang with the thud of iron against oak.

Guenhuifar

Guenhuifar had wept when she learned that it was Medraut who had led Maelcon's teulu in the assault against the lords of the Conui Valley. She had never really given up hope that he would leave Maelcon's side and return to Cair Cunor but now that blood had been shed, things had gone too far for reconciliation.

Arthur had done his best to keep the teulu together in the face of such uncertainty. Although the dragon banner still hung in Cair Cunor's Great Hall, it was officially no longer Arthur's standard. Arthur was a penteulu without a master, a warlord without a cause.

Venedotia reeled in the wake of Medraut's attack. Some would stand with Maelcon, there was no question of that but how and when things would progress was anyone's guess. King Cungen of Eternion had previously voiced support for Maelcon and now contented himself by allowing his bannermen to strike across Rumaniog's southern border in forays, burning and looting wherever they could. It was an indirect act of war and Arthur was convinced that it was designed to draw Mor's attention away from the north, leaving Rumaniog open to attack by Medraut and his newly raised teulu.

Arthur had done what he could to support Mor, riding out with his companies to fend off the raids of Eternion's border lords. But now that the Conui Valley had fallen, the question on everybody's lips was; would he go to war with Maelcon's new Penteulu?

It was a question Guenhuifar knew her husband was reluctant to answer. Rumaniog could not stand alone against Maelcon but by marching against the crown he had spent so many years defending, Arthur would be openly declaring himself a traitor. And Guenhuifar knew that deep down, Arthur had no desire to fight Medraut. The flame of family still flickered faintly in his heart however hard he tried to smother it. Medraut had not just been his son and nephew. He had been Arthur's warrior; a member of his brotherhood. And she knew that Medraut's refusal to remain by Arthur's side stung him far deeper than he would ever admit.

Maelcon's execution of his own uncle had caused a shiver of revulsion. It also served to remind everyone of their suspicions surrounding Owain's mysterious death at the beginning of the year. If eyes had looked to Arthur to stand up to Maelcon before he had taken the Conui Valley, then they looked to him harder now. Nobody criticised him, at least not within Guenhuifar's hearing, but she could sense the mood in the fortress. *What is he waiting for?* It said.

It was on a rainy afternoon that the visitor came to Cair Cunor. Arthur had recently returned with Peredur and his company, their cloaks soaking and their mail and shields splashed with blood. Another of Eternion's raiding parties had met its end.

The stranger wore dry clothes which he had evidently changed into as his horse was being stabled. They were rumpled from being carried in a saddlebag but were of good cloth and embroidered with gold thread. He wore no ornamentation and did not carry weapons. To look at him, Guenhuifar assumed him to be an envoy of some wealthy lord or perhaps a minor member of a noble family. He travelled alone and looked as if he had not had a good meal in days.

"What lord do you serve and why does he send you to a traitor like me?" said Arthur, as the man was brought to him in the praetorium.

"My name is Ithoc mab Munio and my lord is Dylan mab Hueil of the Conui Valley."

"Indeed? How fares your lord? We have heard nothing of the valley bannermen since Medraut's attack and feared that few survived."

"I am afraid that is the truth, my lord. Those few who did survive were held prisoner by Medraut until Maelcon pardoned them. On one condition; that they swear allegiance to him. My lord Dylan did so else he would still be in irons or dead perhaps."

"So," said Arthur, his voice suggesting that imprisonment or death might have perhaps been a more honourable choice. "Why does your lord send you to me now that he is my enemy?"

"Your enemy in name only. Should it come to battle, perhaps the faith of Maelcon's allies might prove to be a little thin. As for my lord sending me to you, he didn't. I came of my own volition."

"Why?"

"After my lord was imprisoned, our lands were ransacked by Medraut's men. Food, livestock, horses and arms were seized to add to Maelcon's war effort. The rest of my lord's servants and I were lucky to escape alive. As we fled, we came across two women travelling alone. They were terrified and we allowed them to travel in our company for safety. One of them wore very fine clothes while the other appeared to be her handmaid. I assumed we had found a young bride fleeing an obnoxious marriage. I was surprised to find out that I was right and that the two women were fleeing the very same thing we were."

"Medraut?" Arthur asked, one eyebrow raised.

"Maelcon," said Ithoc. "This young chit of a girl was the Lady Guallen, daughter of Afall, lord of the valley. After Maelcon slew him, he claimed the poor girl for his bride. She and her handmaid escaped her father's stronghold that very night and fled east where they crossed our path."

"Where is Afall's daughter now?" Arthur asked.

"Further misfortune befell her, I am afraid to say. Yesterday afternoon, we were set upon by a band of rogues out of Eternion. I recognised the sigil of Boron mab Geraint. We did our best but we are servants, not warriors."

"They took her?" Guenhuifar asked.

"Aye, and her handmaid. There was nothing we could do. They bore them off with the rest of their spoils. My mind on the matter is that old Boron will seek to ransom her for he will not know the girl's identity, else he would hand her over to Maelcon and win his favour. I just pray the girl and her handmaid have the sense to keep her true name a secret."

"Why come to me with this information?" Arthur asked.

"My lord, I was hoping that you might intervene. Boron's stronghold is just over the border. A quick show of force would easily be enough to make him hand the girl over …"

"I am just entering into a war," said Arthur irritably. "I have done my best to halt these rogues from Eternion but my true foe lies to the north. I have need of every man and more. Besides, if I storm over the border into Eternion and start accusing King Cungen's bannermen of kidnapping girls, I would soon be fighting a war on two fronts. Driving off interlopers from Rumaniog's borders is one thing, but Cungen has been very careful not to openly declare war on me. I would keep that balance, at least for now."

"Husband," said Guenhuifar, "I believe this servant came with this news not merely because he sympathises with the girl, but to offer you an edge in the approaching conflict."

Arthur eyed her curiously. "How so?"

"Maelcon is clearly besotted with this Guallen, or else desires her on political grounds. Either way, he wants her and she has escaped. If you were to take her in to your care, it might serve as a balm for the enmity between you and Maelcon and negotiations could be made smoother."

"You mean if I hand this poor girl over to the man she detests so he might marry her, he would cease hostilities against me?" Arthur said. "You surprise me, Guenhuifar. I would have thought you might have a touch more sympathy for the girl. But I know why you would go to such lengths to avoid conflict."

With Medraut? Guenhuifar thought to herself. *Yes. I would go to great lengths.* But that was not all of it. She had a deal of sympathy for the girl and knew that she would be better off with them at Cair Cunor than a prisoner of some thief and reiver in Eternion. Whether or not she would be handed over to

Maelcon as a mere bargaining chip was an argument for another day.

"But as I said, I will not risk war with Eternion until the threat in the north has dissipated."

"What if we were to acquire Guallen by non-violent means?" said Guenhuifar. "Any ransom we could offer would surely dwarf the expectations of a hedge robber like Boron mab Geraint."

"Ransom …" Arthur mused. "To ransom her he would have to know who she was …"

"Yes, that is a kink in the plan that needs ironing out," said Guenhuifar, pleased that he was at least considering the idea. "We must somehow convince him that Guallen is the daughter of a nobleman allied to you, perhaps fleeing an undesirable marriage as Ithoc suggested."

"This is a dangerous ploy that would require one of my known envoys such as Gualchmei," said Arthur. "And I can't spare him. I can spare no one, truth be told, for I will have need of my entire teulu if we march to confront Medraut."

"You can spare me," said Guenhuifar.

Arthur glanced sharply at her.

"I am well-known as your wife. Even Boron would recognise me for I would recognise him having seen his ugly face at the Samhain festivities two years ago. That would guarantee my safety for though you may be reluctant to engage in hostilities in Eternion, Boron would know that you would march on him with your entire teulu should anything befall me while I was in his company."

"That is still trusting the sense of a wild reiver," said Arthur. "I would send somebody with you, but I have no warriors to spare."

"Send Ithoc with me," said Guenhuifar. "He knows the girl and is an envoy in any case."

Arthur eyed Ithoc. "No. It's not that I don't trust the man, but everything we know about this girl and Boron's kidnapping of her comes from his mouth; the mouth of a man we have just met. I would be a fool to send you with him into danger. I mean no offense, Ithoc."

"None taken, my lord," replied the youth. "I'm no warrior and although I am known to Guallen, I would be no help in rescuing her if it should come to a fight."

"A fight is something I wish to avoid at all costs," said Guenhuifar. "But there must be someone, Arthur, some spearman from the ranks you could send as a token guard of my person."

Arthur rubbed his bearded chin, deep in thought. "No, I will send no lowly spearman to safeguard my wife. I will send Guihir, my master of tongues who is as fine an envoy as Gualchmei. And his blade is as keen as his tongue when pressed to it."

Guenhuifar smiled. Guihir was known to her of old. He had been one of the seven who had arrived at the old Lys so many years ago when the name of Cunedag and his kin had been as ashes in her mouth. It was the dedication of those seven warriors that had changed her mind as they had fought the Gaels together and embarked upon a mad mission to steal the Cauldron of Rebirth from Arthur's sister. "Guihir will do just fine," she said.

Once Ithoc had been sent to get a hot meal, Arthur turned to Guenhuifar. "I know why you're doing this," he said. "You seek to turn us away from war by returning Maelcon's bride to him."

"Is that so bad a thing?"

He smiled. "No, truly it is not. I have no more desire to fight Medraut than you do. But it may all come to naught. Even if you bring Guallen to us, we may have overestimated Maelcon's desire of her, leaving us with nothing more than a couple of extra mouths to feed. And if Maelcon wants her back, we will be sending a girl into the hands of a monster who seeks to marry her against her will. How does that truly sit with you?"

"None of this sits well with me, Arthur," she told him. "As for sending the girl to marry Maelcon … I just don't know. If we can save her from that fate, then we must do so."

But deep down she knew that if it meant averting war between Arthur and Medraut, she was prepared to sacrifice far more than the happiness of some nobleman's daughter.

They set out the following day, Guihir on a dun gelding and Guenhuifar on her favourite dappled mare. She rode side-saddle after the Roman fashion, knowing that she was in her role as wife of Arthur and Lady of Cair Cunor. That was also the cause of her gown and fur-trimmed stola although she wore women's riding boots rather than slippers, for the ground was muddy and she had no servants to help her down off her horse.

They followed the Afon Deva westwards before heading away from its rushing waters across the deep valleys and cloud-flecked hills of Eternion. Boron's fortress was a stone-walled ring surrounding several thatched halls and a few roundhouses in the old British style. A wooden watchtower presided over it.

"The way I see it," said Guihir, "there are two ways things could have gone for Guallen once she was brought within those walls. She and her handmaid could have kept their mouths shut as to her identity, in which case things may have gone hard for them. Old Boron won't be above mistreating a girl if he thinks she knows something he doesn't. I don't think Guallen will be too much harmed but the handmaid might have fared worse. The other scenario is that they gave Boron a false name, in which case we'll have a job of it figuring out who we are supposed to be paying the ransom for."

It was that last scenario that most bothered Guenhuifar. She prayed to the Great Mother that the women had not been harmed but on the other hand, strolling into Boron's home and offering to pay the ransom for somebody she did not know the name of was foolhardy to say the least. During the journey she had concocted a false identity for Guallen – Rhiannon, daughter of Rhys mab Meirion; a bannerman in the commote of Cair Cunor – but that would be no good if Guallen had already given Boron a false name. And if she had indeed given him no name, even under torture, how could Guenhuifar pass this new identity to her? There were so many ways this plan could go wrong that the only true course was to remain flexible; use her wits to adapt to the situation – whatever it was – within those stone walls.

It was early evening by the time they had climbed the steep path to the hilltop. The wind moaned bitterly and from within the settlement they could hear the sound of raucous laughter. The smell of roasting meat drifted up from the smoke hole in the thatch and the yellow glow of the hearth fire could be seen from the Great Hall's doors.

After Guihir had wrangled with the porter on the subject of his lady's identity and her business, their horses were stabled and they were admitted to the Great Hall. The porter led them in and they were hit by a wall of noise, warmth and the smell of ale and cooked food.

It was clear that a celebration was in progress. The spoils of war lay heaped in the corners: tapestries, rich cloths and amphorae of wine lurked in the shadows. Gold and silver in both plate and cup caught the flickering light of the hearth. All these trophies, Guenhuifar surmised, had been looted from the settlements of southern Rumaniog but the costliest trophy was not on display with all the other trinkets.

Boron's booming voice filled the chamber with his shout for more ale. He was massive in every sense of the word and a thick, black beard streaked with white hung down from a ruddy face to rest on a broad chest.

The tail end of a jest was causing gales of laughter at the other end of the hall. The men were drunk and songs and oaths poured freely from lips, almost as freely as the drink in the jugs the scurrying servants carried between the tables was poured into foaming horns and cups.

In the far corner, almost apart from the festivities, sat a monk in his habit nursing a mug of ale. He watched the proceedings with a pale face and one hand kept wandering to the cross about his neck. The presence of a man of the clergy was not a surprise to Guenhuifar for, though Boron was a robber and a raider, he was a Christian, at least nominally.

"The Lady Guenhuifar of Cair Cunor," announced the porter in a voice that barely carried over the roister.

A word in Boron's ear caused him to turn his great bull-head around and focus his drunken eyes upon the newcomers. A wide grin split his bearded face and he bellowed; "Lady Guenhuifar! The wife of our disgraced penteulu deigns to grace my hall with her presence!"

The hall fell silent as Boron, with some difficulty, heaved himself to his feet and raised his drinking horn in her direction.

"My lord," said Guenhuifar, inclining her head slightly.

"And to what do we owe the honour?" Boron drawled. "Surely you have not tired of your husband's bedchamber and come to Eternion seeking a real man?" He barked with laughter and the hall joined him, making the rafters echo with their guffaws.

"If I was tired of my husband I would hardly find better in a man who has refused to ride with the teulu these twenty years past," said Guenhuifar. "And if my husband were here you would not be so bold in your humour."

That stilled their mirth somewhat for, disgraced though he may be, Arthur was still a powerful lord and insults to a lord's wife were not taken lightly in that part of the world.

"It is not for the lord of a commote to ride with the dragon teulu," said Boron, his face sobered somewhat by the implied insult to his honour. "And I have sent more than my share of men to your husband over the years. My obligations are fulfilled and now that Arthur is no longer Venedotia's penteulu, I would say that I owe him nothing! Your adopted son, Medraut, is now the man I must send men to, by all accounts."

"I did not come here to squabble over obligations," said Guenhuifar.

"Then why did you come? Unless it was our fine company you sought?"

"There have been many attacks on the southern marches of Rumaniog. Settlements raided. Gold and grain looted. Women carried off."

Boron grinned. "Aye, so I've heard. Dreadful business. And I hear also that your husband has a job of it fending these wolves off with what little men are left to him. Helping his friend, King Mor, one assumes. It's nice that he finds work for his idle hands now that he is no longer required at Court."

Guenhuifar ignored the barb. "I point no finger of blame in your direction, but word has reached us of a young nobleman's daughter and her handmaid who, while fleeing an undesirable marriage, somehow ended up in your hands."

"What if they did? I'm not below providing refuge for poor wandering souls."

There was a chuckle around the hall at this.

"This girl is kin to a good friend of my husband. He would be most grateful if she were returned to him."

"How grateful?"

Guenhuifar sighed. "There are some, far less honourable men than yourself, who would seek to ransom the girl. What would you think such a ransom might amount to?"

Boron narrowed his eyes at her. "What family did you say the girl came from?"

Guenhuifar had been worried it might come to this. There was nothing for it but to lie and to lie well. "Her father is Rhys mab Meirion, a bannerman of the commote surrounding Cair Cunor. He has been a loyal supporter and friend to Arthur these many years but, in arranging a union between his house and another, he lost his daughter. I'm sure you can appreciate a father's desperation and fear for his family's good name. Now, you tell me, how generous should such a man be to see his daughter restored to him?"

Boron examined her for a moment and then broke into uproarious laughter. It was a bellow of mirth that was taken up by his companions and by the time he was finished, tears were rolling down his cheeks.

"By Christ on his cross but that was a beautiful moment there," he said, wiping his eyes with the palm of his hand. "To see the noble Lady Guenhuifar lie through her back teeth! Truly the wife of a disgraced lord!"

Guenhuifar gritted her teeth and let the humiliation wash over her.

"You can pack in the pretence, Guenhuifar," said Boron. "I know Arthur seeks the daughter of Afall mab Maeldaf so that he can dangle her in front of Maelcon as a sweetener to any deal he has hopes of. It was the handmaid who told me, after I threatened to whip the hide off the young lady for telling me one too many lies that didn't add up." He turned to a man loitering by the end of the table who must have been his steward. "Bring out the young lasses so our ladyship can get a look at them!"

The steward disappeared into the series of chambers at the rear of the hall and re-emerged with the two young ladies. It was clear to see that they were terrified. They were of the same age and both very pretty. Guallen wore a gold embroidered tunica over a long dress that, while made of fine stuff, was muddy and torn at the hem. Her hair was dark and fell in two plaits on either side of her pale neck which she was visibly trying to hold erect in a posture of mild defiance. Her handmaid wore a hooded cloak that almost concealed hair of reddish gold. She looked at the ground, the light of the hearth fire illuminating the freckles that lightly dusted the tops of her cheeks.

"Well?" Boron demanded. "Is she not a fine maid? And a fatherless one at that! I've a mind to marry her myself and make Maelcon green with envy!"

"Would it be wise to taunt the Pendraig?" Guenhuifar asked. "Maelcon is not the type to give up on that which he desires, nor is he a man to forgive a slight."

"As you and your husband are due to find out," said Boron with a grin.

"I will die before I marry a man such as you!" said Guallen, and she hawked a glob of phlegm and spat it at Boron's feet.

"Ha!" Boron barked. "Then I shall first tame that wild spirit of yours with a birch switch!"

"You'll never manage it," said Guenhuifar. "Girls like that cannot be tamed."

"I assume you speak from experience," said Boron. "The word is that you lead Arthur around Cair Cunor on a leash!"

There was more guffawing at this.

"Let us speak sensibly," said Guenhuifar. "You know as well as I that Maelcon will never let you keep this girl for yourself. He might just be mad enough to go to war with Eternion over it. Do you really think Cungen will want bad blood with his new overlord? He won't protect you. Not for a girl you fancy for your bedchamber. He'll throw you to the wolves rather than get on Maelcon's bad side."

The hall fell still at this and Boron's face grew remarkably sober.

"Would it not be more preferable to profit from this girl while you have the chance?" Guenhuifar continued. "Ransom her to me and let my husband earn Maelcon's enmity, or what little there is left to earn. You will have a full purse and get to keep your lands. And your head."

"How much?" said Boron, apparently keen to talk business at last.

Guenhuifar told him. There was a murmur across the hall.

A smile crept across Boron's face. "Your husband must really want her. Perhaps he plans to keep her in his bedchamber while you continue to run errands for him."

"Are we back to insults?"

"I want half as much again."

"Then you can keep her and my husband will find another way to pressure Maelcon. While you try to find another buyer for Maelcon's chosen bride."

Boron's eyes darted from Guallen to his men and then back to Guenhuifar. He knew he had been outmanoeuvred. He was holding hot property and selling her to Guenhuifar was the only way he was going to see any profit for it. "Done!" he said. "Take her! You may stay the night but I want the lot of you gone by sun-up!" He turned to his steward. "Take the prisoners back to their quarters. The Lady Guenhuifar does not get them until she leaves my stronghold with them."

The girls were hurried off looking rather glad of what had transpired, despite the notion of being bought and sold like chattel. Guenhuifar and Guihir were offered a place at the tables and were served meat and drink. Guenhuifar found that she was ravenous after the day's journey and was pleased with herself for achieving what she had set out to do.

Her sense of triumph was to be short-lived, however, for before the night grew very late and the hall's occupants stumbled off to their beds, a second visitor appeared at the door, flanked by two warriors who bore the sigil of the red dragon.

Maelcon's men, thought Guenhuifar with a sinking stomach. She did not recognise the envoy nor his escort but that was not surprising given how many new recruits Maelcon had drawn to him recently. She wondered if they had been trained by Medraut.

"Siarl mab Goronui, my lord," announced the porter. "Envoy to Maelcon mab Cadwallon."

"What brings men of Ynys Mon to my hall?" asked Boron, doing his best to conceal the concern in his voice.

"Not from Ynys Mon, Lord Boron," said Siarl. "Haven't you heard? The Pendraig has moved the royal seat back to Cair Dugannu."

"I had heard," said Boron. "But I had not heard that he had been already crowned."

The envoy shrugged. "A mere formality. The coronation will take place as soon as Maelcon has his bride returned to him."

"What bride might that be?" said Boron.

"Don't play dumb, Boron. It is known that she and her handmaid fled east and were picked up by one of your raiding parties. It is also known that the traitor Arthur dispatched his wife to retrieve her." He levelled his eyes at Guenhuifar. There was no mistaking the noble woman with the tawny hair at Boron's board. "I am glad to see that I am not too late. It would have been a shame if I had to ride her down on the road and take the Pendraig's property back by force."

"And how highly does Maelcon value his pretty little maid?" asked Boron.

Siarl narrowed his eyes at him. "Surely you don't intend to ransom your high-king's bride to him?"

"Well, the Lady Guenhuifar here has already agreed to pay me for her. Why should I be out of pocket just because your horse was too tardy getting you here?"

Oh, you fool, Boron, thought Guenhuifar.

"Had you already ransomed the girl to *Lady Guenhuifar* here, it would have gone very badly for you, Boron," Siarl answered. "Maelcon is engaged in talks with your king as we speak and it looks like Cungen is keen to be his ally. He will have need of all you border lords in the war to come and if it became known that you aided the enemy, you would be neither a favourite of Maelcon nor Cungen."

Boron swallowed heavily, looking like a cornered rat with no clear idea of how to escape.

"But if you hand the girl over to me," Siarl continued, "I may neglect to mention your previous deal to the Pendraig. Now, it is late and we are tired. Kindly see to our bed and board and we will be out of your beard in the morning. *With* the young Lady Guallen."

Boron glanced almost apologetically at Guenhuifar, no doubt lamenting his own loss more than hers. Guenhuifar watched in dismay as Siarl and his men sat down on the opposite side of the hall and called for food and drink.

Arthur

The ground was wet and soft beneath Arthur's feet. He looked down and saw that it was a carpet of leaves. Dead leaves; rotten and black with mould. One of them stuck to the toe of his boot. He tried to kick the slimy thing off.

The trees around him were skeletal things, black and twisted against a leaden sky. Some of them bore shrivelled fruit, and when he inspected one of them he saw that it was an apple or had been once. As he looked at it, it dropped off the branch and landed with a wet splat. The impact split it open and squirming, glistening maggots spilled out.

He shuddered and turned from it. He knew this was a dream. Not a regular dream for he dreamt so seldom these days. He used to be bothered by nightmares. He used to see the faces of all the men he had killed screaming soundlessly at him as he closed his eyes every night but no more. Perhaps he had grown used to it. The old warriors said that the nightmares disappeared in time. War had a way of numbing you eventually. It might take years but eventually you learnt to forget.

The woman was there in the rotting orchard. He knew she would be changed. The last time he had seen her she had been a beautiful woman in a red dress who had pointed him in the direction of the old Roman temple to Sulis Minerva where he had found *Caledbulc*. Now she couldn't have looked more different.

She first appeared to him as a shadow in the tail of his eye; a black blot that hung there. He turned and at first thought he was looking at a bundle of old rags caught on a tree branch. But there was a form to those rags and as she lifted her head beneath the black hood, he saw wispy white hair, wrinkled skin and a toothless grin.

"You're ... so *old*," he couldn't help himself from saying.

"Aye, not so pretty as the last time we met, am I Arthur?" she said. She sucked her teeth and glanced around at the blighted landscape. "And neither is the land."

"But this is Annun," said Arthur, "not the real world."

"You still don't understand do you, boy? Annun, Albion. They are one and the same. One a reflection of the other. Oh, the apples might look red and ripe in your world but there is a sickness that has set in. And all is ripe for change."

"Maelcon," said Arthur.

The old woman made a movement with her bony shoulders that approximated a shrug. "Some roads come to an end. Others are just beginning. Change is imminent. And you must beware, Arthur. Beware."

"Beware what?" he asked her, but she turned from him and was hobbling off through the trees, her black, hunched form disappearing into the mist that had begun to creep across the orchard.

He awoke to the sound of the camp stirring to life. It was cold but the bright blueness of dawn was blinding. He got up from his pallet and splashed his face with water from the basin that stood next to his armour rack, ruffled Cabal's ears and then he went in search of Menw.

"Modron has taken on her final form," said the bard after Arthur had explained his dream to him.

"Guenhuifar said that the Morgens dress in black now."

Menw nodded. "You are not the only one the Great Mother speaks to."

"But what does it mean?"

"Death. Change."

"Whose death?"

"That is a question known only to Her," said Menw. "Take my advice, Arthur, don't worry too much about who or what. Focus only on your duty, on the task Modron has charged you with."

"Protecting Albion ..." said Arthur. "But am I failing? Is that why the orchard is blighted and the goddess and her priestesses dress in black? Have I failed her?"

Menw sighed. "Albion is changing, there is no doubt of that. But do not forget, your part in this has not yet been played out. Take comfort in that, Arthur. She has use for you still. We all do."

Arthur tried to take comfort in his old friend's words but it was not easy. Since Guenhuifar had left things had gone from bad to worse. King Mor had left his chief hill fort with whatever men he had left and had joined Arthur at Cair Cunor. Together they chased down as many of the border lords of Eternion as they could but once they had scurried back across the border, Arthur dared not follow for fear of drawing Eternion into the war.

That had been a waste of time for news soon reached them of Maelcon's alliance with King Cungen. Eternion had invaded Rumaniog and now marched on Cair Cunor. Arthur had ridden out to meet them and had blocked the Roman road that led between the mountains to the north-west and the moors of Eternion to the south-east.

Word had come down from the north that Maelcon was cementing his rule and proclaiming Arthur as Venedotia's true enemy. He was using the uncertainty of the times to gain control of the whole kingdom.

"He says that you seek to take the crown for yourself," said Gualchmei. "He claims that you call yourself *King* Arthur now."

"*King* Arthur?" said Cei, with a grin. "Can't say it has much of a ring to it but it's worth a thought …"

"No it bloody well isn't," said Arthur. "I'm a warrior. I don't want to spend the rest of my days polishing a throne with my arse. Leave the ruling of kingdoms and seat-polishing to some other bugger. Just not Maelcon, for the sake of all the gods."

He couldn't believe how Maelcon had managed to turn Venedotia against him in so short a time. This was the land that had hailed him as a hero for so many years. His name had been spoken across Albion with the same reverence as the name of the Teulu of the Red Dragon and Venedotia was home to them both. Now, Venedotia was set against him, calling him 'traitor' and 'enemy'.

He supposed Bishop Dubricius had something to do with it. By all accounts he filled his sermons with accusations and polemical fury directed at Arthur. He attacked his pagan followers, calling them serpents who must be driven out and that Arthur was of the devil's brood for leading them.

News of Medraut and Guenhuifach's baptism had also reached them. Now it was a Christian teulu against a pagan one, or at least that was how Maelcon and Dubricius were putting it.

"There's as many Christians as pagans in the teulu," said Cei. "To say we are one howling horde of pagans is a damned lie!"

"This is Maelcon trying to divide Venedotia more than it already is," said Arthur. "He uses men's faiths as weapons along with lies and deceit. These are his tools."

And it was working. True, there were many Christians in the teulu, including three of his four captains. But the lies of Maelcon and Dubricius were beginning to make many of them question their loyalties. Arthur was left with few enough warriors as it was but now that their faith was being called into question, he risked losing even more.

"You have never professed your own faith," said Beduir one evening when they were eating their rations around the campfire. "It might be prudent to claim yourself a Christian. Prove Maelcon a liar."

Arthur glanced at his shield emblazoned with the image of the ambiguous lady holding a babe. It had served him well in the past. The Christians under his standard saw the Virgin Mary and the Christ child while the pagans saw Mabon the blessed Mother and Modron the eternal youth.

"I hear you, Beduir," he said. "You who have known me almost as long as Cei and Gualchmei, know that I have always been torn between two faiths. My mother was a Christian while my father was of Cunedag's line and upheld the pagan beliefs of the north. It may seem simpler to choose one, but I cannot. All who are currently under my standard have been the very loyalist of warriors, despite their religious differences. I cannot abandon one to win the hearts of the other. This teulu is Albion. I care not which holy mother they see on my shield, only that they fight to protect what is right and good in the world."

Beduir nodded thoughtfully, the flames of the fire deepening the lines on his scarred face and glinting off the polished wooden right hand that rested in his lap.

"I know that you and all the other Christians would rather that I embraced what you consider to be the true faith but I cannot let myself be swayed on this," Arthur continued. "I must remain a beacon to all – pagan and Christian alike – a beacon of hope and light against darkness."

"And that you are, Arthur," said Beduir. "It matters not to me, I just want to see this thing ended. But know that the Christians under your banner fight for you, regardless of your faith. We fight for what you represent."

"Thank you, Beduir."

The following day brought news of a great host approaching from the east.

"Cungen marches upon us," said Cei, "All of Eternion is emptied."

Arthur sent his captains to rouse the camp and form battle lines. "We hold this pass and let them bounce off us like hail off a shield," he said. "Small though we have become, we are more than a match for anything Eternion can muster."

The teulu was roughly four-hundred strong with nearly two-hundred auxiliaries. These, Arthur placed at the front centre while he sent two cavalry companies to protect each wing. They marched eastwards at a steady pace, leaving their camp behind them. Arthur intended to block the pass just before the point where his men would be stretched too thin.

Cundelig returned with one of his scouts, Hebog the falcon clinging to his wrist, gnawing a scrap of meat. His face was grave. "Sire, they number nearly six-hundred. And that's just riders. They have wings of spear and bowmen making them nearly a thousand strong."

There was a stunned silence from the ranks as they all processed this. Cabal whined softly at Hengroen's side. "A thousand strong?" said Arthur. "How on earth did Cungen rally so many? There aren't that many warriors in Eternion ..."

"Powys rides with them," said Cundelig, and as soon as he said it, Arthur knew he was a fool for not foreseeing this. Cungen was the nephew of the king of Powys who had long despised the Venedotians. It was only due to old King Etern dying with no sons to succeed him that had led to a marriage between his daughter and Cungen. Now the aging King Ridfet of Powys enjoyed a far more favourable neighbour.

Arthur called an immediate halt and summoned his captains.

"Maelcon isn't daft," Cei grumbled. "He sees in Cungen the source of a far greater ally. It's not just him we're fighting now but all of bloody Powys!"

"My lands are lost," said Mor through gritted teeth. "For we can't stand against them. Not now they're bolstered by Ridfet's warriors. There is no way we can hold this pass!"

"But if we fall back to Cair Cunor," said Beduir, "We'll be under siege before sunrise tomorrow. It would be a death trap to flee now."

"But what can we do?" cried Mor. "We'll be slaughtered to the last man if we hold our ground here!"

"Peace!" said Arthur. "I'm thinking."

His companions held a respectful silence while Arthur rubbed his beard and considered his options. To his mind there was only one road to take. It was a dangerous one, but they were out of options.

"We must march west," he said at last. "Past Cair Cunor, empty the fortress on the way and head to the moors above the Afon Maudach. From there we can march north to Din Emrys and meet with Efiaun. Our approach will be screened by the mountains and our enemies, many though they are, will not be looking for us in the west. Dunauding is friendly territory. We can make good progress and hopefully bolster the teulu with fresh warriors along the way."

"To what end?" Menw asked, as he regarded Arthur with a quizzical eye.

"Once we have reached Din Emrys," said Arthur. "I intend to head through the Pass of Kings, just as Cadwallon did during the civil war, and fall upon Cair Dugannu by surprise."

"By all the gods, how many times must we fight the same battle?" said Mor in exasperation. It was a feeling shared by all; a feeling of history repeating itself.

"It's our only move," said Arthur. "The Conui Valley is blocked to us. We cannot fight Cungen, nor can we hold Cair Cunor. If we move fast enough we could kick Maelcon out on his arse before he knows what has hit him. His eye will be upon Medraut and his progress through Rumaniog, not on his own back door. As for Cungen and his Powysian friends, we shall disappear before them like mist on a sunny morning."

Arthur's gift for rousing men in to action worked once again and soon the teulu was doing an about-face and heading back to Cair Cunor at a breakneck march. It was not a speed they could keep for very long but the fortress was a matter of miles off and there was so much to organise. Arthur did not intend to leave a single soul for Cungen and the Powysians to find.

The burning worry for Arthur was not only for his two sons but also for Guenhuifar who was somewhere in Eternion. If her plan had worked she would be making her way back to Cair Cunor with two girls slowing her down. He could not wait for her. They had to march immediately. It was impossible that she was not aware of Eternion's invasion of Rumaniog by now and he had to hope that she was lying low, making slow but steady progress and avoiding roads and way stations. She was smart. He armoured himself with that knowledge. Soon this war would be over before it had properly begun and he would be back at Cair Cunor with her in his arms.

To leave her felt like the worst of betrayals but there were more important things at stake. He knew she would understand that but a deep, black worry had set in and he knew he would not be free of it until he saw her again.

They reached Cair Cunor before sundown and Arthur immediately ordered the decamping of the garrison and the loading of food and supplies. Every cart and wain that had its wheels was loaded with salted meats, barrels of fish, grain and live poultry. It would be slow going – agonisingly slow – with such a baggage train and such a gaggle of civilians. But he did not trust their enemies not to put his people to the sword and so everyone was coming along with as much food as they dared carry to feed them.

They worked through the night and set off at daybreak. Cundelig's scouts reported that Eternion's teulu had entered the pass during the night and were now camped in the same spot they had occupied the previous day. It was unbearably close. Arthur would have to keep a company at the rear of the baggage train in case the enemy followed them beyond Cair Cunor. Right now, haste was everything.

Amhar rode his stout pony with Lacheu sitting in front of him. They would get saddle sore but for now every saddle had to be filled and the numbers of passengers slowing down the wains had to be kept to a minimum. The image of the older brother with his arm around the younger, protecting him, keeping him from falling made Arthur's heart nearly burst with pride. *If only your mother could see you now*, he thought.

They made good progress despite the size of the convoy and by the following evening, they had passed through the green hills that transitioned to the bleak, brackish moors. To the south lay the greenish-grey haze of the great forest that straddled the Afon Maudach and the border with Meriauned.

The vanguard rode several leagues ahead of the baggage train. The auxiliaries stumbled through the thick, yellowish grass and ferns while the cavalry companies took turns following ridges and high parts to keep an eye on the surrounding landscape.

It was a desolate and barren part of Venedotia and they met nobody. There were no settlements up here on the windswept moors although they did spot the occasional standing stone or ancient cairn signifying that there had been people here once, long ago. Now, this was a land of ghosts.

As they splashed through a shallow, stony brook, Arthur caught sight of a figure upstream. She wore black and she was washing clothes in the gushing water, beating them against rocks and soaking and wringing them. As they passed, she glanced up at them and Arthur felt a chill as he saw her face. It was old, haggard and more than a little familiar. It was his mind of course, playing tricks on him. His fears for the safety of his people, for Guenhuifar and his sons, made him paranoid. But the woman was there, nonetheless, and he couldn't help but think that the stare she fixed on them was for him and him alone.

"The Afon Camlan lies ahead," said Menw. "We'll have to head north to its source to find a suitable crossing point."

Arthur looked up at the leaden sky. It had threatened rain constantly ever since they had climbed up on to the moors but so far the clouds had held. Dark was several hours off and he hoped to cross the Camlan before making camp. It had been a good first day. Tomorrow they would curve north and press on for the mountains and the stronghold of Din Emrys.

A scout came galloping up the ridge, nearly breaking his horse with the exertion. "Sire!" he cried. "The enemy await us!"

"Which enemy?" Arthur demanded.

"Medraut, sire! He and his teulu are camped on the other side of the Camlan. They are five-hundred strong at least! And they block our way!"

Medraut

The escape of Maelcon's chosen bride was an embarrassment to them all. Medraut felt it more than others for it had been his men who had been guarding the young Guallen. He had wormed out the weak culprits and seen that they had been suitably punished but he feared it was a blow to Maelcon's confidence in him.

It was the first time Medraut had seen Maelcon lose his temper. On all other occasions, he was the very picture of restraint and control, dispatching orders and controlling all the pieces in his power with the cool confidence of a man who knew exactly what he was doing. But Guallen's escape had caught him off guard and shamed him. His roaring could be heard behind closed doors and everybody was strangely frightened by the young man's wrath for it had never revealed itself before.

Naturally, Medraut had dispatched riders to hunt the fugitives down, but several hours had gone by before their escape had been noticed and with no idea in which direction they had gone, finding them was proving to be more than a little problematic. And there was plenty else to do besides.

Maelcon was in correspondence with King Cungen of Eternion, putting whatever pressure he could on the outsider king to become his ally. If Eternion's teulu marched across Rumaniog's southern borders, and Medraut's teulu moved down the Conui Valley from the north, Mor's kingdom would soon fall and then ...

Yes, then. That was what occupied everybody's minds at present. The only thorn remaining in Maelcon's side was Arthur. He still commanded a strong teulu, made up of traitors as it was. A battle between Medraut and Arthur was inevitable and none failed to pick up on the dramatic implications of a war between father and son, uncle and nephew.

For Medraut's part, he just wanted it over and done with. If he had to fight Arthur and many of his old comrades, then so be it. But this waiting around in Afall's stronghold while Maelcon gathered support and cut deals was excruciating for him.

He was ready. His teulu had nearly doubled in size since they had set out from Cair Dugannu. Many members of the old teulu had made their way up the Conui to pledge allegiance to the new penteulu and the new Pendraig. Medraut's old companions, Sanddef and Morfran, had arrived and it felt wonderful to have most of his old patrol back.

Medraut had immediately set them to work training the new recruits and they quickly became respected names in the teulu. So much so that Medraut had made them captains. They were young, it was true, but this was a young man's teulu. A young Pendraig, a young penteulu and a young warband fit to run rings around Arthur and all his old loyalists.

Another thing that lifted Medraut's spirits no end was a visit from Guenhuifach. She arrived at the stronghold with a wagon train of supplies from the coast. Medraut met her in the courtyard and held her tight as he kissed her.

"Thank you for coming," he told her. "I've missed you."

"And I you," she said, but he detected some reservation in her that was unusual.

"What is it?" he asked. "We are man and wife now. No need for coyness."

"I'm all right. Just tired from the journey."

"Starved too, I don't doubt. Come on, there's plenty of food from Afall's stores."

He took her to table with Alan, Lonio, Sanddef and Morfran. Alan's new wife was there too. They had recently married now that Alan had been made a captain and he supposed Lonio and Sanddef would be next. Lonio had a sweetheart and Sanddef was always followed by fawning women who were drawn to his fair features. Poor Morfran had less luck for few women could stomach his grotesque face but that was by the by. He was a captain like the others and, as such, had the right to take a wife.

Medraut was toying with the idea of repealing the old rule and allowing any man in the teulu to marry. It was an archaic rule that was a product of the old days. Of *Arthur's* days. Love could not be constrained and Medraut could not see that he or any other man had the right to keep two lovers apart. He would have to put it to Maelcon, of course, but he was confident he could be brought around to the idea.

"Dubricius is rushed off his feet," Sanddef was saying, chewing on a chicken bone. "I'll bet he's never baptised so many heathens in his life! I saw another batch of them up to their waists in the river this morning while he did his bit in Latin."

"The Church is making up for lost time here in the north," said Alan. "For too long have the pagans held sway over Venedotia. Maelcon brings a new dawn."

"About time too," said Morfran. "Maybe we can start winning some wars now with the one true god on our side."

"We won enough battles under Arthur," Medraut reminded him. "So I'm not sure that we were entirely without God's favour." The others had been Christians since birth, but for Medraut it was a recent conversion and he felt that men all too often let themselves be persuaded by their faith so that they saw only the good and ignored the bad. Or vice versa.

"Aye, but who did the fighting in Arthur's battles?" asked Lonio. "Us Christians for the most part. And you know that Arthur always paid some lip service to the Church."

"So a little lip service is all it takes to earn God's favour?" Guenhuifach asked. "Perhaps we needn't have been baptised after all."

"You know that was more political than spiritual," said Medraut. "And besides, Arthur *was* baptised. His mother was a Christian after all, even if his father wasn't. Perhaps God saw more in him than you think, Morfran."

"Well, anyway," said Morfran, wiping droplets of ale from his bristly face with his sleeve, "Venedotia is on its way to becoming a Christian land and that can only be a good thing as far as I'm concerned."

"Maybe Maelcon will finally do something about those nine witches on Ynys Mon," said Lonio.

Alan cleared his throat and his son suddenly remembered himself. "Sorry, Medraut, I meant only …"

"It's of no concern," said Medraut, waving aside the apology. The table had fallen into silence. "I learned to distance myself from my mother long ago. Even if nobody else did. Her connection to that vile cult has plagued me from the cradle. And my grandmother was no better, even if she were an outcast. She would have started her own order if she had been able. No, you're right, Lonio. It would be best if Maelcon drove them all into the sea. I, for one, will be happy to do the job for him."

He felt Guenhuifach stiffen at his side and he glanced at her curiously. Something was clearly preying on her mind but he knew she would never mention it in front of his men.

When dinner was over, he took her back to his quarters and poured them both a cup of wine. They drank together and then, setting the wine cup down on the table, he advanced on her, pushing her back onto the pelt that covered his bed. She twisted away from him and he sat up, frustrated. "What is it?"

"Medraut, tell me that you haven't lost yourself."

"How do you mean?"

"Tell me that no matter how strong your loyalty to Maelcon is, you are still your own man; the man I fell in love with?"

"Of course I am. Maelcon has just freed me. Freed *us*. Without him we would still be prisoners, forced to love each other in secret."

"I know. But tell me that if he asked you to do something you knew was wrong, you'd have the courage to say no?"

He stared at her. "What are you trying to say?" He had a good idea what she was trying to say but he wanted her to say it.

"Did you kill Owain?"

He let silence reign for a moment, just to let her know how awful her question was. "Why on earth would you ask me that?"

She sighed. "People are saying things."

"That I murdered Owain?"

"Yes."

"That's madness."

"Is it?"

"You know me, Guenhuifach. You know that I'm not a murderer."

"Then it's lies? All of it?"

"I was there the night Owain died. It was awful. Elen woke up to find him gone and raised the alarm. We thought he had wandered off. Then, they found him. I helped drag his body out of the river." He held her and kissed her on the forehead. "Listen to me. I will fight Maelcon's war for him. I will lead his teulu, but I am not a murderer."

She softened a little in his arms and they lay down together for a while, neither moving.

"I know it was an accident," she said. "I'm sorry for asking you. It's just … first Owain and now Afall. Maelcon's enemies are dropping like flies."

"Be prepared to see them drop all the more frequently," he told her. "Afall was a traitor. So is Arthur and any man who stands against the Pendraig."

"I know, it's just so awful. I can't believe Arthur or my sister. Why can they not swallow their pride and listen to reason?"

"They have had their chance."

"Is it too late? Must you fight him?"

"I don't know. It depends on Maelcon. Perhaps if Arthur submits to me, he may be allowed to retire and live out his days in peace. But I do know this; enemies of Venedotia cannot be allowed to live. Our future is too important for that."

The following morning Maelcon called for him. "My lord, my men have not yet returned with news of Guallen …" he began by way of apology. Every day that passed was a further embarrassment to him. It had been his men who had let the damned girl escape so he had the responsibility of finding her. However difficult that may be.

"I know," said Maelcon. "Forget about the girl."

"My lord?"

"I have more important duties for you. I have just received word that King Cungen will support my claim to the throne. With all Eternion mustered, my bride-to-be will be quickly recovered if she has wandered east."

"That's good news."

"It certainly is. That traitor, Mor, will be caught between me and Cungen. And through Cungen, I have secured further allies."

"Who?"

"His uncle, King Ridfet of Powys."

Medraut blinked. "Powys is with us? They have long been our enemy …"

"My *father's* enemy," Maelcon corrected him. "The time of our fathers is over, Medraut. The world is changing. Powys is with us and I intend to use them to drive Arthur right into your arms."

"Do you think he will try to storm us here?"

"No, he is too canny for that. You know him best, Medraut. What do you think he will do when he receives word that the combined teulus of Eternion and Powys march upon Cair Cunor from the east? Will he wait out a siege?"

Medraut chewed his lip. "No. He despises siege warfare. To sit at Cair Cunor with that many men marching on him; it would be like digging his own grave."

"Where will he go?"

"Not north. He knows the Conui Valley is too narrow for his cavalry to do much good. Arthur likes to fight in wide open spaces. Moors, hills and flat terrain."

"West then?"

"Perhaps. Efiaun has long been his friend. He may seek to cross into Dunauding."

Maelcon smiled. "Every time I test you, Medraut, you always fulfil my expectations."

"How do you mean?"

"I've been toying with you. I know exactly where Arthur will go, and so do you. He will go west and seek to sneak around us, filling out his ranks with Efiaun's men as he does so. Then, he will attempt to march from Din Emrys through the Pass of Kings and come upon Cair Dugannu from the west. Just as he and my father did."

Medraut nodded, surprised by Maelcon's insight. But he was absolutely right. The plan was Arthur to a tee.

"Then you know what I require of you."

"What?"

"You must take the teulu west at daybreak. Make great haste for time is now short. March straight past Din Emrys. You needn't worry about Efiaun; he'll be cowering in his mountain stronghold at your approach. Head south and cut Arthur off before he enters the mountains."

Medraut was silent. He had been waiting for these orders so eagerly and now that he had them, he didn't know what to feel.

"I know this is hard for you, Medraut," said Maelcon, patting his shoulder. "He was as a father to you. But that is why it must be you. Nobody knows him better. It will be cavalry against cavalry in open terrain, just as Arthur likes it. Use everything you know about him to your advantage. You are young, he is old. *Outwit* him. God will be with you. Arthur, along with my late father, represents the old ways, the barbarian ways. Go now, bring an end to those days and help me usher in a new era for Venedotia; an era of peace. An era of God."

Guenhuifar

The appearance of Siarl and his demands had put a dampener on the previous night's roistering and Boron's warriors soon began slinking off to their beds. Siarl and his men did not stay at table for long. Once they had eaten their fill, they asked to be directed to their quarters. Drinking with a common border lord of Eternion was something an envoy of Maelcon saw as beneath him.

"What are we going to do?" Guihir asked Guenhuifar, as she sipped her wine slowly, watching the hall begin to empty.

"Play the only card we have left," she replied in a low voice. "Boron's greed."

Once Siarl and his men had left the hall, Boron rose, apparently also keener for his bed than another horn of mead. Guenhuifar rose too and followed the tables around to intercept him before he left.

"We have both been done out of our prize this evening," she said.

"Aye, miserable luck, but there it is," Boron replied.

"But we needn't let ourselves lose all to bad luck. Not if we use our heads."

"You heard him. He knows Guallen is here."

"But does he know what she looks like?"

It took a moment for Boron to comprehend her meaning and when he did, his face turned from befuddlement to sly revelation. "A switch? Perhaps it could work. But surely, Siarl will want to take both maid and handmaiden. What good would swapping them do us if we are to lose both in any event?"

"We must find an excuse to keep the handmaid here. Say that you want her as compensation for losing out on the deal with me."

Boron rubbed his bearded chin. "A hard thing to convince him of. He knows that he has me by the balls."

"True, but what is a handmaid to him? Another mouth to feed on the journey north, another aid in any escape the young lady might attempt. Put your skilful way with words to good use and persuade him that it would be better if the girls were separated and then, when he is riding north with what he thinks is Maelcon's bride ..."

"You return to your husband with the real Guallen. And I receive my pay-out for the lass."

"You have it exactly."

It had taken some wrangling but Boron had pulled it off. The following morning, Siarl was persuaded that one captive would be more than enough for the three of them to escort back to Cair Dugannu. The holy man Guenhuifar had seen at table the previous night was summoned. He was a Deacon called Sebastianus and Boron instructed him to convince the girls to swap clothes.

"Only tell them what they need to know," said Boron. "Those fools will likely give the game away if they know they are to be separated. Just tell them it's for their own safety."

Sebastianus had done as he was asked but, when the two girls were brought out and it became apparent to them that they were to be separated, Guallen, in the plain clothes of the handmaid, had put on a great show of grief at losing her loyal servant. She wailed and fought against the guards who restrained her as the handmaid, dressed in her fine clothes, was taken to her horse. "Don't take her from me, I beg you!" she cried. "To separate us is death to me!"

"A nice performance," Boron muttered to Guenhuifar, as they watched from the steps to the Great Hall. "Young Guallen would have made a fine mummer in another life, I'll give her that."

They watched Siarl and his men lead their prize through the gates and off down the path while Guallen wailed and beat her fists at Boron's guards.

"Take her inside and give her a cup of wine," said Boron. "She's worked herself into hysterics and forgotten who she is."

Guenhuifar watched with growing concern as the girl was taken indoors. She glanced at Sebastianus who also showed some disquiet. Boron took Guenhuifar by the arm.

"Come, let us discuss the payment of the ransom. Then you can take the young lady to your husband once she has calmed herself. I will have your horses ready."

But Guallen did not calm herself. She was escorted to her chamber and the door was bolted. Her screams and pleas could be heard across the settlement and it was most unnerving. Eventually she exhausted herself and apparently fell asleep. Guenhuifar gave her an hour before paying her a visit in her chamber.

The guard unlocked the door and she found Guallen on her bed, red-eyed and utterly broken.

"Guallen?" Guenhuifar said softly. "How are you feeling?"

The girl sat up and rubbed her palms into her eyes. She sniffed. "I'm not Guallen. I had no idea we were to be separated or I would never have gone through with it! That deacon should have told us!"

A chill crept over Guenhuifar. She didn't know why she hadn't seen it before. All the clues had been there: Guallen's apparent disregard for her own safety, her gentle comforting of her handmaid as if she were the one looking out for the both of them. It had been the handmaid who had been looking out for them all along.

"You swapped clothes before you were apprehended by Boron, didn't you?" she told the girl.

The handmaid nodded. "Before we fled Maelcon and his thugs. It was my idea. I couldn't let anything befall my lady so it seemed safer for her to be the handmaid and I the lady. And now look! I sit here, a captive …"

"While the real Guallen is being swiftly carried off to her fate," said Guenhuifar. She could have cursed herself for a fool but there was no time. Siarl had a good hour on them. She had to think and act quickly or else all would be lost.

She left the handmaid in her chamber and hurried out into the Great Hall where Guihir was having a casual conversation with Sebastianus. She looked about to see if Boron was nearby. He wasn't. That was good.

"We've given away the wrong girl," she announced in a low voice.

Both warrior and deacon gazed at her uncomprehendingly.

"They swapped roles before they even crossed Boron's threshold," she explained. "They were too afraid to say so when we surreptitiously switched them back and now Guallen is on her way to her wedding with Maelcon while her handmaid lies back there weeping."

"I can catch up to them!" said Guihir. "They'll be taking their time with a captive. I could ride fast and come upon them and …"

"And get yourself killed?" Guenhuifar said. "Just how would you convince them to hand Guallen over to you? You are one and they are three. No, we must use our heads." She turned to Sebastianus. "Are you a fast rider?"

"I keep a good pace," said the deacon.

"Then you must take my horse. She is the white mare and a far finer beast than any of the sturdy little things Siarl and his men rode in on."

"You can't mean that I should go chasing after armed men!"

"Your word would carry a great deal of weight. They are Christians, after all."

Sebastianus looked flustered. "My lady, what could I say that would persuade them to hand over their charge to me?"

"The truth. Tell them that Boron has cheated them. Tell them that he ordered the girls to switch clothes before he handed them over to you. Swear it on the cross you carry around your neck."

"And if they ask me to swear that the girl isn't Guallen?"

"Use your cunning. Say only that he ordered them to swap clothes. Convince them that Boron sought to play them false without giving the game away. They'll believe you and will turn right back around and head back here to stop Boron ransoming Guallen."

"And then what?"

"Leave that to me. Persuade Siarl to let you accompany the girl back here yourself. He will no doubt be eager to make all haste. Take Guallen north and meet us at the ford on the river. Then we shall be away with both Guallen and the handmaid while Siarl and Boron are too busy snarling down each other's throats."

"This is very risky …"

"It is our only chance to get Guallen safely out of Maelcon's clutches."

The deacon nodded, bolstered somewhat by this thought. Guenhuifar tried to ignore her own guilt. By Siarl's hand or by Arthur's, the poor girl would most likely be delivered to Maelcon anyway.

"I will do my best and meet you at the ford," said Sebastianus.

"Good man."

As he headed for the stables, Guihir regarded Guenhuifar curiously. "What of us? Do we sit here until Siarl rides in with foam at his mouth?"

"No. We must give Boron the bad news and see to it that he acts upon it."

"You mean to tell him the truth? Just as Sebastianus is to tell Siarl a portion of it?"

"The truth will serve even better than lies in this case. But we must give our good deacon a head start."

They waited until enough time had passed for Sebastianus to be well on the way to catching up with Siarl before seeking out Boron. He was found admiring his falcons in the yard behind the Great Hall.

"My lord, I have grave news," said Guenhuifar, as they approached him.

"That you are still here is grave enough for me, Lady Guenhuifar," he replied. "I would have hoped that you might be on your way to your husband now to arrange the transport of the ransom to me."

"There will be no ransom for the real Guallen is on her way to Maelcon as we speak."

He whirled to face her, the sudden movement making the startled peregrine flap its wide wings in protest. "What trickery is this?"

"Trickery that has outwitted us both. The real Guallen was dressed as the handmaid the entire time. We only switched them back to their rightful roles. Now we have lost her and kept the handmaid."

The falconer stepped forward to hastily take the bird from Boron's wrist as he began to shake with rage. "If I find that you had some part in this trick, woman …"

"Speak sense, Boron! Why would I want that girl to be taken by Siarl? I need her! *Arthur* needs her!"

Boron bit his knuckle. "Three men and one captive on a mountain road …" he mused.

Come on, come on! Guenhuifar thought. The man was clearly weighing up the ransom against the danger of crossing Maelcon but his indecision was infuriating.

"Accidents do happen …" he said. "And there are bandits about in the hills these days …"

"Such a mishap must happen quickly if it is to benefit us …" Guenhuifar prompted.

Boron pounded his fist into his gauntleted hand. "Yes! It can be done!" He strode off to bark orders at his fastest riders to ready their mounts, bear arms and strip themselves of all sigils. They were to be as unidentifiable as hill bandits.

He sent six of them on ahead before riding out himself to take custody of the prisoner personally once Siarl and his companions had suffered their mishap. It was just as Guenhuifar had hoped. She and Guihir were alone in the fort with the handmaid and Boron's men. An escape could be pulled off. *Now, if only that deacon does his bit, we shall be home free.*

They headed back indoors and gathered their things together. "The main gate will be watched too closely for us to sneak out that way," Guenhuifar said. "But I did spy a secondary gate."

"Aye, the small one that leads to a trackway down the north side of the hill," said Guihir. "I saw that too. It's narrower than the main trackway but less steep. Boron probably uses it for having goods delivered."

"That was my thinking too. There is a single guard posted there. I want you to go and procure a jar of wine and strike up a conversation with him. See if you can get him a little on the merry side."

"Not a problem, my lady. What will you be doing?"

"Seeing to our horses. We'll need to steal one to replace my mare I lent to Sebastianus. I want to be out of here by noon."

"Then I'd best get a move on and see how drunk I can get that guard."

He headed off towards the kitchens. Guenhuifar hurried along to see to the handmaid in her chamber and ready her for the journey.

She found her in a similar state to what she had left her in. "Come, now girl," she told her. "I have put a plan into action that might see you reunited with your lady."

The handmaid looked hopefully at her. "Really?"

"We have a chance. A slim one, but it's all we have. Now, what's your name?"

"Iona," she sniffed.

"Iona, you are brave, I know that. I saw how you placed yourself in danger to keep Guallen safe. I need that bravery now. We are to escape and meet Sebastianus on the road with Guallen if he has managed it. Then you are both to come with me to Cair Cunor."

Iona's tear-streaked face broke into a grateful smile.

"Save that," Guenhuifar warned. "We're not out of the woods yet and must not give Boron's guards any idea that something is amiss. Come on now, get your things together."

They remained in Iona's chamber until the sun had passed over the fort's thatched roofs before emerging. The settlement was quiet. With their blustering lord and several of his warriors chasing Siarl in to the hills, everybody seemed to be having a relaxing day. As they passed through the Great Hall, they saw at least two warriors slumbering on skins by the dying embers of the hearth.

Outside, the sun was glaring and there was little activity in the compound. Guards could be seen leaning on their spears atop the palisades and from the houses and workshops came the lazy hum of a slow, quiet day.

They made for the stables and found them empty but for a few horses twitching their tails and blinking away flies. Guenhuifar saddled Guihir's horse and then set about examining the remaining beasts in their stalls. She decided upon a dun mare that was a little smaller than she was used to but could still bear two. After saddling it, she and Iona led the horses out of the stables and down to the small gate in the northern wall.

From a distance she could see Guihir and the guard playing at dice on the hard-packed dirt in the shade of the wall a few yards from the gate. The wine jug stood nearby, its rim glistening.

"Come on!" Guenhuifar hissed to Iona and they quickly crossed to the section of wall on the other side of the gate, keeping well out of sight of the guard whose attention was fixed on Guihir's most recent throw of the dice.

Guenhuifar crept forward and placed her hands on the gate mechanism. The guard stood with his back to her, his attention still diverted. She succeeded in unbolting the gate and managed to swing it open without too much noise. At a beckon, Iona led Guihir's horse through the gate while Guenhuifar went back for her own.

But the horse didn't know her and was a little on the cautious side. She tugged gently on its reins and it let out a snort; a small one but a snort nonetheless.

The guard whirled around, lunging drunkenly for his spear that was propped against the wall. "What goes on here?" he demanded. "Where are you taking those horses?"

Guihir lifted up the wine jug and brought it down on the guard's head. Pottery shards and the remnants of the wine cascaded over his shoulders and he slumped to the ground, unconscious. Guihir dragged him by the heels under the thatch of one of the workshops that had been built against the wall.

"Nicely done, ladies!" he said, as he caught up with Guenhuifar and Iona who were leading the horses onto the path.

"Likewise," said Guenhuifar. "It'll be a couple of hours before he'll be missed I should think. That gives us the time we need. Now, onwards to the ford and, if Sebastianus hasn't let us down, to Cair Cunor with Maelcon's blasted bride!"

Arthur

As Arthur strode through the camp, Cabal trotting at his heels, he did his best to acknowledge each and every one of his warriors who nodded and saluted him. They were tired, hungry and nervous. The march had exhausted them and now they had found themselves cut off in one of the bleakest parts of Albion. The food was running short and there were no settlements for miles around. There was some hunting to be had but most deer had moved off the moors at the advance of the teulu. Time was not something they had much of.

The Afon Camlan ran between the two camps, its gushing waters the perfect excuse for either side to go no further, almost as if it had been set between them by the gods as a way of halting their inevitable meeting. Its churning flow reminded Arthur of the old washer woman he had seen on the march; the woman in black from his dream. He almost physically shuddered every time he thought of her. In years past, he had felt an attraction, almost a love, for the woman in his dreams whom he had always seen as both his protector and guide. Now he felt a revulsion for her and a deep dread he could not explain.

But Guenhuifar had returned to him and with her perhaps their only hope; a chance to force Maelcon to call Medraut off. He met her on the camp perimeter where she was accepting a cup of wine from one of his men. Her white mare stood nearby.

"Thank all the gods!" he said, as he hurried to embrace her. "I am so sorry, Guenhuifar. We had no choice but to abandon Cair Cunor. I would have ridden through Hell to fetch you but Eternion and Powys combined marched on us …"

"I know, Arthur," she said. "All Eternion is roused. We had a job of it avoiding capture on the way west."

"We? Then you and Guihir …"

"Succeeded in our mission, yes. I left Guihir with our charges at a nunnery on the edge of the forest not far south from here. We have a deacon with us – Sebastianus – who led us to it. He was most helpful in getting the girls out of Boron's clutches but it was a long trek back to Cair Cunor. When we saw men bearing Eternion's sigil foraging so close to the fortress I guessed that you had moved west. I knew you would not go north."

"So Medraut and he managed to head us off. But you may have saved us from battle."

"Medraut … is he …"

"Across the river, yes. We have been staring at each other across the water for three days. I don't believe he wants to attack me any more than I want to attack him. We have been sending envoys back and forth. Ithoc is with him now."

"Ithoc? The lad who brought us news of Guallen?"

"Aye. He's turned out to be quite the honey-tongued diplomat. He is a trained envoy after all. I sent him with Gualchmei the first time and Gualchmei came back singing his praises so I sent him alone the next time. Menw would have gone too but the damp on these moors does not agree with his bones and he'd rather keep to his tent."

"He's not sick is he?"

"Menw? No. It'll take more than Albion's dismal weather to bring that old mage down. He is just getting old, that's all and he feels the ache of age. And so do I." He rubbed an old wound on his right arm. Guenhuifar clasped it.

"But your aches are the aches of war on a young man's body."

He smiled. "Not so young anymore."

"What do we do with Guallen now? How do we end this?"

"I'm not sure that it can be ended. Maelcon is hardly likely to give up the throne for the sake of a girl who has taken his fancy."

"No, but he may be brought to heel. Some of his more aggressive policies might be reined in."

"We won't know until we ask him. But first Medraut must be placated."

"And in the meantime, I want to see our sons. Where are they?"

"I'll take you to them. They've been asking after you three times a day at least. I think it would be best if you took them and a few other innocents to this nunnery of yours. A battle camp is no place for children."

Amhar and Lacheu were overjoyed to see their mother and the four of them enjoyed a rare private meal in Arthur's tent. They talked and laughed and they almost forgot their surroundings. But, as was always the case, a bellowing horn brought Arthur back to the here and now and he rose from his family and pulled back the tent flap.

"What is it?" Guenhuifar asked, her voice concerned.

"Someone approaches," said Arthur.

Men were running through the camp in an easterly direction and all about was the feeling of alarm.

"Wait here," he told Guenhuifar.

Buckling on his sword, he hurried to join the flow. He spotted Beduir and hailed him. "What goes on?"

"Riders from the east!" said Beduir. "A whole host of them!"

What now? Arthur wondered.

Upon reaching the edge of camp, he found Cei marshalling a line of spearmen. In the distance the perimeter sentries could be seen escorting a group of horsemen towards the camp. A banner fluttered above them, its sigil instantly recognisable to those in the teulu who had fought Cerdic's West Saeson in the south years previously.

"Dumnonia!" Arthur cried ecstatically. "King Cador of Dumnonia comes!"

Cei bellowed for the line of spearmen to stand at ease and Arthur pushed his way through them to greet his old ally. King Cador swung himself down from his horse and embraced Arthur.

"Cador!" Arthur said. "Your coming is most timely! But why? How?"

"Do you think the rest of Albion is deaf to Venedotia's cries?" Cador asked. "Dumnonia was grieved to hear of the passing of Cadwallon and of how things have gone from bad to worse. When I heard that this whelp, Maelcon, took the throne and declared war on his father's most loyal allies I could do naught but muster my bannermen and ride north to your aid. Just as you fought alongside me against Dumnonia's enemies, so too shall I fight alongside you against the tyrant who holds Venedotia in his grasp!"

"Thank you, old friend! How many warriors have you brought?"

"Two-hundred horse and three-hundred foot."

"The very sight of them will lift my men's spirits to the very heavens. Bring them in! Pitch your tents alongside ours. We shall extend the perimeter. Cei?"

"I'll see to it, Arthur," said Cei, and he strode off to bark orders.

A second man Arthur recognised climbed down from his horse, only this one did not fill his heart with half the joy seeing Cador had.

"Abbot Petroc," said Arthur. "I did not expect to see you make such an arduous journey north with Cador's teulu but I am glad of your company. You are most welcome."

"I thank you," said the abbot. but his face did not look pleased. He no doubt remembered their quarrel over certain donations to the war effort Arthur had wrung out of the holy houses of Dumnonia. "I ride with Cador as I ride with God and will see that the work of both is done here in the north."

Arthur smiled. "Well, come to my tent, all of you and we shall toast the rekindling of old acquaintances. And you can tell me all of what goes on in Dumnonia. How is the Lady Esyllt?"

"She fares well, and our son too," said Cador, as they walked through the camp.

"Young Constantine must be, what, seven now?"

"Eight. And as lusty and boisterous a prince any king could ask for. He has his mother's temper, there is no doubt about that!"

They supped and toasted one another in Arthur's tent and the day was turning to dusk when Ithoc crossed the river back into camp. His eyes lit up when he was admitted into Arthur's company and he saw Guenhuifar.

"What news?" Arthur asked him.

"Medraut is biding his time although I do not believe he will wait forever," said Ithoc.

"His purpose is to block our way," said Arthur. "Surely he will not attack me unless provoked?"

"I don't know, sire. His men seem restless."

"Did you learn anything about his captains? Of his teulu's organisation?"

"His captains seem to be a man called Alan who is closer to your age, begging your pardon. There were two others in his tent, young men. One fair and handsome. The other ugly as sin."

"Sanddef and Morfran," said Arthur. "Hardly surprising. They were his old comrades when he led a patrol under me. So, he gives out high-ranking positions to his friends rather than those with more experience. Foolish, but predictable of him."

"His teulu does seem to lack men of experience," said Ithoc. "I barely saw a lad over twenty years of age."

"Medraut represents all the un-tempered rages and follies of youth," said Arthur. "You only have to look at the would-be-king he serves. Maelcon promises an unattainable dream and Medraut carries the battle standard for all young men's grievances against their fathers and uncles. They think he will overturn the old and herald a new dawn for all of them. But before they know it they'll be old themselves, fighting down a new generation of hotheads eager to chase them into their graves."

The tent fell silent at his morose words. Ithoc took the opportunity to speak to Guenhuifar. "My lady," he said. "Did you …?"

"Free Guallen? Yes. She and her handmaid are safe and sound at a nunnery south of the moors."

"Speaking of which," said Arthur, "you should go and prepare to join them. Take the boys with you. I will come and see you off."

"I think we shall take our leave of you also, Arthur," said Cador, as Guenhuifar hustled Amhar and Lacheu out of the tent. "I must see to the building of our camp."

Arthur was soon alone with Ithoc. "Now then, lad," he told the envoy. I want you to return to Medraut on the morrow and tell him that we have Maelcon's bride. If his master truly wants her returned to him, then he will have to allow us to cross the Camlan and deliver her to him personally. I intend to camp my teulu on the coast within sight of Cair Dugannu and discuss terms with him. We'll stop this war yet."

Ithoc blinked at him. "You don't really mean to hand Guallen over to him as if she were a bargaining chit?"

Arthur clasped his shoulder and poured the young envoy a cup of wine. "I know you protected the lass for a while and it stung to have her stolen from you but she is no longer your responsibility. It's a miserable thing to have to do but there it is. We can't wager the lives of thousands on the marriage choices of a girl."

"But Maelcon is a monster. I have heard you say it yourself."

"A monster that might yet be tamed."

"And what about Guallen? Don't her wishes count for anything?"

Arthur frowned. He believed that Ithoc had developed quite a shine for the girl while she was under his protection. "I know it's hard but we all suffer hardships for the greater good. Guallen is our chance to end all of this."

Ithoc looked at the ground. "I suppose … if battle is to be avoided …"

"That's the spirit, lad. Now, go and find something to eat and get some sleep. I want you back across that river at daybreak."

Once he had gone, Arthur went over to the perimeter to see Guenhuifar and his sons off. His mind lingered on Ithoc. The envoy had done well but his recent emotional state made Arthur question his suitability. Once he had delivered his message to Medraut he would relieve him of his duties and send him on his way. With any luck they would be striking camp and preparing to march north by noon tomorrow.

He kissed Guenhuifar and his sons goodbye and watched as they rode off across the moors. He breathed deeply and allowed himself a small smile. At last, things were going to plan.

Medraut

Medraut could see the banner of the red dragon fluttering over Arthur's camp from his position on the western bank of the river. It stood out like a red flame, taunting him; so close, separated from him only by a thin river.

Arthur's audacity was outrageous. To still carry that standard with him – the standard of the Pendraig – after he had abandoned all it stood for was a direct insult to Medraut. *That banner is mine*, Medraut thought every time the tail of his eye caught its redness across the tops of the tents and through the drifting smoke of campfires. *And I will reclaim it for Venedotia.*

He had been awoken early by Alan who told him that Arthur's camp had grown in size during the night. A large force, it seemed, had arrived to bolster his ranks. From the west bank, Medraut could see the large cluster of tents beyond Arthur's camp but could make out no banners or sigils. *What allies did Arthur have left?* It crossed his mind that King Edelsie, whom they had aided against the Saeson the previous year, was now repaying the debt but he couldn't imagine that old man would be fool enough to leave his borders unguarded and open to reprisals from Wintra or Afloeg. Whoever it was had made any attack on Arthur's position a deal riskier.

It would be a blow to his men's morale, there was no escaping that. Their enemy had grown considerably in size. But Medraut would not let himself be concerned. He had gone over his plan of attack a hundred times in his head. A three-pronged attack was the only way. The main crossing over the

Afon Camlan lay right before them; large blocks of stone heaved into the water to create a fording point by a people long since vanished. Further upriver, close to the Camlan's source, the river was narrow enough for riders to cross it. A third crossing lay concealed in the woods to the south where the Camlan emptied into the series of waterfalls known as the Black Falls. It had been there that Cadwallon had held back the advance of Meriauned in the Civil War. Arthur would know of that crossing but it was well screened and Medraut was confident he could send a third of his teulu across the river at that point without detection. Besides, he would ensure that Arthur's attention would be wholly focused on the battle unfolding on the northern part of the river so that he would be unaware of Medraut's third company coming up on his left flank.

As he walked through his camp, he saw the sigils of many houses and families: painted on shields, sewn on tunicas and on banners that fluttered in the breeze. Many bannermen had pledged their support to Maelcon and had joined the teulu with their sons and retinues. There had been a feeling of great optimism as they had marched south, a feeling that they were doing God's work and ridding Venedotia of the last vestiges of paganism. They had picked up an abbot along the way – Ceduin, another of Iltud's students – and he was currently holding mass for a large group of kneeling warriors at the rear of the camp.

A large crucifix had been constructed and plated with beaten iron, polished so it caught the sun's glare. It stood above the congregation, more prominent than any battle standard. These men fought for God just as much as they fought for Maelcon. Bishop Dubricius's words of fire and brimstone had succeeded in doing what no Venedotian king had yet done. He had united the people in a common cause that transcended borders and banners. All that mattered to the people now was that good triumphed and evil was destroyed.

But Medraut's ambitions were not so lofty. He didn't care if Arthur was sent by the devil as Dubricius claimed. He had a pretty good idea that he wasn't. All he wanted was to defeat him and to ride home with the dragon banner, back to Maelcon, back to Guenhuifach, triumphant. He wanted to finally become everything Arthur had tried to stop him from being. *That* was what *he* fought for.

Alan hailed him. "That envoy is back, the little rodent-faced one. And he has a man of God with him."

"What does he want now so soon after yesterday's wrangling?" asked Medraut impatiently. "Arthur merely seeks to buy himself time with his feeble attempts at parley. And what does he mean by sending me a holy man? Haven't we enough?"

"I imagine men of the cloth are hardly welcome amidst that pit of heathen savages," said Alan. "Maybe he's been kicked out."

"Come on, let's see what they want now."

The holy man introduced himself as Abbot Petroc. Ithoc stood by while this newcomer stated his business.

"I came north to tend to the Christian needs of Arthur's warriors and to do what I can for the lost souls in his retinue."

"And how have you fared with them?" Medraut asked him.

The abbot sighed. "In truth, not well. They are a barbarous lot with altogether too many different faiths between them. Even the Christians don't seem to mind sharing hearths and meals with pagans."

"You would find better company amongst my own men," said Medraut.

"Abbot Petroc here insisted that he accompany me this morning," said Ithoc. "He wished to see if there was anything he could do for the souls of your followers."

"We already have an abbot to tend to our Christian needs."

"Indeed?" said Petroc. "Who is he?"

"Ceduin of Iltud's school."

"I do not know him but I know well his tutor's name. Iltud's school is spoken of with great reverence even in Dumnonia. I should very much like to meet him."

"Then you shall. Alan, please send for Abbot Ceduin." He turned to Ithoc. "And now, while our holy men have matters of spirituality to discuss, let us turn to more practical talk." He led the envoy down the length of his river defences while they talked. *Let him see. I have nothing to hide. Let him return with tales of my strength.*

"I fear I bring a rather sterner message than the one I carried yesterday," said Ithoc.

"Oh? And what has changed that Arthur should take a different tone with me?"

He knew very well what had changed and why it had bolstered Arthur's confidence. The sudden addition of a new ally and what looked to be at least five-hundred men did wonders for morale.

"Perhaps you have seen, there are more tents in Arthur's camp than there were this time yesterday," said Ithoc.

"Indeed I have. Who is his new friend?"

"King Cador of Dumnonia arrived early yesterday morning along with Abbot Petroc. He has pledged to aid Arthur."

Ah! Cador of Dumnonia. That was before Medraut's time. "Goodness, how strong some friendships are. That not even seven years and two-hundred miles can break them."

"Indeed. So perhaps you will understand when I give you Arthur's message, that it comes from one who is confident that he can win this battle."

"Win? We'll see about that but do go on. What is Arthur's message to me?"

"That if you stand aside and allow him to pass unmolested, he will forgive the quarrel between the two of you or, to be more exact, the quarrel between your respective wives. Once he has claimed the throne of Venedotia, he will reconsider allowing you into the teulu."

Medraut took a moment or two to digest these words so incomprehensible they were to him. "He? Forgive *me*? Forgive *Guenhuifach*?" Rage boiled inside his gut. "This quarrel was entirely of his and Guenhuifar's making! He dares to presume that we are the cause of it? And reconsider allowing me in to the teulu? *I* am the penteulu now! He is just an imposter!"

"He said that you would act just so, begging your pardon. He warned me to expect an outburst."

"Outburst!" Medraut roared. "Just what exactly did he say?"

Ithoc looked a little flustered and more than a bit embarrassed. "Know, sire, that these words come from Arthur and I am just an envoy …"

"Yes, yes, out with it!"

"He said that you were ever a temperamental boy given more to wild impulse rather than logic and that is why you were unfit to be a captain and are now unfit to lead a teulu. You are playing at being him, he said, and that he partly blames himself. He promises that if you give up this nonsense and return to his side and help him in his war against Maelcon, then he will ensure that you are given command of a company."

The rage that had threatened to erupt within Medraut settled to a dull, heavy anger like a glowing lump of red-hot iron deep in his chest. He did not explode. He did not rage. He *seethed*. He did not understand it fully but somehow he felt as if Arthur's words no longer mattered. If there had ever been any hope of reconciliation between the two of them then Arthur had now just severed it and ground it into the dirt. And Medraut thanked him for it. He felt his mind was clearer than it had been in weeks. His uncle and adoptive father were finally dead to him and he knew exactly what he was going to do next.

"Return to Arthur," he told Ithoc. "Tell him that he is a relic of a dead age. His words are feeble and his teulu is feebler still. *I* will be the one to offer *him* his life if he surrenders. Go, now!"

Ithoc nodded and left him standing there alone. Medraut looked up at the clouds drifting overhead. *The time has come,* he thought. *Now, I end it.*

Arthur

The attack came as suddenly and without warning as a thunderbolt from a clear blue sky.

"That he should attack now when I hold Maelcon's bride?" Arthur marvelled, as horns bellowed and warriors hurried to muster themselves. "Has he lost all his senses?"

"Perhaps he knows you are not capable of harming her," said Cei, buckling on his helm.

"Aye, but what's to stop me sending her away, hiding her someplace where Maelcon will never find her? Medraut is taking an awful risk if he thinks to storm our position and take her by force."

"I have sent all our spearmen to form a funnel at the edge of the ford," said Cei. "Bowmen have been mustered in two wings on the higher ground. What are your orders for the companies?"

"Medraut is no fool. He will split his forces and send a detachment north to cross the river at its narrowest point thinking to fall upon our right flank. I want you and Cador to take your companies north and meet them."

"The other captains?"

"Will remain here. I am merging Gualchmei and Peredur's companies and they shall form our left wing. Beduir and I, our right. Mor will keep his own riders in reserve at the rear of the spear line, ready to reinforce whichever wing begins to falter first. Between us we will hold the ford and you shall smash Medraut's flanking manoeuvre. He will rue his impulsiveness this day!"

Cei saluted and hurried off to prepare his company. Arthur strode towards Hengroen who was being walked up and down by one of his grooms. Cabal trotted alongside him.

"Well, old friend?" he said to his white stallion. "Are you ready for one more battle?"

Hengroen blinked and looked away. Arthur swung himself up into the saddle and rode off to join Beduir who was marshalling the right wing. He passed Cador and his riders on their way to join Cei and they saluted each other.

The front lines had been bolstered significantly by the spearmen of Dumnonia and they stood three lines deep, painted shields overlapping in a long wall that bristled with iron-tipped spears. In the distance Arthur could see Gualchmei and Peredur galloping south at the head of their companies, skirting King Mor where he sat with his own small company behind the centre of the spear line.

Medraut's men had mustered on the far bank and were beginning to cross the ford. He was sending his cavalry across first, hoping to break through Arthur's spearmen, opening up a gap for his footmen who would be able to wreak havoc with sword and axe once the formation was broken. But it was a hard man who sent horses against spearmen.

As soon as the enemy riders wetted their mounts' fetlocks in the river, they were within range of Arthur's bowmen who began loosing arrows down upon them. With shields upraised, the riders pressed on through the churning river as arrows thudded into oak, mail and horse flesh. Some riders were thrown from their screaming horses into the foaming water which quickly became streaked with blood.

It was not enough. Arthur simply had not the bowmen to halt their advance and the cavalry slammed into his spear lines like a thundering wave. The men stumbled backwards but held the line, stabbing and thrusting, giving no ground. *Hold*, Arthur silently willed them. *Hold!* He was waiting for just the right moment.

The ford was a natural bottleneck. The waters were too deep on either side of it for Medraut's cavalry to skirt the press of battle. They had to wait until either the riders in front of them had broken through the spear lines or had died trying.

"Let's give them a little room," Arthur said to his horn blower. "Signal them to fall back ten paces."

The aurochs horn bellowed out the signal and the weary spearmen gladly gave up ground, marching backwards, fending off the blades and spears of the enemy cavalry every step of the way.

The ends of the line halted while the middle section continued for a few more paces, forming an inverted wedge. Medraut's riders filled the V shape, the ones at the back urging their mounts up out of the river, their flanks dripping, as they sought to fill in the edges and widen the line of assault.

Arthur turned to Beduir who sat astride his black stallion. "Take your company into the breech. I will signal to Gualchmei and Peredur to do the same on our left."

Beduir nodded and galloped off to the head of his company. Soon they were off at a charge, skirting the ends of the spear lines and slamming into the enemy's left flank. It was cavalry against cavalry and, as Arthur leant forward in his saddle to get a better look, he found that he did not miss the hot mad press of horses' flanks, of dodging and shielding blows from wavering riders on horseback with no way out but on, forward at all cost, trampling the fallen under hoof.

"Sire!" cried his standard bearer.

Arthur followed his outstretched arm and could see some disturbance way over on their left flank where Gualchmei and Peredur should be leading their own charge. There was much jostling in the ranks, particularly at the rear and the signs of what looked to be a fight.

A rider came galloping towards them. "Sire! Lord Arthur! The enemy has fallen upon our left flank! At least three-hundred horse!"

"Three hundred?" Arthur exclaimed. How was it possible? They held both crossing points. How could the enemy have crossed unless Medraut had sent a company way south …?

The Black Falls.

He remembered with a sudden queasy feeling Cadwallon's first battle in the civil war all those years ago. Cadwallon had engaged Meriaun's teulu at the Black Falls while sending a company under Cunor west to cross the Afon Camlan as it entered the woods. He had been a fool to forget! Medraut had sent a three-pronged attack against him and he had only prepared to fight on two fronts!

"King Mor has seen them," said the rider.

Arthur watched in desperation as the small company of Rumaniog's riders charged down the line to reinforce his left flank. "They are too few! We must join them. Follow me! Ride now!"

With the bellowing of the horn in his ears, he drew *Caledbulc* and kicked Hengroen into a gallop. His company followed close as he pushed them on, desperately trying to catch up to the fleeting sight of Mor's riders. They were stretched thin now, with all reserves occupied. If anyone faltered there would be no cavalry companies to reinforce them. *Keep the right flank, Beduir*, he thought as he rode. *And don't let anyone slip by you to fall on our rear, Cei.*

Guenhuifar

The nunnery was a lonely, windswept place of limewashed stone and thatch. Several wattle huts housed the necessary industries that supported the sisters and there was a chicken run at the back as well as a couple of goats for milking. It was situated by a stream that ran off the moor and disappeared into the woods to the south which loomed like a dark haze.

The nuns had prepared a simple meal of broth and bread and they ate in the tiny refectory at a single oak table. Guenhuifar was glad of the warming meal for it had been a cold, damp morning's travelling. As she dipped bread into her broth she eyed Guallen. The girl wasn't touching her food.

"You should try some," she urged her. "You have been through an ordeal and must keep your strength up. Besides, we do not want to offend our hosts." She looked down the table at the small gathering of nuns who ate their own meal in silence, occasionally paying them a suspicious glance.

"An ordeal?" said Guallen bitterly. "My ordeal is yet to come. I had been better off Boron's prisoner."

"He would have handed you over to Siarl and you would have been married to Maelcon all the same," said Guenhuifar with a sigh. Perhaps it had been a mistake to tell the girl exactly what was to happen to her on the morrow. Arthur and Medraut were likely hammering out the details of the handover as they ate their broth. Ignorance of the future would have been better for the girl but Guenhuifar could not keep up the lie any longer. Not when she had returned to the nunnery and seen the look of hope on Guallen's face.

"And you had the audacity to call yourself our rescuer," said the handmaid called Iona with a look of hard reproach in her eyes. "You and your husband are no better than that Medraut or Boron. You'll barter a girl's happiness for your own gain all the same."

"None of this is for my gain," Guenhuifar lied. The mention of Medraut's name still stung her. "You are being returned to Maelcon in order to save thousands of lives."

The handmaid glanced at Sebastianus who was silently drinking broth from his bowl. "And you, you will just sit by and let this unchristian behaviour unfold around you?"

Sebastianus set his bowl down uncertainly. "My dear, there is really little I can do. I thought to save you from your fate but forces far bigger than me now exert their influence." He looked at Guenhuifar and she detected reproach in him too. Gods, was this all her fault? All she wanted was for this damned war to end. Was that really so terrible? If she could find any way to save Guallen from marrying Maelcon then she would do it but there seemed to be no other choice.

"I really thought he would come for me," said Guallen, looking at the door as if she half-expected the wind to swing it open and carry her away. "I know he still loves me, wherever he is."

"If there was any way at all," said Iona, placing her hand gently on her arm for comfort, "then he would have come. Perhaps it is best that he did not for he would surely now be dead and the result would be the same. Instead, let us be happy that he is alive and free."

"I miss him so much," said Guallen. "If only Father had let us marry last year none of this would have happened."

"Who's this?" Guihir asked. "You had a lover?"

Guallen looked at the tabletop, a tear welling in her eye.

"Aye," the handmaid answered for her. "A nobleman's son from the neighbouring commote. "Ithoc was his name and they were to be married. But your blasted wars put a stop to all that."

"Ithoc?" said Guenhuifar, feeling a sudden chill that froze her to her bones.

"Aye, Ithoc mab Munio. Why? Does the name mean aught to you?"

"Is he a small fellow, dark hair and pointed features?"

"That's him. And what he lacks in height and strength he makes up for in goodness of heart."

"And was it this Ithoc who met you on the road after you escaped Maelcon? Did he conduct you east only to lose you to Boron's raiders?"

Guallen and Iona looked at her in confusion.

"I have not seen my dear Ithoc for a month," said Guallen.

Guihir glanced at Guenhuifar. "Ithoc has been playing us false," he said.

"Aye, and now he plays as intermediary between Arthur and Medraut."

"What?"

"My husband saw the merit in a trained envoy and so sent him to Medraut to talk terms."

"God help us …" said Guihir. "Does he know Arthur intends to hand his lady love over to Maelcon?"

Guenhuifar nodded and rose from her seat.

"Where are you going, my lady?" asked Sebastianus.

"Back to Arthur. I must leave immediately."

"My lady, let me go," said Guihir.

"No. I have been there and back already today and know the way. You remain with my boys."

She ran from the refectory and made for the stables. Her white mare which she had lent to Sebastianus had been fed and brushed and she quickly saddled him. It was already past midday. If she rode fast she might reach the Afon Camlan before dusk. *Will I be too late?*

A terror had gripped her that spurred her actions. Ithoc was a live spark in a haystack, threatening to ignite a blazing inferno at any moment. She *had* to get there and stop whatever he was planning to do.

As she led her horse out of the stables, several of the nuns had emerged from the monastery along with Guihir and Sebastianus. Amhar and Lacheu wandered in tow. They all looked on her with concern. She ignored them, swung herself up into the saddle and kicked her mount in to a gallop, spurring it on, up towards the moors.

Medraut

The spear line that guarded the ford had broken in most parts and the footmen were falling back from Medraut's press of cavalry. The river was littered with the dead and its waters ran red around the lifeless forms of men and horses. It had been a costly attack but they were through at last. Arthur's front line had been pushed back from the river affording space for Medraut's reserves to reinforce their comrades.

Medraut led them himself, yelling a war-cry at the top of his lungs as he charged into the river. Up ahead he could see only a fraction of Arthur's cavalry fighting on the left flank. Amidst the chaos he could make out Beduir on his massive black horse. *So, Beduir holds their right.* He glanced downriver and saw a cluster of horsemen charging into the fray caused by Sanddef and Morfran's flanking manoeuvre. Two banners wavered above the outnumbered host; one bearing the raven sigil of Rumaniog, the other ... *the red dragon!*

Arthur was reinforcing his left flank himself! That was more than Medraut could have hoped for. He had assumed Arthur would have remained at the ford to help repel the initial assault but he had instead charged into the most dangerous part of the battlefield to rescue whomever he had sent to guard it. *Cei? Gualchmei? Peredur?*

The dragon banner called to Medraut across the heaving mass of battle like a warm flame in the coldest winter. He was irresistibly drawn to it. To strike down Arthur and raise the banner of the red dragon high above his own teulu was all he cared about in that moment and so he made the decision to chase it.

The left flank needed help against Beduir's company. The right line of Arthur's spearmen still held although the left was wavering visibly. Medraut wheeled his horse and led his men towards it.

It was a dangerous thing to attempt but no less dangerous than what he had asked of his first wave of cavalry. They smashed into the spear line and Medraut hacked aside an outthrust spear with his sword, severing its tip before swinging down at the man who wielded it.

His sword clanged off the iron boss of an upraised shield but the man was now unarmed. The press of his own men behind him pushed Medraut forward and the spear line bent under the impact. Medraut thrust his sword in through a gap between the shields and felt hot blood spatter across his forearm.

The man was down and the spear line had its weak link. Medraut urged his horse on, fending off spear jabs with his shield while hacking and slashing with his sword.

The gap widened and more and more of his riders pushed themselves in. The spear line was broken and quickly disintegrated into small clusters of men or single warriors who were quickly speared, cut down or trampled by the dense press of horses.

They were through! Arthur's last defences of the ford had been broken and nothing now stood between Medraut and the battle on the right flank. He yelled triumphantly and wheeled his sword around in a circle above his head, sending droplets of blood spraying everywhere.

"With me! On! On to victory!"

And he led the charge towards Arthur's position.

Arthur

Arthur gritted his teeth as he fought on, his grime-smeared face streaked with tears of grief. He had seen Gualchmei fall just as he had joined the battle. Peredur was already dead. The company he had formed to guard the left flank had been too small for Medraut's flanking manoeuvre and had been decimated before he and Mor had been able to reinforce them. Simply too many horses had charged them from the south, emerging from the woods like avenging demons.

He had no idea if Medraut had led the assault but he scanned the helmed heads of the enemy for him. He spotted Sanddef's fair face, spattered with blood and, far down the line, Morfran's ugly head could be seen roaring as he hacked and slashed from his saddle. Arthur knew that if he got the chance this day, he would kill Medraut.

"On our right!" he heard Mor cry.

Turning, he just had time to see a second company of enemy cavalry charge into them from the direction of the ford. This time he was in no doubt. Only Medraut would be so reckless as to plough through a line of spearmen just to lean more heavily on an enemy wing that was already outnumbered and weakening fast.

So be it, Medraut, Arthur thought. *Killing me is more important to you than saving your men. Very well.*

He forced Hengroen around to face the newcomers. The enemy that had outflanked them was still too strong but if he could only reach Medraut ...

Cabal, loyal hound that he was, saw his master's intention and turned to face the enemy himself. He had already torn the throats out of a couple of fallen riders and his jaws and chest were red and matted with gore.

As Arthur turned his back on the enemy, a sword stroke clipped his helm with enough force to make him see stars. He reeled in his saddle and turned to fend off a second blow with *Caledbulc*. Cabal, seeing the danger, turned back and leapt at the enemy rider.

The man screamed as the hound sank its jaws into his thigh and began to tug and heave, pulling the man from his saddle.

A second rider galloped up to aid his comrade. This one carried a spear and he thrust down at Cabal, skewering him between the shoulder blades.

"No!" Arthur screamed. He had lost too many comrades today. The man Cabal had savaged was between him and the hound's killer and Arthur abandoned the fight to ride around him and slash at the mounted spearman.

The man's spearhead was lodged in the writhing hound and he could not bring it up in time to defend himself from Arthur's blow. *Caledbulc* sheared through the bone and sinew of the neck, decapitating the man. The head tumbled from the shoulders and the headless corpse swayed in the saddle for a moment before tumbling from its horse.

The other rider followed up the attack and came at Arthur, sword swinging. Arthur grunted as the jarring pain caused by iron on iron vibrated up his arm to the elbow but was able to offset his opponent's balance enough to get in a low thrust at the belly. *Caledbulc's* sharp tip punched through mail and cloth and sank deep into the man's guts. Arthur ripped it free and kicked the man from his saddle.

He wheeled Hengroen around to look for Cabal. He saw him dead in the mud, the enemy spear still lodged in him.

Horns bellowed from somewhere and Arthur glanced over the heads of the seething mass of warriors. Through blurry eyes he could see more horsemen were joining the fray, this time from the north.

"It's Cei!" he shouted, upon recognising the man who led them. "Our brothers come!"

Any hope of a victory that day had left him and any victory to come would always be bittersweet after having lost so many comrades but Arthur allowed himself to take heart in the return of his friend. Between them they had Medraut pinned. They may not survive this battle but neither would Medraut.

Arthur called his remaining riders to him and they pushed forward as one. He could see Medraut now, his dark face iron-hard amidst the frenzy.

The shockwave of Cei's charge caused a shudder throughout Medraut's company and many of them turned to fight the oncomers. They were distracted now, unsure of themselves. Arthur pressed on but he could feel Hengroen's strength flagging beneath him. Many horses had been killed and their riders now fought on foot. The formations were loose and disorganised. The battle was now a brutal match between individuals.

Arthur called the nearest of his men to him; a young warrior who had already lost his mount. "You, lad, what is your name?"

"Cunuil, my lord!"

Arthur swung himself down from Hengroen's saddle. "Take my horse. See that he is removed from the battlefield."

"You want me to ... retreat?" There was a reluctance in the young warrior's eyes.

"I have lost too many friends today, lad," said Arthur. "I don't want to lose this one as well. Take him and survive this day!"

Cunuil nodded and climbed up into Hengroen's saddle. Arthur watched them go and knew he had made the right decision. To lose that white horse whom he had rescued as a foal from a hawthorn bush all those years ago would be too much for him to bear today. He gripped *Caledbulc* with both hands and hacked his way into the fight ahead.

He fought and fought until his arms screamed with fatigue. Although he stayed clear of the mounted warriors and gravitated only towards those on foot, there seemed to be no end of enemies. Somewhere, at the rear of the mass of warriors in front of him was Cei. Would that they could meet and stand side by side! But he felt utterly alone. Mor was in some other part of the fray and he recognised the few warriors around him only by face.

Even his standard bearer had been struck down. The dragon banner, under which he had spent his whole life fighting, now lay trampled into the mud and blood of the battlefield.

"Arthur!" cried a voice.

Arthur looked about. A mounted warrior approached him. It was Medraut. He swung himself down from his horse and ran at him. Arthur brought up *Caledbulc* and parried.

A circle began to form around the two warriors as they fought, the gravity of the fight making them forget the larger battle and focus only on the battle between uncle and nephew, father and son.

There were no words to be spoken; the time for talk had passed. All that remained was the brutal blow-by-blow struggle for dominance, one generation versus another in a desperate fight for victory.

Arthur felt himself tiring. Medraut was younger, fitter and fresher than he was. But he was also impulsive and likely to put a foot wrong if Arthur could somehow let him …

He began to rein in his blows and take only the defensive stance. It was the only way to beat Medraut's raw aggression. He parried and dodged and circled and sidestepped. His non-comital tactics drove Medraut to frustration and even greater efforts.

Medraut yelled as he swung and thrust. He was a fine warrior, there was no doubting that, but he was constantly blocked or offset by Arthur who drew upon every ounce of his experience.

At last, Medraut faltered and put a foot wrong. Arthur switched suddenly to the offensive. Medraut desperately parried the blow but was off balance and Arthur would give him no chance to recover it. He swung and chopped, putting every last bit of his strength into this final assault. It was now or never.

Panic showed on Medraut's face as he was buffeted backwards by a blow from *Caledbulc*, his sword arm flailing wide. Arthur swung hard and batted Medraut's blade out of his hand. It landed in the mud with a spatter.

He did not think. He did not feel. He did only that which he knew he must do. He ended it.

Caledbulc's tip slid into Medraut's sternum, erupting from his back, bursting through mail links which soon began to seep blood. Medraut sucked in an agonising lungful of air and slowly sank to his knees. The onlookers were silent. Somewhere Arthur heard a raven caw.

He pulled his sword free from Medraut's guts and glanced around at the awestruck faces of enemy and ally alike. Some would cry out in jubilation while some would wail their grief but not yet. It was too early. Time seemed to have slowed to a trickle and Arthur thought he could see a face passing behind the heads of the gawking crowd. It was a hooded face but within its shadows he could see wrinkled skin, wispy white hair and eyes like green fire. The old woman smiled at him and he felt a deep revulsion as he remembered the old washer woman at the ford.

A sharp pain seared through his right thigh. A collective gasp went up from the crowd. He looked down. The dagger had passed straight through his leg and its red tip was poking through the other side, dripping blood. Medraut removed his hand from the dagger's hilt and sank back onto his haunches. With a roar, Arthur swung *Caledbulc* down upon his head, splitting him to the chin.

He reached down and pulled the dagger out of his thigh with a slow gasp of pain. Blood pulsed from the wound, soaking his breeches. He glanced up at the stricken battlefield of broken banners, riderless horses and still corpses. The ravens were already beginning to descend on their feast. He staggered and felt the arms of his comrades catch him as he fell. *It is over*, he thought. *It is over at last.*

Guenhuifar

Guenhuifar pushed her horse on and on across the moors, through streams and along crumbling ridges. The sun was a dying glow in the west as she approached the eastern fringes of Arthur's camp.

She could see the tents but there were no fluttering banners. *The teulu has marched! I'm too late!* She galloped through the camp, past burnt-out cookfires and cooling forges. Camp followers idled in small groups and the whole place had the air of tense patience.

As she left the camp on the side that faced the river, she saw that she was well and truly too late. The river was a silver streak in the distance under the setting sun and between her and it lay the desolation of a dying age.

The dead littered the moor. Ravens had descended in their droves and were picking their way through the grisly remains. Small clusters of survivors were gathering horses and equipment while others merely wandered about in an exhausted daze.

Guenhuifar clamped a hand over her mouth as the tears started in her eyes. How many had died? Who was left?

She urged her mount on through the horror and it shied and reared at the stench of blood and opened bowels but she forced it on. The sigils of a hundred houses and families lay amidst the slaughter, fouled and smeared with blood. If there had been a victor that day it was not apparent who it was.

She hailed a group of warriors bearing the red dragon sigil. "What company are you?" she asked them.

"We are Beduir's men, my lady," said one of them.

"Where is Beduir?"

"He rode to the left flank to join Arthur after we pushed Medraut's men back to the river."

Guenhuifar looked across the grim length of the river to the far southern side of the battlefield. There appeared to be the highest concentration of standing men there and her heart filled with hope. The victors had rallied around Arthur it seemed.

She wanted to gallop but had no desire to trample corpses for they littered the ground like a carpet, and so her journey across the battlefield was a slow and ugly one. All about she heard the cries of the wounded and they tore the heart from her breast for she could do nothing for them.

At last she came within sight of men she knew and she could hold it no longer. Swinging down from her saddle she ran the rest of the way to where she could see Beduir and Cei standing around looking lost and utterly broken. Two dead men lay at their feet and Guenhuifar let out a cry of anguish when she saw who they were.

It was Cei who came to hold her as the strength gave out in her knees. She could do nothing, say nothing but mouth soundless cries of agony at the sight of Arthur and Medraut lying side by side, their beautiful bodies blood-soaked and smeared with the dirt of battle.

"Arthur lives, but barely," said Cei.

"He lives?" Guenhuifar managed.

"He is wounded deeply in the thigh and has lost a lot of blood. Menw has done what he can for him."

"Let me go to him!" She wriggled free of Cei's grasp and ran to kneel at her husband's side.

He was deathly pale but there was some movement behind his eyelids. A linen cloth had been bound tightly around his thigh but the blood had already seeped through it. She touched his face and whispered into his ear; "Arthur, I am here."

His eyelids fluttered and he looked at her with glassy eyes. "Guenhuifar ... I am ... so sorry."

She kissed his forehead and wept.

"He is at death's door," said Menw. "The thigh is one of the worst wound places. It bleeds out quickly. When one loses that much blood it is in the hands of the Great Mother whether or not they shall pass into Annun or turn back from its gates."

"Guenhuifar," said Arthur. "You must ... take me to Ynys Mon."

Guenhuifar glanced up at Menw who looked upon Arthur with grave concern.

"Why?" she asked him.

"She is calling to me. I must go to Her. Take me ... take me to the Morgens."

"He will not survive the journey," said Menw. "It is too far. Besides, we have to pass through Maelcon's territory to get there and then there are the straits to cross ..."

"Do it!" said Arthur, his voice husky. "I must meet my end upon that isle ..."

Guenhuifar looked around at the ruinous battlefield. The Teulu of the Red Dragon had been utterly decimated. And Medraut's teulu? Here lay Medraut, his shade already in Annun. Maelcon had won but only barely. He had no teulu. And he would not be expecting survivors of this slaughter at Camlan to head north. *It can be done. If Arthur can survive it.*

She rose and looked at what was left of Arthur's companions. Cei and Beduir's faces were streaked with tears. "Where are Gualchmei and Peredur?"

"Dead," said Cei.

"Mor too," said Beduir. "Medraut's men outflanked us. I held the right flank while Arthur and Mor rode to aid them even though they were outnumbered."

"Cador fell also," said Cei. "We were able to smash Alan's company as it tried to cross the river north of here. Most of his men had deserted him when they saw our combined companies heading off their approach. We slew Alan but not before one of his men speared Cador. Dumnonia weeps with us this night."

Guenhuifar squeezed her eyes shut against the tears that started afresh. Now was not the time for mourning. Now was the time for planning else none of them would get out of this alive.

"Muster what is left of the teulu at the camp," she told Arthur's remaining two captains. "Menw shall tend to Arthur and prepare him for the journey north."

"I tell you, he cannot make it," said Menw. "He can barely be moved as it is."

"He'll make it," said Guenhuifar. "Or die on the way. Either way we must try."

"Will you have us march on Cair Dugannu with a fraction of the teulu's strength?" Cei asked her.

She looked at him. "I no longer care about the fate of Venedotia. Maelcon can have it for all I care. But I *will* honour Arthur's wishes and you *will* help me. We will march north as one and see what we face. Maelcon no longer has a teulu to speak of. Perhaps we will meet with no resistance. Then you can continue your bloody war for that damned crown. I go to Ynys Mon with my husband. I'm going home."

Once Arthur had been moved back to camp and made comfortable, Guenhuifar rode south. Darkness had fallen by the time she reached the nunnery and she had to hammer on its door. The Mother Superior admitted her warily and she went straight to the quarters where Amhar and Lacheu slumbered.

She got into bed with them and watched their little faces as they slept by the moonlight shining in through the window. So peaceful. She wept while they slept. She wept for Arthur, for Medraut and for the future of her sons.

She awoke with the dawn and roused Guihir and told him of what had happened at Camlan. He took it well although with a deathly silence and a pale face.

"Will you come north with us?" she asked him at length.

"Yes. For as far as I am able. While Arthur lives he is still my penteulu and I will do whatever he or you command of me."

"Thank you, Guihir. We shall have need of loyal friends in the days to come."

They packed quickly and ate a hasty breakfast with the nuns before setting out. Guallen and Iona emerged from their chamber looking as concerned as when Guenhuifar had departed the previous day.

"Good news, girls," said Guenhuifar. "You are free. Medraut was killed yesterday and his teulu scattered. My husband no longer has a use for you."

They broke in to smiles of joy that turned Guenhuifar's stomach. "You can go and find your beloved Ithoc if it so pleases you. But know this: if I find him first, you will be mourning his death instead of marrying him."

They looked confused at this and Guenhuifar left them then and mounted her horse. Before the sun was fully up, they were heading up onto the moor towards Arthur's camp.

Arthur's condition had not improved. Menw was spooning him some broth when she arrived. Some effort had been made to clean his face and comb some of the crusted mud and blood out of his hair.

"I gave him a sleeping draught last night and he passed the night well," said Menw. "He is still very weak. The bleeding has stopped but he will be extremely susceptible to illness in his weakened form."

"Then we shall have to take care of him as best we can on the road north. How go the preparations?"

"The camp is more or less ready to be struck. Cei and Beduir await your orders."

"How many men have we?"

"Around a hundred and fifty. Twenty or so horses. Then there is the baggage train. Most of the camp followers have already left. Nobody wants to follow a defeated teulu."

"No, I don't suppose they do. Just as well. We need to move swiftly and without detection if at all possible." She took the spoon from Menw and continued to feed Arthur while the bard left the tent to pack his own things.

A visitor came to the tent and Guenhuifar stepped outside to meet him. He was a youngish warrior who held a fine white stallion by the bridle. Guenhuifar immediately recognised Hengroen.

"Arthur gave me charge of him at the last," said the warrior who introduced himself as Cunuil. "It was his wish that the horse should survive. Perhaps I did wrong to follow his orders … Perhaps he would …"

"You did well," Guenhuifar told him. "Arthur knew what he was doing and if he had the strength he would thank you. But I must thank you in his stead. Will you do a further service for Arthur?"

"Anything, my lady."

"Continue to keep good care of Hengroen. We have lost many of our grooms and servants and the warriors must take care of their own horses. Will you safeguard him for Arthur on the road north?"

Cunuil's face broke into a grin of pride. "It would be an honour, my lady!"

Guenhuifar would let nobody but Cei and Beduir carry Arthur out of the tent and lay him upon the wagon that was to serve as his sick bed for the duration of the journey. Once he was made comfortable and draped with a sheepskin, the small convoy set out and headed north towards the mountains.

They made for Din Emrys, but before Dunauding's mountain fortress came into sight, a large company of riders approached bearing the sigil of King Efiaun.

"A fine time you lot choose to come down from your hill," said Cei bitterly. "The war is over and lost. Medraut is dead but Arthur lies dying. We sorely needed your spears."

"And it grieves me that I only learned of the battle yesterday," said Efiaun, as he rode forward to the head of his company. "I received word of Medraut leading his men south through Dunauding but as to his destination or the location of you boys, I had no idea. I mustered my teulu at once and we have been following Medraut's trail ever since. Is it over then? I truly am sorry."

They camped within sight of Din Emrys that night. Efiaun offered them refuge but Guenhuifar wanted to push on. "It's the first place Maelcon's followers will look for any survivors friendly to Arthur. Besides, I dare not take him up that steep hill and move him into the fortress."

Arthur had spent most of his conscious moments of the journey in conversation with Menw about deep and spiritual matters. When Guenhuifar questioned the old bard he told her, "Arthur has made his peace with the Great Mother now. All his life he has been unable to decide between her and the new faith. He has now decided and wants to die on the sacred isle where his shade will be close to that of his sister."

"He spoke of Anna?"

Menw nodded, then shrugged. "Perhaps he has made his peace with her too. I don't fully understand his reasons but there is a deep sense of homecoming about his words. I think Modron is calling him to her and he wants to meet her where it all this started. Where he met *you*."

Arthur died in the night. When dawn broke over the Venedotian mountains, grief rose with it to consume the small band of companions like a thick fog. All they had known and loved had been taken from them leaving them lost and aimless. Guenhuifar wept with her sons by Arthur's side. They had wrapped him in the dragon banner, stained with blood and mud as it was. He had given everything for it in life and now he would be the last of the line of Cunedag to bear it. Maelcon would never get it.

Efiaun came down from the fortress to pay his respects. He brought news also. "Maelcon is to be crowned Pendraig at Cair Dugannu three days from now. Word has it he has recovered his runaway bride, the lady Guallen."

"How did he manage that?" Guenhuifar asked feeling a sudden pang of guilt at having left the girl where she thought she would have been safe.

"Bands of Medraut's men who survived the battle have been looting and raiding across my kingdom. Word is that they helped themselves to the stores of a nunnery and there they found a girl in noble clothing with her handmaid. It wasn't too hard to guess that it was Guallen."

"So he will have his queen on his coronation day after all," said Guenhuifar bitterly. She raged at the world. Had absolutely everything been for nothing?

"All the kings have been summoned to the coronation," said Efiaun.

"Will you go?" Cei asked him pointedly.

Efiaun shook his head. "I failed Arthur in life. I will not dishonour his memory by supping with his enemies. I don't know what your plans are other than to convey Arthur to Ynys Mon but you have my full support and I hope that you know you will always find shelter at Din Emrys."

"You know that Maelcon will come after you next should you defy him?" Guenhuifar said.

"Yes. But currently he has no teulu. Arthur saw to that. Perhaps it was his parting gift to us; to ensure that we have a fighting chance against Maelcon. I don't know what will happen, but we will be ready, no matter what."

They continued onwards, skirting the Giant's Cairn and entered the Pass of Kings that would take them out on to the northern coast of Venedotia. Scouts returned with news of a company of warriors entering the pass on its northern side.

"Men from Cair Dugannu," said Cei. "We can take them." But there was a lack of confidence in his words that was most unfamiliar to all who knew him. It was a small company that approached to be sure, but they were also few in number and none really had much fight left in them.

"Cei, I don't want another battle," said Guenhuifar. "There must be some other way …"

"Aye, there is," Cei admitted. "We draw their attention and lead them south while you head north and make for the straits with Arthur's body."

"Are you thinking of leaving us, Cei?" asked Menw.

"To give us the time we need," said Guenhuifar. "Thank you Cei."

"This is probably goodbye then," said Cei. "If we can outrun these dogs, then I will make for Cair Cunor, if any of it is left standing. If Efiaun can hold on to his ancestral home then perhaps so can I. And who knows? If there is to be a new alliance against Maelcon, they'll find my spear ready."

Guenhuifar embraced Cei and kissed him. "Will you see Arthur one more time before you go?"

He shook his head. "Never been too keen on corpses besides those I make myself. I prefer to remember him as he was. As a bear of a man who lived. As my brother. I wish you well, Guenhuifar."

"And I you," she replied, feeling a lump rising in her throat. She hadn't always seen eye to eye with Cei over the years but to lose him now was like losing another piece of Arthur.

"I will remain with you, if that's all right," Beduir told her.

"You would accompany us to Ynys Mon?" she asked. "But why?"

"My fighting days are over. Cei has enough men to draw the enemy. I … just can't leave him. Not yet."

Guenhuifar smiled. "He always thought so very highly of you, Beduir. And we would be glad of your company."

Cei mounted up along with every other able-bodied rider while Beduir led the small baggage train of three wagons into a narrow pass that broke off from the wider one. Here they would hide until the enemy had passed by, drawn by Cei and his companions. Guenhuifar sent Cunuil to join them upon Hengroen.

"The time has come for rider and horse to be parted at last," she told him. "Arthur goes where Hengroen cannot follow. Take him and be good to him. He has earned his retirement."

"I shall treat him as a brother," said Cunuil, tears in his eyes. "Goodbye, Lady Guenhuifar."

As Cei led his men back down the valley, they gave one final salute to their fallen chieftain. Twenty spears were raised in the air to a man they had loved in life and now honoured in death.

Guenhuifar tore herself from the scene and followed the wagons up the steep defile where they would be out of sight from the pass.

They did not have long to wait before the company of Maelcon's riders galloped down the pass in pursuit of Cei and the others who had loitered long enough to let themselves be seen. Then, they were all gone in an instant and Guenhuifar felt more alone than she had felt in years. Beduir, Menw and a handful of others were all that was left of Arthur's great following.

Dusk had settled before they dared emerge from their hiding place and continue the journey north. By the time they reached the coast it was dark.

The ferry point had grown up again in the year following the great pestilence. The tavern was open once more and the ferryman awaited passengers on their side of the straits.

"We must go on alone," said Menw, glancing at the small band of followers who were stabling the ponies and goods for the night before heading indoors in search of food and beds.

"The three of us, the two boys and Arthur," said Guenhuifar. "Beduir, can you carry him?"

"Of course." The big man lifted Arthur's form out of the wagon despite his missing hand and carried him over to the ferry. The ferryman required extra payment to take them across at the next low tide rather than wait for the morning for he had his mind set on a tankard of ale and his bed but it was arranged at last and they clambered into the small vessel.

Once they had crossed to the far side, dawn was only a few hours off. They bedded down in the woods and caught some sleep. Guenhuifar awoke shivering with Amhar and Lacheu in her arms, a thin blanket over them as the dawn broke over the island.

They continued wordlessly, Menw leading the way to the sacred lake of the Morgens. *Where it started*, thought Guenhuifar, *so shall it end*.

The small settlement took them in and fed them. While the boys slept in one of the huts with Beduir to watch over them, Guenhuifar and Menw went down to the lake to speak with the nine sisters.

"An age is over," said the high priestess once they had told her that they came bearing Arthur's body. "And a new one begins." She looked at Menw. "He was the Mabon, you do realise that?"

"Yes," said the bard with a nod.

"For years we followed the one called Anna who was once our high priestess. She was convinced that her son was the blessed youth who would bring about the turn of the wheel. His name was Medraut …"

"It was Medraut who slew Arthur," said Menw. "He is also dead."

"Just so. Perhaps Anna had some truth of it. Two Mabons in conflict; a light and a dark. And now, both gone and Mabon may not be reborn for many years."

"We came here because it was Arthur's wish," said Guenhuifar.

"He fulfilled his purpose and now, Modron will carry him to Annun where he will wait until she has need of him again."

Guenhuifar had long ago given up trying to understand the riddles of the Morgens. She had done what Arthur had requested. That was all. Now, she wanted to sleep next to her boys and not dream for a hundred years.

The Morgens took Arthur's body into their great roundhouse and washed him and combed his hair; preparing him for the funerary rites. Guenhuifar was glad that they had taken over for she did not feel she had it in her to organise his funeral. But, on the other hand, as soon as those women in their black robes had carried him away from her, she felt as if she had finally lost him forever. His journey would continue but she would play no part in it.

"Arthur's sword," said Menw to her that night. She glanced at *Caledbulc* in its sheath in the corner of the hut. Beduir had cleaned and oiled it and kept it safe for his friend since they had left Camlan. "Modron gave it to him. He no longer needs it."

"Then what should be done with it?" Guenhuifar asked. She had no desire to keep it as an heirloom for her sons – *may they never hold swords for as long as they live* – yet she could never bear for it to fall into the hands of some other warrior as if it were a simple tool to be given a new owner.

"It should be given back to the goddess."

"How?"

"I'll show you."

When dawn broke, Menw led her and her sons and Beduir down to the lake shore. "I have not the strength in my arms," he said to Beduir. "Cast it as far as you can into the centre of the water."

"Throw it into the lake?" Beduir asked, looking down at the beautiful weapon with its golden serpents on the hilt.

"It belongs in Annun," said Menw. He looked out across the still waters to the shimmering reeds on the other side. "It is not the first weapon this lake has received. Such was the warrior's way in the old days. These watery depths hold many secrets."

Beduir looked uncertain. Guenhuifar gripped his wrist. "I know this does not sit well with your Christian beliefs," she told him. "We are in pagan company and you have already done so very much for

Arthur that you did not have to. Will you do this one last thing?"

Beduir nodded grimly. "Aye," he said. "I'll do this for him."

They stood back as he unsheathed *Caledbulc* and cast the scabbard aside. The morning light glinted along the blade's length. Then, they stood back as Beduir began to turn, spinning around three times, the blade whirling about before he let go.

They watched the sword flail through the air and descend almost dead centre in the lake. The water erupted upon impact and the sword immediately vanished from sight.

Later that morning, the Morgens made ready to take Arthur to the Isle of the Dead where he would be laid to rest in a tomb where the ancients lay, forever sleeping. They assembled on the shoreline and watched the small boat set out, nine figures surrounding the corpse of Albion's hero wrapped in the banner of the red dragon.

Guenhuifar refused to cry, even though Beduir did. She had wept enough. Now was the time to be strong for her sons. She held them close as the boat drifted out across the water, through the mist of morning towards the mysterious isle of tombs and standing stones that even the Romans had feared.

The rising sun flecked the sea with gold and began to burn away the mist but not before the little boat was swallowed by it. When the mist cleared, there was no sign of the boat or the Morgens. Arthur had completed his final voyage. Guenhuifar turned from the shore and led her sons away.

EPILOGUE

The Caledonian Forest, 575 A.D.

The bard looked up at the sky through the wavering pine tops and listened to the sighing of the wind through those venerable boughs. He breathed the woodland air deeply, inhaling the scent of life, of moss and earth, of bark and needle. The vast forest was the most peaceful place he had ever been and he understood at last why the man he sought had retreated deep into its shaded solitude and not ventured out of it for two years.

He pressed on, following the directions Guentuid had given him. She occasionally visited her brother and brought him food and drink. Her grief had not stopped her from loving him, nor had it prevented her from defying her husband who had called for his death.

The bard was on a spiritual mission. He had spent his life collecting legends and scraps of folklore concerning Arthur, the greatest hero of the Britons. He was compiling his masterpiece; a poem that told of Arthur's voyage to the misty island of Annun to steal the magical Cauldron of Rebirth.

Such tales kept the spirit of the Britons alive in dark days. And they had been dark days indeed since Arthur had left them. With the absence of its champion and the Teulu of the Red Dragon, Albion's enemies grew in strength and courage. Cerdic of the West Saeson broke the treaty Arthur had brokered and with Cador of Dumnonia slain at Camlan, there had been little to stop them winning a decisive battle over the young King Constantine. In the north, King Edelsie had died and his wretched grandson, Afloeg, claimed Lindis at last. But even he had only held it for a while. His old ally Wintra of the North Angles betrayed him and took Lindis for his own. He, in turn was usurped by Wehha of the South Angles who conquered the territories of the North Angles, merging them with his own to form the new kingdom of East Anglia.

And what were Albion's heroes doing during these transgressions? The ruthless ambitions of Venedotia's new overlord kept many eyes turned inwards. Maelcon had got his wish of ruling Rhos as regent until his cousin, Cunlas, came of age and, even when he did, he was ever Maelcon's puppet. Together the two of them waged war on their own kin, swallowing up the kingdoms Cunedag's sons had founded until Venedotia was one whole kingdom ruled by Maelcon, supported by an increasingly corrupt and power-hungry clergy.

In all this turmoil, one man's name stood as a paragon of all that the Britons had lost, a name that stood for a lost age when the Britons had been inspired by courage and not paralysed by fear, of when they held honour to be the highest virtue and did not fight each other over the scraps from their enemies' tables. That name was Arthur and it was the word for a dream that was quickly vanishing.

The bard followed the ridge of woodland and turned down in to a dip carpeted with pine needles. There, at the bottom of the dip, just as Guentuid had said it would be, was a large wild apple tree. Beneath its splayed branches a small bower had been constructed. Smoke drifted from a cookfire nearby and beyond it a simple pig run had been constructed from crudely woven wattle. The little beasts oinked and snuffled about as the bard approached and their stirrings awoke the bower's occupant.

He shambled out of the tiny abode looking like a beast himself rather than a man. His clothes were little more than rags and he wore some poorly-cured animal skin as a cloak into which had been woven many ornaments of wood, bone and feather. His grey hair was lank and greasy and hung in great tendrils on either side of a shaggy beard.

This was what was left of the great bard, Merdin. This wild man, dressed in filth and scraps, had once been the court bard of King Guentoleu whom he had grown up with. His sister had been married to King Riderch of Ystrad Clut; that great bastion against the Gaels of Dal Riata and the Picts of the northern fringes.

Riderch now cursed his brother-in-law's name with a hot vengeance. The marriage of Merdin's sister had been an attempt to heal years of strife between Ystrad Clut and the small kingdom Guentoleu ruled on its border. But due to a personal matter concerning insult and honour, Merdin kindled strife between the two kings, thinking only of his own pride.

That strife resulted in the Battle of Armterid; a battle of such futility that it nearly rivalled Camlan in its senseless slaughter. Guentoleu was slain as were many others. It was only when Merdin saw the mangled, blood-spattered corpse of his own nephew amongst the slain that he suddenly understood the implications of his actions.

Riderch and Guentuid blamed Merdin for their son's death for he had brought about the battle knowing his own nephew would be on the opposing side. Riderch in his anguish, called for his head and Merdin fled into the Caledonian Forest to escape his wrath. There he remained, seeing no one but his sister who, although she pitied him and brought him food, would never forgive him.

The bard looked into those haunted eyes and saw a wildness and a wretchedness that almost made him wish he had not come. *Is there any sanity left in the old man?*

Those crazed eyes looked him all over, savouring every last detail, lingering at the harp he carried in his crane-skin satchel and hovering over the crucifix he wore at his throat. "Why have you sought me out?" Merdin asked at last.

"For instruction," said the younger bard.

"What instruction can a wretched old fugitive like me offer a bard who, by the grey in his hair, I surmise competed his training long ago?"

"People say you were trained by Menw, the bard of Arthur himself."

Merdin smiled. "Aye. I was trained by Menw, though he was blind and half-mad even when I was a boy. He taught me everything he knew."

"Then you are the last person alive who knew one of the men who, with Arthur, stole the Cauldron of Rebirth."

Merdin regarded him curiously from beneath his heavy, white eyebrows. "Who are you and why have you run me to ground to learn of Arthur and the Cauldron?"

"My name is Taliesin and I too have been a fugitive but that was many years ago."

"Oh? Then do tell me of your wild youth for I thirst for new tales here in my seclusion."

Taliesin breathed deeply and began. "The man who adopted me was called Elffin, one of the sons of Guidno, brother of King Maelcon."

"So you hail from Venedotia, just as Arthur did?"

Taliesin nodded. "When I was just a child, Maelcon's son, Rhun – who was just as debauched and depraved a youth as he is now a king – lusted after my adopted mother. She refused his advances and in his rage, Rhun had poor Elffin incarcerated at Cair Dugannu.

"Although I had barely seen ten winters, I journeyed to Maelcon's court at Cair Dugannu and pleaded with him to release the only man I had ever called 'Father'. I was laughed at and not least by Maelcon's own bard, a man called Heinin."

"Aye," interjected Merdin. "I knew him."

"Then you will know that he was an arrogant fool. I saw that much even then and so I made a deal with Maelcon. A contest. If I could beat old Heinin in a battle of words, then he would release my father."

"You're not telling me a ten-year-old matched words with Heinin?"

"Aye and thrashed him soundly before the whole court. Words of satire poured forth from my lips that struck at the very heart of the old fool until he was rendered dumb and could utter no more than nonsense syllables. Maelcon was enraged and banished Heinin from his court but he had to honour our bargain. My father was released to me and we made ready to leave. But I had a final word of parting for Maelcon. I predicted that he would die before the following year's snows fell."

"I can't imagine he took that well," said Merdin. "To foretell a king's death is a dangerous thing. But let's see, Maelcon died when you were a youth, what year was this?"

Taliesin smiled. "The year before the last great pestilence swept Albion and claimed Maelcon's soul along with many others."

Merdin gazed at him in awe for a time before speaking. "Are you telling me that you too have the gift of the *awen*?"

Taliesin nodded. The awen was the gift of prophecy; the divine inspiration from the world beyond their world, be it the Christian Heaven or the pagan Annun, it was all the same to a bard.

"Then we are as two kindred spirits. Who trained you in the ways of prophecy?"

Taliesin shrugged. "Nobody. I occasionally get ... *visions*."

Merdin blinked at him. "You mean to say that you do not voyage to Annun through the means of a trance?"

Taliesin shook his head.

"You do not enter a cave or some dark, isolated place and let your mind find its way to Annun? You do not chew on raw flesh or drum or rattle some instrument in order to make a connection with the awen?"

"No. It just comes to me, sometimes in dreams but sometimes when I am awake."

"Tell me, you say that you were adopted. Who were your real parents?"

"I had none. Elffin found me as a baby in a hide coracle that had been swept into one of his fishing weirs."

"You came from the sea …"

"Apparently so."

"And perhaps from even farther away. You may be even more powerful in the gift of prophecy than I am. What can I teach you?"

"I cannot command the awen on a whim as you can. I require guidance in the taming of my gift."

"But what do you *seek*?"

Taliesin thought for a moment. "I seek Arthur."

"Why? Arthur was a mere man. Now his body lies in its tomb, wherever that may be. He is lost to us forever."

Taliesin nodded. It was rumoured that Maelcon had the Morgens put to the sword in his campaign to stamp out the remnants of the old faith and with their deaths, none now knew where Arthur's final resting place lay. Only through song and tale did Arthur's deeds continue to inspire any hope in the people. *And there it is.*

"Hope," he said at last. "I seek hope from the awen for there are some who say that Arthur will return to us. I wish to seek him out wherever he dwells in Annun."

Merdin smiled sadly. "Hope is something that has become increasingly elusive to me. You see, the awen does not speak to me as much as it once did."

"You ... have lost your gift?" Taliesin asked, feeling a rising panic at a potentially wasted journey.

"Not completely, at least not yet. I hear whispers now and then but it has been many moons since I trod the soft grass of Annun. But perhaps the two of us might make the journey together. Our combined gifts might be powerful enough to lift our boat and carry it through the waves to the isle of apple trees."

"Yes!" said Taliesin. "Let us open the books of awen together!"

"Come into my bower," said Merdin. "I will make the preparations."

The small hovel was cramped for the two of them and Taliesin sat down on a yellow ox skin while Merdin went back outside to fetch something. He heard a squeal and, presently, the old bard returned with a dripping chunk of flesh.

"I hate to slaughter one of my dear little piglets but their flesh is sacred and will suit us best."

"The chewing of raw meat ..." said Taliesin, eying the red lump Merdin set on a flagstone between them with distaste.

"One of the easiest ways to connect with the awen. We chew and chew and let the spirit of the pig enter us. We close our eyes and awake amidst apples and the soft breath of maidens. At least, that is how it used to be ..." His voice trailed off, laced with sadness.

"Let us try," said Taliesin, feeling strangely as if he were now the master leading the apprentice.

Merdin nodded and drew a knife at his belt. He cut the meat into two pieces and popped one of them into his mouth. Taliesin did the same and he bit into it, feeling the still warm blood fill his mouth, tasting the iron, the lifeforce of the pig ...

They chewed and chewed with their eyes closed for what felt like hours. When Taliesin opened his eyes, he found himself facing a river that glinted gold in the fading sunlight.

He looked around him. Merdin was nowhere to be seen. Before him a massive host was facing the river, all spears focused on a narrow ford across which an enemy host was embarking. Taliesin glanced at the standard held by the defenders.

A red dragon.

And beneath it sat a man in helm and cloak astride a fine white stallion. Taliesin knew that he looked upon Arthur himself.

The enemy charged. They carried round shields and bore long-bladed knives. Their leaders wore boar-crested helms and above them the banner of a white dragon fluttered. There was no mistaking them. These were the Saeson.

They gouged into Arthur's host, overwhelming them on all sides, surrounding the defenders which were gradually whittled away to a small band.

Taliesin forced back the urge to look away. Tears stung his eyes to see his countrymen cut down. *What battle was this? Badon? The Black River in Lindis?* Arthur had never suffered such a defeat save at Camlan and that had not been against the Saeson. *This is not how it happened!*

But wait! A third host had entered the battle and was riding down hard upon the enemy's rear. Men in mail coats astride massive war horses were bearing down upon them, trampling the Saeson. They carried large kite-shaped shields and wore helms with prominent nasals. The Sais host disintegrated in to confusion. Ranks broke and men died by the hundred.

They are defeated! Albion's age-old enemy had been entirely subdued by these new conquerors! But now these proud horsemen with their long shields continued towards the ford, thundering into the water towards Arthur's host with the same gusto with which they had decimated the Sais ranks.

But now Arthur was nowhere to be seen. The dragon standard remained but the man in its shadow had changed. And he changed still as the Britons fought these new warlords back and forth, first advancing, then retreating and on and on it went.

A great push from the Britons' side forced the enemy back across the ford and Taliesin noticed that the banner had switched to a golden one. This golden dragon was carried deep into the enemy ranks before being surrounded and fighting a retreat back to the ford.

It had changed now, back to a red dragon and was being carried forward once more. It crossed the ford and the enemy fell back from it. The man who rode under the dragon banner received a crown upon his head and …

The vision faded.

Taliesin awoke on his back in Merdin's hut, the older bard leaning over him with a concerned face.

"What did you see?" Merdin demanded.

"How … how long have I been asleep?" Taliesin asked, as he rubbed his aching limbs which felt like they had not moved in an age.

"A long time," said Merdin.

"I saw …" Taliesin began, recalling the images of his dream which already felt like old memories to him. "I saw the Saeson conquered by men on large horses with strange shields. Then these new conquerors turned on us and we fought them and fought them …"

"We?"

"The Britons. The men of the red dragon. The *Cymry*." It was an old word that meant 'compatriots' and had begun to be used for all Britons of the old blood who now fought Sais, Pict and Gael on every front.

"Go on!" said Merdin excitedly.

"A hero will rise, not Arthur, but somebody like him. This hero will carry the fight to them, across the ford. He will retreat and be succeeded by another, and another until …"

"Until?"

"Until he wears the crown of both peoples on his head."

Taliesin sat back, stunned. The awen had shown him Arthur reborn, not once but countless times over. *Or was it Arthur?* Arthur had been merely a man. The bards of the old faith like Menw had named him 'Mabon' the eternal youth, son of Modron the Great Mother. Was She still working her magic through men? The Christian bards now equated Mabon with the Christ, the son of the divine Mary. Did such cycles repeat on and on until the world was but dust? In that case, Arthur would come again, not in the flesh, but the spirit of his courage and defiance would be reborn in others; others inspired by Arthur's legend.

Far from being wiped out, hundreds of years from now – *no, thousands* – the small group of survivors who claimed descent from Arthur and others before him, still stood. This brave band of compatriots who now called themselves *Cymry*, still held out. And the banner they carried before them bore the sigil of a dragon, a red dragon, still defiant, still feared.

Merdin regarded him in silence for a long time. Then he said, "The awen speaks to you now, Taliesin. It has closed my mouth and shut my book at last. Therefore, this task is given to you. Rejoice in it and continue Arthur's tale so that he might never be forgotten."

Taliesin nodded. He understood now. Whenever there was tyranny, whenever there was a *gormes* to be overturned, the Mabon would be reborn and the people would rally to his standard. The standard would be different each time but its meaning would never change: resistance, hope, *freedom*.

Taliesin understood that it wasn't about Arthur. It was about hope. That hope had to be kept alive in the Mabon's absence. It must be gathered and kept warm like a glowing ember that would one day kindle a blazing fire that would sweep across this Island of the Mighty. Bards like he and Merdin were the custodians of that ember. They could keep it alive with their tales and their song. And the song Taliesin would sing would be a song of Arthur, hero of the Britons. Arthur of Albion. *Arthur of the Cymry*.

AUTHOR'S NOTE

Whatever went on in the region of Linnuis, it seems to have been a lengthy and bloody campaign for Arthur who fought no less than five battles there according to the 9th century *Historia Brittonum*. Linnuis is generally taken to mean the Romano-British kingdom of Lindis, named after the town Lindum Colonia (Lincoln) which later became the Anglo-Saxon kingdom of Lindsey. The first battle mentioned took place on the river 'Glein' and the remaining four on the river 'Dubglas' which possibly means 'dark' or 'black'. Neither of these rivers have been positively identified.

One academic who has written extensively on post-Roman Lincolnshire is Dr. Caitlin Green. Her examination of the medieval tale of Havelok the Dane first recorded by Geoffrey Gaimar in his 12th century *Estoire des Engleis*, was a particular influence on this part of *Field of the Black Raven*. She suggests that the story of Havelok (Afloeg to give him a British name) may have been influenced by local legends concerning the post-Roman kingdom of Lindis passing into Anglo-Saxon hands due to the marriage of a British princess to a Germanic king.

Green also explores the possible presence in the region of the cavalry unit *Equites Taifali* (Taifals) who were a people of Germanic or Sarmatian origin that supplied mounted auxiliary troops to the Roman army. She suggests that the Taifals remained to protect Lindum after much of the Roman army had left Britain and the presence of their descendants is reflected in the name of the nearby town Tealby.

Maelgwn (Maelcon) is frequently mentioned in Welsh records and literature and rarely in a good light. Gildas calls him the 'Dragon of the Island' in his polemical *On the Ruin and Conquest of Britain*. This may seem a compliment but Gildas was drawing parallels between him and four other British 'tyrants' to Biblical beasts from the *Book of Daniel* and the *Book of Revelation*.

He tells us that Maelgwn spent time as a monk and indeed, he seems to have been a staunch supporter of Christianity and was a patron of many churches both in Gwynedd and other parts of Wales suggesting that his influence extended beyond the borders of Gwynedd.

His time with the clergy did not last long, much to Gildas's disapproval, and he berates Maelgwn for usurping his uncle 'with sword and spear'. While this uncle may have been his father's brother, Owain, the Latin term 'avunculus' usually refers to a maternal uncle meaning that it was probably an unnamed brother of Meddyf. Darrell Wolcott of The Center for the Study of Ancient Wales identifies this man as Afallach, whom the genealogies name as the father of Maelcon's wife, Gwallwen (who bore him his son and heir, Rhun). This suggests that, after usurping his Uncle Afallach, Maelgwn took his daughter (his own cousin) as his wife.

Gildas claims Maelgwn tired of his first wife and even murdered her before pursuing the wife of his nephew (whom he also murdered) and then married her. Who this second wife was is up for speculation.

As well as Gwallwen, two other women are named as Maelgwn's wives: Nest and Sanan although, like Gwallwen, little is known about them.

The *Annales Cambriae* claim that Maelgwn died of a 'great mortality' in 547. This along with a reference to the 'yellow plague of Rhos' in the Welsh Triads possibly suggests that the Plague of Justinian which originated in the Eastern Roman Empire in the mid-6th century, made its way to Britain.

The Battle of Camlan is a monumental event in early Welsh literature but its references are cryptic and its causes are shrouded in mystery. First mentioned in the *Annales Cambriae* as a 'strife' that claimed the lives of both Arthur and Medraut, its location is not given. Neither is it made clear if Arthur and Medraut were fighting against each other or on the same side.

The Welsh Triads expand a little on this but not by much. In these sources it is clear that Arthur and Medraut are on opposing sides (although no familial connection is made). Camlan was one of the 'Three Unfortunate Counsels of the Island of Britain' due to 'the three-fold dividing by Arthur of his men with Medraut'.

A rather tantalising cause for the battle appears to have been a quarrel between Arthur's queen and her sister, Gwenhwyfach (who is first mentioned in the tale *Culhwch and Olwen*). Camlan, one of the 'Three Futile Battles of the Island of Britain', was apparently brought about 'because of a quarrel between Gwenhwyfar and Gwenhwyfach' while the second of the 'Three Harmful Blows of the Island of Britain' 'Gwenhwyfach struck upon Gwenhwyfar, and for that reason the Battle of Camlan happened afterwards'.

An entirely different cause for the battle is given in the otherworldly tale *The Dream of Rhonabwy* in which Iddawg, the messenger, admits that he is responsible because he delivered insults to Medraut instead of Arthur's words of peace. He claims to have done penance for seven years as recompense although his reasons for stirring up trouble in the first place are not given.

Other individuals are named in connection to Camlan. *Culhwch and Olwen* names three survivors of the battle as Morfran ail Tegid (who survived because of his ugliness), Sandde Bryd Angel (because of his beauty), and Cynwyl Sant (who was the last to be parted from Arthur by taking his horse Hengroen).

While not mentioning Camlan, the 'Three Unrestrained Ravagings of the Island of Britain' refer to an ongoing quarrel between Arthur and Medraut after the latter 'came to Arthur's Court at Celliwig in Cornwall; he left neither food nor drink in the court that he did not consume. And he dragged Gwenhwyfar from her royal chair, and then he struck a blow upon her.' This late triad is apparently influenced by Geoffrey of Monmouth's fictional *The History of the Kings of Britain* which has 'Modredus' as Arthur's traitorous nephew who seduced Arthur's queen 'Guanhumara' and tried to usurp the throne while Arthur was away, prompting the battle of Camlan.

Whatever the original cause of the Battle of Camlan, Geoffrey of Monmouth has forever shaped it in to a conflict between Arthur and Mordred, uncle and nephew. The aforementioned *Dream of Rhonabwy* calls Medraut Arthur's foster-son and the 13th century Vulgate Cycle made Mordred Arthur's son *and* nephew via an incestuous encounter with his sister Anna/Morgause and this tradition has continued in most modern retellings.

Although I have tried to use only pre-Galfridian (Geoffrey of Monmouth) sources in writing this trilogy, I have allowed myself the indulgence of making Medraut Arthur's nephew and adopted son. The relationship and resulting conflict is an indelible part of the modern perception of the Arthurian legend and to me it was an interesting way to present Camlan as part of the age-old conflict between the old generation and the new.

Printed in Great Britain
by Amazon